VINTAGE **CLASSICS**

THOMAS SAVAGE

Thomas Savage was born on 25 April 1915 in Salt Lake City, Utah, to a large sheep-ranching family. His parents divorced when he was two years old, and on his mother's remarriage Savage moved with her to Montana. He studied at the University of Montana and worked as a ranch hand for several years, but when an article he wrote on horse-breaking was published in *Coronet* magazine in 1937, Savage enrolled at Colby College in Maine to study English. He went on to have a variety of jobs, including welder, insurance man and plumber as well as teaching English at Brandeis and Vassar. His first novel, *The Pass*, was published in 1944 and he went on to write twelve more, including *The Power of the Dog*. He was awarded a Guggenheim fellowship in 1980. Thomas Savage died in Virginia on 25 July 2003, aged eighty-eight.

OTHER WORKS BY THOMAS SAVAGE

The Pass

Lona Hanson

A Bargain with God

Trust in Chariots

The Liar

Daddy's Girl

A Strange God

Midnight Line

The Sheep Queen

Her Side of It

For Mary, with Love

The Corner of Rife and Pacific

THOMAS SAVAGE

The Power of the Dog

WITH AN AFTERWORD BY
Annie Proulx

VINTAGE BOOKS
London

3 5 7 9 10 8 6 4 2

Vintage
20 Vauxhall Bridge Road,
London SW1V 2SA

Vintage Classics is part of the Penguin Random House group of companies
whose addresses can be found at global.penguinrandomhouse.com.

Penguin
Random House
UK

Copyright © Thomas Savage 1967

Afterword copyright © Annie Proulx 2001

Thomas Savage has asserted his right to be identified as the author of this
Work in accordance with the Copyright, Designs and Patents Act 1988

First published in the United States by Little, Brown in 1967

First published in Great Britain by Chatto & Windus in 1967

www.vintage-books.co.uk

A CIP catalogue record for this book is
available from the British Library

ISBN 9781784870621

Penguin Random House is committed to a sustainable future for
our business, our readers and our planet. This book is made from
Forest Stewardship Council® certified paper.

MIX
Paper from
responsible sources
FSC® C018179

Printed and bound in Great Britain by Clays Ltd, St Ives plc

For my wife

Deliver my soul from the sword
My darling from the power of the dog.
                                   — Psalms

1

Phil always did the castrating; first he sliced off the cup of the scrotum and tossed it aside; next he forced down first one and then the other testicle, slit the rainbow membrane that enclosed it, tore it out, and tossed it into the fire where the branding irons glowed. There was surprisingly little blood. In a few moments the testicles exploded like huge popcorn. Some men, it was said, ate them with a little salt and pepper. 'Mountain oysters,' Phil called them with that sly grin of his, and suggested to young ranch hands that if they were fooling around with the girls they'd do well to eat them, themselves.

Phil's brother George, who did the roping, blushed at the suggestion, especially since it was made before the hired men. George was a stocky, humorless, decent man, and Phil liked to get his goat. Lord, how Phil did like to get people's goats!

No one wore gloves for such delicate jobs as castrating, but they wore gloves for almost all other jobs to protect their hands against rope burns, splinters, cuts, blisters. They wore gloves roping, fencing, branding, pitching hay out to cattle, even simply riding, running horses or trailing cattle. All of them, that is, except Phil. He ignored blisters, cuts and splinters and scorned those who wore gloves to protect themselves. His hands were dry, powerful, lean.

I

The ranch hands and cowboys wore horsehide gloves ordered out of the catalogues of Sears, Roebuck and Montgomery Ward — Sears and Sawbuck and Monkey Ward, as Phil named those houses. After work or on Sundays when the bunkhouse was steamy with the water for washing clothes or shaving, fragrant with the odor of bay rum on those about to go into town, they would struggle with their order blanks, hunched over like huge children, biting the end of the pencil, frowning at their crabbed handwriting, puzzling over the shipping weight and the location of their postal zone. Often they gave up the struggle, sighed and turned the job over to one more familiar with writing and numbers, some one among them who had got as far as high school, one who sometimes wrote letters for them to fathers and mothers and remembered sisters.

But how marvelous to get the order into the mails, how delicious and terrible to wait for the parcel from Seattle or Portland that might include with the new gloves, new shoes for town, phonograph records, a musical instrument to charm away the loneliness of winter evenings when the winds howled like wolves down from the mountain peaks.

Our very best guitar. Play Spanish-style music and chords. Wide ebony fingerboard, fine resonant fan-ribbed natural spruce top, rosewood sides and back, genuine horn bindings. This is a real Beauty.

Waiting for their order to get to the post office fifteen miles down the road, they read again and again such descriptions, reliving the filling out of the order blank, honing their anticipation. Genuine horn bindings!

'Well, you fellows looking over the old Wish Book?' Phil would ask, standing by the stove and stamping the snow off his feet. He would look out into the room, spraddle-legged, his bare hands clasped behind him. Over the years a few of the young men tried to imitate his habit of going bare-handed, maybe seeking his approving smile or nod, but their imitations went unnoticed and at last they took up their gloves again. 'Looking over the old Wish Book?'

'Sure thing, Phil,' they'd say, proud to call him by his first name, but closing the catalogue under cover of conversation that he might not see them lusting after the pert women who modeled corsets and underwear. How they admired his detachment! Half-owner of the biggest ranch in the valley, he could afford any damned thing he wanted, any automobile, Lozier or Pierce-Arrow, say, but he desired no car. His brother George had once expressed a wish to buy a Pierce, and Phil had said, 'Want to look like some Jew?' And that was the end of it. No, Phil didn't drive. His saddle, hanging by a stirrup from a peg in the big long log barn, was a good twenty years old; his spurs were of good plain steel — no fancy silver inlays, not such spurs as crowded the dreams of others; he wore plain shoes instead of boots, scorned the trimmings and trappings of the cowboy, although in his younger days he was as good a rider as any of them, a better roper than George. With all his money and family, he was just folks, dressed like any hired hand in overalls and blue chambray shirt; three times a year George drove him into Herndon for a haircut; he sat in the front seat of the old Reo stiff as an Indian in his stiff town suit, his imperious nose hawklike under the slate-gray fedora, his jaw jutting. So he sat in Whitey Judd's barber chair, his long, thin, weathered hands motionless on the cool arms of the chair while his accumulated hair fell in piles to the white-tiled floor around him.

A drummer, a natty dresser with a flashing stickpin, had once chuckled and questioned Whitey.

'Wouldn't laugh, if I was you, mister,' Whitey remarked. 'He could buy and sell you fifty times over, or anybody else in the valley except his brother. I'm proud to have him sit in my chair, mighty proud.' Snip, snip, snip. 'Him and his brother are partners.'

Just so they were, and more than partners, more than brothers. They rode together at roundup time, talked together as if they'd met for the first time, talked of the old days in high school and at a California university where George, as a matter of fact, had flunked out the same year that Phil was graduated. Phil recalled tricks he'd played on other students, friends they'd had — high jinks. Phil had been the bright one, George the plodder.

It was something of a joint decision when they sold their steers each fall or bought a Morgan stud to improve the saddle stock. Each year Phil looked forward to hunting in October when the willows along the creeks had turned a rusty red and the haze from distant forest fires hung like veils over the mountain peaks. You saw the two of them with their packhorses riding across the flats toward the mountains, Phil with his stubby carbine, or with his thirty-caliber. It was not unusual to see such a relationship between brothers, Phil tall and angular, staring with his day-blue eyes into the distance, then at the ground close by; George stocky and imperturbable, jogging along on a stocky and imperturbable bay horse. They made wagers — who would sight and shoot the first elk? How Phil did relish a meal of elk liver! At night they made camp below timberline and sat cross-legged before the fire talking of the old days and of plans for a new barn that never materialized because that would mean tearing down the old one; they unrolled their beds side by side and together listened in the dark to the song of a tiny stream, no wider than a man's stride, the very source of the Missouri River. They slept, and woke to find hoarfrost.

So it had been for years, Phil now just forty. So too they slept in the room they had as boys, in the very brass beds, rattling around now in the big log house since those Phil referred to as the Old Folks had taken off to spend their autumn years in a suite of rooms in the best hotel in Salt Lake City. There the Old Gent dabbled in the stock market and the Old Lady played mah-jongg and dressed for dinner as she always had. Closed off, the Old Folks' bedroom gathered dust kicked up by the automobiles — more and more of them every day — that putt-putted up the road out front. In that room the air grew stale, the Old Lady's geraniums died, the black marble clock stopped.

The brothers kept Mrs Lewis, the cook, who lived in a cabin out back, and she found time to clean the house after a fashion, complaining at every movement of the broom. Gone now was the girl, last of a series, who had waited table and slept upstairs in a tiny room. Her presence might have looked strange in a bachelor establishment, but still the brothers comported themselves with almost shocking modesty as if women still stalked the house. George bathed once a week, entering the bathroom fully clothed, locking the door behind him; silently he bathed, with small splashing and no song; fully clothed he emerged, but followed by the telltale steam. Phil never used the tub, for he did not like it known he bathed. Instead, he bathed once a month in a deep hole in the creek known only to George and to him and, once, one other. He looked around before he went there, should there be prying eyes, and he dried himself in the sun, for carrying a towel would have cried out his purpose. In the fall and spring he had sometimes to break a crust of ice. In the winter months he didn't bathe. Never had the brothers appeared naked before each other; before they undressed at night they snapped off the electric lights — the first in the valley.

Nowadays they ate their breakfast with the hired men in the back dining room, but took their dinner and supper as before in the front dining room off white linen, and the tools they used were sterling. It is not easy or desirable to slough off old habits, or to forget who you are, a Burbank with the best connections in Boston, back East in Massachusetts.

It sometimes worried Phil that George got a far-off look, rocking in his chair, for George's eyes would suddenly stare out across to the mountain called Old Tom thirty miles away and twelve thousand feet, a beloved mountain, and George would rock and rock and rock, looking across the flat.

'What's the matter, old-timer?' Phil would ask. 'Old mind wandering again?'

'What's that?'

'I say, your mind wandering again?'

'No, no.' George would slowly cross his heavy legs.

'How about a little cribbage?' They had kept careful score over the years.

To Phil, George's trouble was that he didn't engage his mind. George was no great reader, like Phil. To George, the *Saturday Evening Post* was the limit; like a child, George was moved by stories of animals and nature. Phil read *Asia*, *Mentor*, *Scientific American* and books of travel and philosophy the fancy relatives back East sent by the dozen at Christmastime. His was a keen, sharp, inquiring mind — an engaged mind — that confounded cattle-buyers and salesmen who supposed that one who dressed as Phil dressed, who

6

talked as Phil talked, must be simple and illiterate, one with such hair and such hands. But his habits and appearance required strangers to alter their conception of an aristocrat to one who can afford to be himself.

George had no hobbies, no lively interests. Phil worked in wood. He constructed the derricks that stacked the wild hay — timothy, redtop and clover — hewing out the huge beams with adze and plane. With those clever naked hands he carved those tiny chairs no higher than an inch in Sheraton or the style of Adam; his fingers moved like spiders' legs, paused briefly sometimes as if to think, for Phil's fingers had a private intelligence lodged, perhaps, in their padded tips. Seldom did his knife slip, and if it did, he scorned the iodine or Phenol-Sodique, two of the few medicines in the house, for as a family the Burbanks did not believe in medicine. His little wounds healed rapidly once he had wiped them with the blue bandanna he stuffed in a rear pocket.

Some who knew Phil said, 'What a waste!' For ranching was no demanding or challenging occupation, once you had the ranch, and required brawn but little brain. Phil, people marveled, might have been anything — doctor, teacher, artisan, artist. He had shot, skinned and stuffed a lynx with skill that would have abashed a taxidermist. Easily he solved the mathematical puzzles in the *Scientific American*; his pencil flew. From the pages of the encyclopedia he taught himself chess, and often passed an hour solving the problems in the Boston *Evening Transcript* that arrived two weeks late. At the forge in the blacksmith shop he designed and hammered out intricate pieces of ornamental iron, firedogs, pokers shaped like swords and tridents; he wished he could have shared his gifts with George, who never caught fire, seldom even smoked, so to speak, who looked forward no longer even to

7

the trips he made to Herndon in the Reo for the bank directors' meetings and lunch later at the Sugar Bowl Cafe.

'How about teaching you chess, Fatso?' Phil once asked, looking ahead to evenings before the fireplace. The name Fatso got George's goat.

'No, I don't think so, Phil.'

'Why not, Fatso? Think it'd be a little tough for you?'

'I never was much of a one for games.'

'You used to play cribbage. Pinochle, sometimes?'

'That's right, I did, didn't I?' And George would pick up the *Saturday Evening Post* and lose himself in some cheap fantasy.

Phil was a whistler, and a good one, his tone accurate as a flute's; he would whistle a merry tune and go into the bedroom and get out his banjo and pick away at 'Red Wing' or 'Hot Time in the Old Town.' He had taught himself to play and it was fine to see those fingers leaping on the strings. Once it was not unusual, when he played, for George to pad quietly into the room and lie on the other brass bed and listen. But not lately.

Lately after a tune or two, Phil would get up from the edge of the bed where he sat playing, stand straight, put away the banjo and walk the path through the rustling ryegrass to the bunkhouse.

'Well, fellows,' he would say, blinking his eyes against the white glare of the gas lamp.

Once one of the hired hands always rose to give him a chair, some cast-off chair from the Big House.

'Hey — don't bother,' Phil always said, but someone always did bother — and fruitlessly, for Phil would accept neither chair nor gift from anybody. His visitations interrupted some discussion of whores, politics, horses or love and caused a silence that lasted until the *clunk!* of a length of firewood shifting in the stove emphasized that silence, and some man, terrified of silence, felt bound to speak.

'What you think of this Coolidge?' a man might ask, for eventually the *Transcript* found its way to the bunkhouse where it was used as waste and tinder, but only incidentally to read.

Then Phil would frown and roll a perfect cigarette with one hand. He knew the value of the pointed silence. 'Well, I'll say one thing for him.' Lighting the cigarette. 'He's got the gumption to keep his trap shut.' And Phil would laugh, and there would be a halting conversation, perhaps of Coolidge. Then maybe one of the younger fellows, hoping to flatter, would ask advice about ordering a saddle. Did Phil think a center-fire or a three-quarter rig the better? Was the Visalia saddle all it was cracked up to be?

At last Phil would look a little wistful. 'Well, I guess you fellows must want to roll in.'

'Oh, hell no, Phil.' And there would follow more talk, perhaps of the work the next day, the overhauling of the mowing machines if the time was spring, the whereabouts of a bunch of wild horses, or Phil might tell an anecdote of Bronco Henry, that best of riders, that best of cowboys, who had taught Phil the art of braiding rawhide. Recently, having finished telling the fellows a story, Phil looked suddenly out the window over the top of the whispering ryegrass to the lighted bedroom window of the Big House. As he watched, the window went suddenly dark. George had not waited up!

'Well, fellows,' he said with a sad grin, 'got to hit the hay.'

When he had gone, one of the new loudmouthed young cowhands spoke right up. 'Hey — he's sort of a lonely cuss, ain't he? Like about what we was saying before he come in, do you guess anybody ever loved *him*? Or maybe he ever loved anybody?' The oldest man in the bunkhouse stared at the young fellow. What the young fellow had said was unsuitable, even ugly. What had love to do with Phil? The oldest man in the bunkhouse reached down and patted the head of a little brown bitch that slept close. 'I wouldn't want to be saying nothing about him and love. And if I was you, I wouldn't call him a cuss. It don't show respect.'

'Well, hell,' the young fellow said, blushing.

'You got to learn to show respect. You got an awful lot to learn about love.'

In the fall the brothers with their hired hands trailed a thousand head of steers twenty-five miles down the road to the stockyards in the tiny settlement of Beech. Unless the weather was miserable, the rain beating out of the north, the sleet cutting the face or the cold hindering the circulation of the blood, the event had something of the quality of an outing, or picnic; the young fellows thought of the lunches Mrs Lewis the cook had put up to be eaten at noon when the shadows hid under the sagebrush; they thought of the saloon across the highway from the yards and of the rooms over the saloon where the whores lived.

When the sun rose red and the frost fled from the surface of the short, dry grass, the herd was already lined out over the length of a half mile; caught under the bewitching spell of the dark and that holy quality of the dawn that turns men in upon themselves, the cowhands were silent and the brothers were silent, listening to the step-step-step of the cattle and the crackling sound of sagebrush crushed under cloven hoofs; squeak-squeak-squeak of saddle leather and the ringing of German silver bit chains. The new sun rising above the eastern hills showed a world so vast and hostile to individual hope that the young cowhands clung to memories of home, kitchen stoves, mothers' voices, the cloakroom at school and the cries of children let out at recess. Raising their chins, they fixed their eyes now on an abandoned log shack, opened to the weather, where stray horses in summer sought a little shade, where years before a man like them had failed; where the road wandered near a barbed wire fence, a rusty sign peppered with bullet holes urged them to chew a brand of tobacco that no longer existed; ahead, hunched over the pommel of his saddle, rode the oldest man in the bunkhouse, gray, lined of face, one who like them must have once dreamed of a little place, a few acres, a homestead, a few cattle, a green meadow, a woman to be a wife; God knew, maybe a child.

Then the sun loomed higher out of the hills and the new warmth nourished their hopes and they talked, laughed, joked; their plans would materialize; when they got to be old like that fellow up there hunched over his saddle, they would have a little place. They would have their money; they would make plans. In the meantime the nose of their horse was pointed toward the stockyards, to the saloon, to the women upstairs.

The brothers, too, had been silent in the darkness, known to each other only by their shapes, the lean one and the stocky one — by their shapes and the long familiar squeak of the other's saddle. So, thought Phil comfortably, they had always been silent at the beginning of a drive, thoughts turned inward upon the past, and the silence now told him that the past had not changed, not changed much. Yes, he did resent the stage, the dark green Stearns-Knight that nowadays blatted its way headlong through the herd of cattle — much too fast, if you asked Phil. Once the driver had dared sound his horn, and the noise had so frightened the cattle that Phil rode right over to the creeping car and, towering up there on his sorrel horse, he gave the driver a good piece of his mind. You should have seen the passengers in the back seat make themselves small!

'God damn scissorbills,' he growled. 'George, did you hear that son of a bitch honk his horn. Dear good Jesus, they don't give a good hot damn how much weight they run off your stock. Like to see every damn car blowed up.'

But George, loyal to the Reo (as he was loyal to all he owned), looked ahead over the backs of the cattle. 'Hell,' he said. 'Oh hell, Phil, man's got to go with the times.'

'The times!' Phil said, and spit. Ten years before there was a proper stage with a real man there on the box, handling the reins, fine four-horse rig. 'What was the driver's name, Fatso?' Phil asked George. He seldom forgot a name, but here was a way to launch into the new morning's conversation.

'Harmon,' George said.

'By God, you're right.' That got them back into the past, to when they were kids, got them back to where they could reminisce about Bronco Henry, back to the time of the last stinking Indians before the government got onto itself for a change and shipped them off to the reservation. Phil recalled to this day the swaybacked old horses the Indians rode away on, the rickety old buggies the old Indians piled themselves into. All one week the Indians had straggled past the ranchhouse on their way down to the reservation in southern Idaho, stirring up the dust and making the ranch dogs bark. Only the chief was not with them, that shifty old character. He had died.

Phil liked to recall to George the many times while trailing cattle down that his sharp eyes had fixed on Indian arrowheads which he picked up and added to his remarkable collection. He couldn't recall that George had ever found an arrowhead. Phil grinned to himself. How could he? For George always looked straight ahead, as he did now, over the dusty backs of the cattle.

Now exactly, Phil wondered, where should he begin the day's conversation? So special a day, this day. Should he begin with Bronco Henry? Or with an incident of last year — the car, trying to get through the river of cattle, that ran off the side into a ditch? Two women and a man, all in knickerbockers, damnedest thing you ever saw, and then there they gauped at the car tipped almost on its side, them just looking. Phil had been glad that George was in the lead of the herd, for George would have hooked onto the car with his rope and pulled them out, and they wouldn't have learned their lesson.

Or begin this morning with the most important fact, that this was the twenty-fifth year they had been together driving cattle? Twenty-five years! How proud they had felt that time, and how old! To Phil there was some kind of stuff in the fact that they made the first round trip in the nice round year of nineteen hundred, nineteen hundred and naught. Jesus! Jesus! Bronco Henry wasn't older then than he and George were now — not much older, to tell the truth, than the young fellows with them today, dressed up in their fancy duds. They didn't know who the hell they were any more, the young fellows — cowhands or moving picture people. Phil had never seen a moving picture and by God never would, but these young fellows had magazines about the moving pictures in the bunkhouse, and a fellow name of W.S. Hart had got to be sort of their God. Look how they creased their hats now, look at the silk bandannas they knotted around their necks, and the fancy chaps! He'd heard that one of them had sent away for made-to-order boots with fancy inlays — spent a month's pay on some damn thing to put on his feet. And then wondered why they ended up on the county! Well, Phil mused, there you were. The more ignorant people were, the more they felt they had to decorate their backs.

George had sort of moseyed over to the right, and now Phil moved diagonally through the plodding cattle, humming soothingly so they wouldn't get their dander up. 'Well, Georgie boy,' he grinned, 'I guess this is it.'

For brothers, they rode differently, sat so differently on their saddle horses, the one slouching easily, the reins loose in his naked hands; the other straight, rigid in the saddle, gut pulled in, looking straight ahead. 'It?' George asked, turning his head. 'What's *it*, Phil?'

'What's it? What's it, Fatso boy? Today is twenty-five years. Nineteen hundred and nothing. Nineteen naught, naught. Recall that?'

'Fact is, I forgot,' George said.

Now, how could he have forgot, Phil wondered. What had he thought about all year? 'Twenty-five years. Sort of makes it sort of a silver anniversary, or whatever,' Phil said, 'don't it?' In jocular or angry moods, Phil used bad grammer to point up his words.

'Long time ago,' George remarked.

'Well,' Phil said, 'not *too* God damned long.' He had not mentioned the matter to emphasize how long it had been since they were kids. Phil himself didn't feel a year older than when he was twelve and George ten — only one hell of a lot smarter. 'But I'll tell you one thing, George, we had some great old times.'

'I guess we did at that.' George reached in his shirt pocket for his Bull Durham sack; he looped both reins around the saddle horn, removed his gloves and rolled a cigarette; he rolled a thick, funnel-shaped cigarette.

Phil looked at it and snorted. Damned if he was going

to carry the whole burden of the anniversary conversation. What ailed George? Gut hurting him? Swell fellow to camp with this fall! Been funny all summer. 'Say, Fatso,' he remarked. 'You never did learn to roll a smoke with one hand.' And with that, Phil rode abruptly through the herd to talk to the young fellows, moving his lips as he prepared to tell them of how Bronco Henry, sick with fever, had made one of the prettiest rides a fellow ever saw — at age forty-eight. God damn it — sometimes he longed to tell the whole story. One reason he hated booze, he was afraid of it, afraid of what he might tell.

Now a small gray bird whirred out of the brush. Phil's sorrel shied and stumbled. Phil felt a sudden fury, and anguish like nausea. 'God damned old fool!' he cried, yanking up the sorrel's head, giving him a good sharp jab with the spurs. Twenty-five years since he'd ridden side by side with Bronco Henry.

Now the sun was high, the shadows shortened, the hours ahead were hot and long. Yes, and so were the years long, Phil thought, and the shadows they cast.

If the wind was right and your nose was keen, you might smell the stockyards at Beech long before you saw them; they lay close to the river that was almost dry this time of year, shrunk away from its banks and so placid the surface reflected the arching and empty sky, sometimes the magpies that flapped across, searching out carrion, gophers and rabbits dead of tularemia or a calf dead and bloated with what they called blackleg in that country. Yes, if the wind was right and your nose was keen you got the odor of water and of the sulfur-and-alkali stink of the sluggish creek that there at the yards met the river and polluted it.

If the sun was right and your eyes sharp, you sometimes

saw the settlement first appear as a mirage floating just above the horizon, the yards, the stockcars spotted at the chutes, the two false-fronted saloons with rooms upstairs, the shabby white school with the short bell tower — all surrounded by sagebrush and a bare spot where the boys played ball and the girls skipped rope. Across from that bare spot was the building called The Inn, and behind it rose a bare hill on whose slopes thin wild horses grazed, the perpetual wind worrying their tangled manes and tails. Summer and winter that wind howled, shrieking down the slope of the hill over the graveyard at the base where rusty barbed wire and rotting posts kept stray animals from trampling the graves and toppling the fruit jars that often held flowers — Johnny-jump-ups in spring, Indian paintbrush later, but only the recent dead could be certain of flowers. Flowers wilted suddenly in that sun and their message was ephemeral, and quickly the stems festered in the fruit jars.

He was a clever one who thought to decorate one recent grave with paper flowers, and over them to turn a fruit jar upside down, against the rain.

Hearts always beat a little faster in Beech when word got around that someone had seen dust rising off the flat, that a bunch of cattle were being trailed in by a bunch of free-spending cowhands; in the two saloons the bartenders looked to the level of the rotgut in the bottles behind the bar and set out the real whiskey, down from Canada, for those with the wherewithal — the ranchers who liked to make big gestures.

'I'm telling you,' a bartender said to a drummer who had blown in the night before on the train from Salt Lake City. 'Stay off the highway and don't go gawking at the cattle when they trail in, or you'll like to spook them and they'll have trouble gettin' 'em in the yards. Coupla years ago they shot right over the head of a fellow gawkin' around spookin' the cattle. Christ, you should a seen him run for cover, coattails a-flappin'!'

'Sounds like the Wild West,' the drummer said sarcastically. He had meant to sell small electric light plants to the saloons, to the school and to the hotel called The Inn, but had no takers.

'Hell, it *is* the Wild West,' the bartender said. 'Far as I know, the only electric lights in the valley are up to the Burbank ranch. The rest of us use lamps.'

'The Burbank ranch,' the drummer said, and looked at the girlie calendar behind the bar. You could see her garter.

'It's their outfit coming in this afternoon. Thousand head. Eight, ten cowhands. And the brothers. Take my advice and stay inside and don't cause a stampede. What'll it be, Dolly?' he asked a blonde. 'My, but you smell pretty.'

'Thanks,' she said. 'Florida water it is, and my drink is gin as you right well know.'

'The Burbank outfit's on the way in.'

'I seen them from the upstairs,' Dolly said. 'And oh how I dread it.'

'Well, you got your friend now to help out.'

'Lot a good she is. She's sick.'

'Hey? She got the same thing old Alma had, remember?'

'T.B.? Oh, hell no. She's got her usual flowers.'

Hearts beat a little faster, too, in the only dining room in town at the small hotel called The Inn. The dining room was ready and the beds upstairs. The register at the desk was open to a clean new page and beside it, smelling of cedar wood, was a fresh-sharpened pencil.

2

The wind was never idle in Beech summer or winter, nor was the windmill atop the shed behind The Inn. The ratchet and chain to pull the fin that dragged the face of the mill out of the wind-stream had broken long before the Gordons moved there. Winter and summer it turned, the shaft attached to the excentric purposelessly moving slowly up and down, doing no work, attached to nothing, squeaking, squeaking so painfully that sleep was difficult for the infrequent transients trapped in the town. Shortly after the Gordons moved there, Johnny Gordon the husband had tried to stop the thing, following a sharp complaint; he got a shaky ladder up against the shed, climbed up and tried to figure it all out. A sudden mean shift of wind turned the flying blades against him, tore his coat and cut his shoulder. He left it alone, after that.

'We never should've moved here in the first place,' he often told Rose, his wife, and when he told her she would look at him with her great eyes, begging him not to say it again, but saying nothing with her mouth. She was all eyes, that young woman.

Still, it was not only her eyes that had attracted him to her in the first place, in Chicago where he was finishing his internship at a desperate little hospital, mostly colored and charity patients. To escape the pain and the filth and squalor he largely lived with, he began to go in a few nights a week to a moving picture palace. Oh, he thought, if he could meet up with a girl with the warmth and tenderness and fortitude of Miss Mary Pickford, whose smile and whose eyes melted the human heart, her dimples, her glance! Once, a little drunk, he confessed his dream to two young doctors who hooted at him. 'You talk too much,' they advised him. But still he clutched his dream close, embroidered it, so that now in its fruition it included a vine-covered cottage and a white picket fence.

And imagine! He sat one night down front near the piano whose bright tunes and thumping base explained and underlined the flickering drama before him. He was lost in his dream for a few moments after the lights came up. The young woman at the piano touched her hat, fussed at her hair, and fussing with it, turned. Imagine! She had been sitting there not ten feet from him, sitting there every time he'd been there. They stared at each other, and he smiled.

He did not suggest that she come to his room; she didn't look that kind, although his friends would have asked her right off, the ones who hooted at him.

'She could always say no,' they might have told him.

He didn't want it like that. And his hunch was right. Imagine asking a girl to your room who Sundays played the piano in a church.

He said right off he was a doctor, hoping to impress her, to establish himself. 'There's a carnival by the lake,' he offered. 'They say it's swell. You like carnivals?'

'Just one of my favorite things!'

'Say,' Johnny asked. 'What's your *favorite* thing?'

'Flowers,' she said.

'Mmmm.'

'That wasn't a hint. But you asked me.'

Her father certainly looked him over, even after he said he was a doctor. 'We won't be late, sir.' Her father gave him a look and took his newspaper into another room.

'Well, Mr Gordon,' her mother remarked.

'Doctor Gordon, Ma'am.'

'. . . our only child. You understand how it is. Someday you may feel the same.'

'Bet your boots I will.' Breathless, he watched Rose pin the violets he'd brought to her coat; he'd never seen such affection in fingers.

Her mother sighed. 'She's always loved flowers. When she was a little girl, she was always touching people's flowers.'

He'd say one thing for her — she was a game one! Game for all the rides, the roller coaster, and my, your stomach just left you, and the big pendulum you got into that swung and then went clean around. 'Oh,' she said, thrown against him, and he could smell the violets. 'I'll say one thing,' she said when she caught her breath. 'For a fellow who says he hasn't got so much confidence, you have an awful lot to go on these terrible things!'

'Oh, say, I've got plenty when you're around.'

But she would not go into the tents where freaks were shown, and he only suggested it to see how she felt about freaks. He hated it for freaks, especially when they smiled.

Not, then, into the tent of freaks, but rather to hear a young man with a pointed beard sing songs from a new operetta; thus it was that Johnny and Rose emerged humming tunes from *The Red Mill*. Rose was not wearing the pretty little hat he first admired, decorated, he thought, with flowers. She wore instead a scarf tied round her head, sort of gypsylike.

'It's a bandeau,' she told him, and stood back for him to get a good look at it. 'You like it?'

'It looks peachy to me,' he said.

'I got it out of a magazine,' she said. 'It's what Mrs Vanderbilt wears.'

'Oh, hey — I bet it looks better on you than on Mrs Vanderbilt,' he said.

'I'd hardly say that.'

'I would,' he said soberly. He remembered from somewhere a picture of Mrs Vanderbilt walking toward a Rolls-Royce touring car, and do you believe it, Rose did indeed look a little like Mrs Vanderbilt, but a Mrs Vanderbilt the merest breath would blow away. 'You know, you do look like Mrs Vanderbilt?'

'Honestly?'

He laughed. 'Yes, and you think so, too.'

'Now you know my little secret.' That little band around her head was her badge.

'You tell 'em, I stutter!' he said. That's what they all said then. And Johnny laughed.

But when a few nights later she agreed to marry him, her eyes shining and her lips parted slightly like one who knows she is about to be kissed, tears suddenly sprung into his eyes; he felt his life, whatever that might be, was incomplete without her, and he was afraid. Afraid for her, or for himself? He couldn't tell.

'All I can say to you, young man,' her father remarked, 'is always be good to her.'

'I assure you, sir, I always shall,' Johnny said.

'The first time you called,' her father said, frowning, 'you were a little under the influence.'

'You're a perceptive man, sir,' Johnny said. 'I admit to that charge. I took a drink to give me confidence.'

'Liquor is a poor thing.'

'It's just a medicine, sir,' Johnny said, 'if you use it right.'

He was not asked to remain at the hospital when his internship was up; he knew he would not be asked, and yet he was disappointed; but the fact might have pointed up to him his tenuous connection with reality. He felt that if he had met Rose earlier, and put his shoulder to the wheel, as he phrased it, he would have been asked to remain. Why, until he met Rose, he had just gone through the motions, so to speak, or so it seemed to the director.

'But I'll say one thing for you, John,' said the director, and looked across the skull he kept on his desk. 'I have eyes and I have ears, and I know you're probably one of the most naturally kind young fellows I've ever known.'

'Kind?' Johnny asked. 'Kind? I never noticed, sir, that I was kind.'

'Maybe not,' the director said, smoking his pipe as Johnny wished he could smoke one — with authority. 'That's why I said naturally kind. It proceeds, these new psychiatrist fellows tell me, from a certain sensitivity. And —'

'And what, sir?'

'We sometimes have to control sensitivity. Can be dangerous. Not sure it's a trait especially valuable to a doctor. Shame, but there it is.'

'Then what should I do, sir, about getting a job?'

'Some small town, John. Some small town, till you get on your feet.'

It embarrassed him to be called John. He didn't feel like John. He felt like Johnny, and maybe that was his trouble, for who trusts the Johnnys of the world, they who skip through life laughing and crying, but always skipping.

He found the small town. This was it — Beech. This town of which he so often said, 'We never should have moved here in the first place.' And then Rose would look at him.

It had seemed so possible as a place where a young doctor

22

not so sure of himself might settle and make a living. It was on the railroad. He had put Rose up in the hotel in Herndon, the county seat, twenty-five miles north, while he inquired around Beech, and everybody seemed enthusiastic about having a doctor.

'Not for twenty-five years,' they told him in the saloon.

'That's a long time,' Johnny said.

Oh, they told him of the dryland farmers off behind the hill that slipped down to the town, and about the big ranches to the west. They told of talk that a spur of the Northern Pacific might come through and meet the Union Pacific. Beech at the junction was bound to grow, they said. Not months before, they said, surveyors had been working with their instruments, and what a fine bunch of young men they were!

Caught up in the enthusiasm generated in the saloon, Johnny bought another round of drinks for his new friends, and they all toasted a future so vast it left him breathless, vast as the land outside. And what about living quarters for him and his wife?

He had a wife? Now, that was a good thing.

He brought out her picture.

Well, he was fortunate indeed. 'Strikes me,' the bartender said, 'you might take a look at the old hotel. The Inn, used to be called.'

A small hotel of six small identical rooms on the second floor, each with an iron bed, washstand, closet and neat coiled rope beside each window in case of fire. The Inn had been abandoned long enough to have got the reputation among the schoolchildren of being haunted; they had seen lights, they had seen faces at the windows. One of the bolder among them had shied a stone through an upper window, and told how he heard a kind of scream. Especially when the moonlight fell against the weathered brown clapboards, brightened the windows and picked out the bleached white deer horns over the sign that said THE INN — especially then it seemed haunted.

But in the sunlight it looked solid and innocent enough; the windmill that stuck up out of the roof of the shed behind lent the place a practical air, and it seemed to Johnny that until he had established his practice, they might run the place as an inn again — have two strings to their bow. Impractical, was he?

The bank in Herndon owned the property, and he came almost at once to terms with the fellow there. The legacy of the aunt who had wanted him to study medicine covered the initial payment and bought him the secondhand Ford motorcar he'd need for his rounds. Enough remained to furnish an office in one of the rooms on the second floor. A clever metal chair collapsed into an examination table; a human skeleton grinned in a glass case.

Now he was doing the last necessary thing. 'Come on over here and look, Rose,' he said. Smiling, he watched her rise from her knees beside the building where she planted California poppies — one of the few flowers, they said, that thrived in the cranky, sour soil. He still held in his hand the spade he'd used to dig a hole for the post and top-piece, a kind of gibbet that displayed the sign he'd planed and sanded and painted and attached to the top-piece by four eye screws so that it swung free.

JOHN GORDON, M.D.

'My, but there's so much wind here,' she said, watching the sign swing, 'but I hardly hear it now. Oh yes, that does look nice.'

'You get used to the wind,' he said, 'after a while.' Then they went back inside and set to, cleaning up. Lysol and plenty of good hot soap and water put to flight old ghosts.

His son he delivered himself. He himself took his blessed son from the mother's womb, and together they erred in attaching to the child the faintly epicene name of Peter because it had belonged to Rose's father, and that burly man had become Pete.

Johnny thought he had never seen a lovelier sight than his wife lying in the bed, nursing the child; he waited on her, sat beside her and read to her from Byron, enchanted by the wonder and beauty of birth. How everybody congratulated him, and how straight he sat at the wheel of the Ford motorcar, grinning and handing out cigars. Once having caught sight of his own face in a mirror, he continued to stare at himself, thinking. He thought how it was that whenever she looked up from whatever it was she was doing, she always smiled. He wondered if anybody had ever noticed that before.

The poppies bloomed, withered and died; the winter wind screamed down from the distant mountains, and then again the ground was bare of snow, the poppies pushed up and bloomed again, withered and died. Although they did not speak of it to each other, the Gordons were disturbed that the blond little boy was late in walking and late in talking, and when at last he walked — and that was a day! — he walked with a stiff, mechanical gait that depended little on the use of the knee, a gait that hinted that walking was a painfully acquired skill and not a human instinct. And when at last he talked, the boy astounded them by speaking with a faint lisp in measured, adult cadences that assured them he was advanced and not retarded in spite of his slightly enlarged forehead, his wide, innocent eyes, and a disquieting habit of seeming to listen to the distance. At four he was able to read.

Johnny soon learned a curious fact that at first did not trouble him: when the big ranchers and their wives and families needed a doctor, they drove to Herndon and combined the visit with shopping, dinner at the Herndon House or the Sugar Bowl Cafe. They liked to sit in the big green leather chairs in the hotel lobby and greet friends, gaze out the big plate-glass windows at the townspeople on God knows what errands, and at their own motorcars nudging the curb out front; they liked to take a slow turn about the town, marvel at the neatness of the huge lawn that fanned out before the yellow brick Gothic courthouse and the jail behind where the sheriff kept his pet drunks and vagrants; they savored the tree-lined streets in the residential district, stood awed and embarrassed before the rubber trusses in the drugstore window, walked to the station to see the train pull in and stop. How the earth trembled! How the steam deafened! Then back to the Herndon House where they took a room with a bath, indulged in all that luxury, and smiled, anticipating the moving picture show later in the evening. There was no such luxury at The Inn, no such excitement in Beech, there where the wind howled. Nor is it relaxing to stop at a place that smells of despair and failure.

In all the years that Johnny Gordon practiced in Beech he was faithful, totally faithful, to the Hippocratic oath, and never refused a call for help whether he got a fee or not; his patients were the dryland farmers behind the hills whose lives somehow paralleled his; they had been lured West by colored handbills printed by the railroads, promised cheap land which God knew was there and rain God knew was not. Only the big ranchers who controlled the creeks and the river thrived.

But at least the dryland farmers, the Norwegians, Swedes and Austrians, could fail in clean surroundings.

'By golly, Rose,' Johnny used to say, 'but they sure all are clean. Why, you could eat off the floor. Drive on out with me one of these days, and we'll picnic.'

Him they summoned to set broken bones, arms torn and shattered by the teeth of circular saws. Clumsy former city-dwellers, they were kicked in the groin by horses and cows. Their wives gave birth. When Johnny arrived in his Ford motorcar, they had the water boiling so he could clean his instruments; he laughed and complimented them on the babies he pulled forth raging or whimpering at the world around them; sitting at scrubbed kitchen tables, he celebrated with the fathers, joked to draw attention from their women's suffering. 'Why does Uncle Sam wear red-white-and-blue suspenders?' Singing, he went careening back to Beech with a gallon or two of chokecherry wine in the back of the Ford. 'They'll pay up when they can,' he reassured Rose. And they did, when they could.

But now the sign with his name that hung from the gibbet before The Inn had so weathered it was unreadable; the bleached deer horns over the entrance fell one night of the wind; The Inn itself wanted painting, but inside all was desperately clean, the windows shone. It was not Johnny's fees but the drummers passing through with their lines of dry goods and notions, it was the occasional cattle-buyer who stopped for the night and took a meal — it was they who paid the bills.

Peter suffered not only the gamut of childhood diseases but also a myriad of chills and fevers that sapped his strength and left his arms and legs nothing but the merest crust of bone around the vulnerable marrow. Johnny wondered if people might not take his son's constant ailments as a reflection on his own abilities, and if there were not perhaps some paradox in the ancient books — along with that of the shoemaker's child — that the doctor's son is always sick. But Peter never complained nor demanded, and dutifully handled the toys his parents pressed on him. He learned early what it is to be an outcast and looked on living with deepset, expressionless eyes that saw everything or nothing. He played no ballgames, preferred books and solitude, had an aversion to sunlight and on going out into it always paused, squinted, and shaded his eyes.

People blew out their lamps early in Beech — a single puff down the chimney — and so their world was left to the single light behind a sickroom window, to the pale, flickering flames behind the glass in the switches near the railroad station, and sometimes to the moon. It was then Peter liked to leave the house.

'What were you doing?' Rose would ask, or Johnny, and always Peter answered, Nothing.

Nothing, and they took nothing to mean he walked, walked to nowhere. But once the clock in the kitchen moved around and around until two hours passed and Johnny was seized with sudden panic, a twisting in the region of his bowels; for fifteen minutes he sat paring his nails, afraid to communicate his queer terror to Rose. 'I think I'll take a walk out and see what he's up to,' Johnny said.

The land was flat and bright with the moon whose beams caught in the early dew on the sagebrush and defined a path ahead like moon on water; he could think of nothing that might beckon the boy but the river, and nothing on the bank of the river but the single huddle of willows. *There* the boy must be. If he was not there, well, what? As he approached the willows, he slowed his steps.

And there he found the boy, found him sitting with his back against the willows nearest the river where, in the middle, the water parted, disturbed and glittering, around a stump that caught in a sandbar, and the rippling murmur perhaps swallowed up Johnny's careful footfalls, for the boy sat motionless, his face caught in the cool radiance, his bony temple casting a shadow that hid his deepset eyes like a domino. Sensing he was intruding on some mystery, Johnny hesitated. Just so had he hesitated on the several occasions when he'd come on the boy regarding himself in the wavy mirror that hung over the washbasin; Johnny could not tell from the level expression of the eyes whether the boy was searching for something, judging himself, or simply seeking companionship in his own image, and when the boy turned, it was without embarrassment — he seemed unaware of the strangeness or wrongness or whatever it was; it was Johnny who felt the prickles of guilt, and he wanted to share the burden of the several incidents with Rose, but each time he kept silent.

Now something in the fall of the cloth of the coat the boy wore, something in the shadow that obscured the boy's expression and the half-web of black willows that spread fanlike above him suggested the religious, a monk engaged in prayer. Johnny was struck with the idea that perhaps the boy's habitual remoteness was not the detachment of the doctor or scientist but the withdrawal of the mystic, the priest. When he spoke, Johnny was struck with the impropriety of his own voice. 'Peter?'

'I was coming right back.' Unsurprised.

'I wondered what you were doing.'

'I was watching.'

'Watching?'

'The moon.'

★

As poultry in the pen pecks to death the maimed or strange among them, so at school was Peter hazed, taunted and named a sissy — the hiss of the word was everywhere. But only when they named his father a drunk did he turn on them. Quicker than he, they dodged easily and stood in a circle around him, their eyes bright with fun, their mouths making in unison the cruelly lacerating sound of the nasal 'a.' Just so, he knew, in other circles had their fathers stood, and their grandfathers, tormenting some other pariah, some other odd one; just so would their own sons stand.

Doctor Johnny
Is a rummy.

Again he started to lunge, hunching his thin shoulders, but then stood suddenly still, looking at first one and then another, at Fred who rode to school each day on a horse with a fifty-dollar saddle, at Dick the bartender's son who wrote on the walls in the toilet and bored a hole so he could peek at the girls, whose marks in class were very nearly as good as Peter's own; at sly Larry who already weighed nearly two hundred pounds and grinned often without speaking much. And watching, Peter knew with a knowledge as tempered as a sly old man's that he must oppose them on his own terms, not theirs. And he knew it was not only they for whom he harbored this novel, cold, impersonal hatred, but for all those normal, rich, envied and secure ones who might dare insult his private image of the Gordons.

That image began to take concrete shape when he started a scrapbook of photographs, drawings and advertisements cut from old magazines few in that country had ever heard of — *Town and Country, International Studio, Mentor, Century* — all passed on to the school by an unusual woman up the valley, piling up unread over the years in the dark of the cloakroom alongside cartons of unclaimed overshoes and forsaken mittens. The schoolteacher, a kind, phlegmatic lady who thought often of childhood and of a kitten she'd had and loved, saw no reason why they should not be cut up; they had little to do with anything she or her other pupils might find valuable. What characterized the drawings Peter chose and clipped and pasted in with his pale hands was luxury and affluence — scenes of the sailing of ocean liners, the departure of a crack railroad train, collections of jewels, English country houses, heavy draperies, leather luggage, the beach at Newport and the automobiles that brought the fashionable bathers there — Locomobiles, Isotta-Fraschinis, Minervas. But luxury and affluence were not all that characterized his choices: each drawing, photograph or advertisement contained human figures that reminded him of his father or his mother, his mother standing on a terrace gazing across a sculptured lawn, his father checking in at a great hotel. Thus he began a book of dreams raised up against his family's failure and the everlasting whimper of the wind, a blueprint of the world to come. He would bring this world about by becoming a great surgeon, reading a paper before learned men in France, standing aside while strangers spoke of his mother's beauty and his father's kindness.

Now he stood unmoved when at school they said his father talked to a whore.

And so his father had, talked to one who had started in a good house in Salt Lake City. When the bloom was gone and she'd had a few quarrels, she took the train to Herndon and worked there in the Red-White-and-Blue Rooms. In

Herndon she began to pray a good deal, was found kneeling beside her bed many times. She would seek out churches at night (two were never locked) and she was thought to be out of her mind. Had she not drawn attention to herself by all this kneeling and praying, she might have escaped the sharp eye of her current madam who now detected symptoms of consumption. She liked to keep a clean house, and suggested that the sick woman, named Alma, go to Beech where a girl was badly needed and the clientele was not so fussy.

'Maybe God will help you,' the madam suggested. 'You put a lot of stock in Him.'

She arrived in Beech with a cardboard suitcase containing several kimonos, a carton of Milo Violets, and an old photograph of the father who had thrown her out. If only she had listened to him. Had he not loved her, he would not have disciplined her.

It was apparent to Doctor Johnny, in for an early drink, that Alma's trouble was other than consumption — the eyes showed it and the complexion, and the workings of the mind. He had an astounding gift for diagnosis. Years later, in the days of the specialist, he might have triumphed, might have had an office with heavy Spanish furniture and Persian rugs — and so are we sometimes born in the wrong place at the wrong time. When he examined a patient, he seemed to hear a whisper in his ear, perhaps through the stethoscope, and this gift for diagnosis was one he passed on to his son.

Johnny took the whore Alma aside and bought her a drink. 'You shouldn't be working, you know,' he said.

'God told me to work,' she remarked, and sipped her drink.

'Not just because of yourself.'

'I don't owe them nothing,' she said.

'Yes, you do. You know you do, or you wouldn't talk about God. You know what He wants.'

She touched her temple with the flat of her fingers. 'If God's lied to me, what will I do?' She had been in bed for some days and was now tottering.

'Don't have contact with anybody, just for now.' And another month went by, many nights and many dawns.

'It'll be another week, anyway,' Johnny told Rose. 'Maybe a little longer, but she'll never get out of bed; now they say they don't want her to die over there, and anyway, that's one hell of a place to die, in that little room.' He glanced at Rose and took out a Sweet Caporal. 'Of course, some would say she doesn't deserve much.'

'You're very cold, aren't you, John?' Rose remarked. 'I've already fixed a room for her here.'

His smile was crooked, and he went to her and tipped up her chin. 'That's my little Mrs Vanderbilt.'

'No,' she said. 'Mrs Gordon, Mrs John Gordon.'

Now in the town they called The Inn the Whorehouse Inn because a mad, praying whore had died there, and in Herndon and Beech many good women — doctor though her husband might be — felt free to cut Rose dead on the streets. And truly her beauty — useless and careless as a butterfly — was hard to forgive, and so was her quick smile and proud carriage.

'Oh, he'll be a doctor you bet,' Johnny said, making plans. 'How he reads all the time? Eyes open — notice? That's the thing, open eyes. He loves the facts.'

Peter did indeed love the facts, shut in his room with the Britannica; at twelve he was studying the drawings of Vesalius, reading Hippocrates and certain passages in Virgil and the medical journals his father no longer broke from their wrappers.

'Oh,' Johnny said, 'he'll get to places I never got to,' and his heart grew big with pride, his mind swept over the enchanting landscape of his son's future. 'You wait and see.'

'You're a good man, too,' Rose reminded him.

'Good? A man once called me kind, not good. I don't fool myself. That's my virtue. If you notice, it's almost always what a man wants is to have his son better than he is. Rose, I've noticed that. And then, I never had much confidence. But every man lacks something.' And thus do we excuse our failures, by admitting them.

Sometimes when Johnny drank he felt the equal of the big ranchers: they had money, he had education. When they drove cattle into town he'd saunter into the saloon after the dust had settled and the cowhands were in there whooping it up, and he'd talk — horn in, as the bartender put it. He'd stand up there with the best of them in his dark doctor's suit and a starched collar and expound his theories on politics, on education and on Europe.

'You wait,' he'd say. 'They're going to fight over there and then we're going to be in it, you're going to be in it and I'm going to be in it.' They thought him mad. He didn't seem to notice when they edged away from him as his speech grew slurred, when he spilled on himself and impulsively touched people's arms. For the most part they respected him; some pitied him. Some remembered how he'd wandered out on the highway when he'd first come to town, anxious to see his first big herd of cattle, and how a man had shot right over his head and cursed him, and how he'd run and cowered behind the freight depot. Lord, he must have been there hours.

But once Johnny got talking to the wrong rancher. You could see the fellow standing there with his drink, beginning to get riled as Johnny pursued the most recent phantom in his mind — the lack of civic pride in Beech. Why, he wanted to know, didn't they paint the schoolhouse? Why did they just dump their trash back there on the hill where the world could see it, why desecrate the beautiful country?

'Why look right out there now!' he commanded, and looked out the saloon door at the spot on the hill where the sun caught on the most recent cans and broken glass. 'Ten feet and they'd have dumped it in the graveyard. It's an eyesore, that's what I call it.'

The rancher spoke. 'That's what I'd call you,' the rancher said.

'What's that, sir?' Johnny asked, not understanding.

The rancher said nothing, but there was a small appreciative murmur in the saloon.

'Now you take flowers,' Johnny advised. 'You go into a little town, and you see flowers here and there and around and about, and you know the people in that town have what you call civic pride, from the Latin *civatas* meaning city. You take railroad stations, even right there in Herndon, they'll have a nice bed of flowers out there on a neat green lawn there. People in the cars looking out the windows can see them, and they leave that little town with a mighty fine impression. You wouldn't be surprised if sometime people came back to settle in that little town, now would you?' Johnny paused and looked thoughtfully into his drink. The silence in the room encouraged him. 'Now you take flowers,' he began again. 'You take what we did, my wife and son and I.' He and his wife and son had prettied up The Inn, hadn't they noticed? Hopvines climbing up the side of the porch, and you had to have the right kind of twine for them to climb on or they got up there and fell kerbang, a green heap, of their own weight. Well, hopvines, and the California poppies, and the nasturtiums. All grew well there

35

in Beech, wanted only watering. 'You probably've seen us out there watering plants.'

The rancher spoke again. 'Was that what you was up to a few years back when I shot a gun over your head?'

'What's that, sir?'

'I say, was it you out there watering your flowers when I shot a gun over your head?'

'So it was you did that? Well, I will admit, sir, I had it coming. I didn't know much about customs in those days.'

'That a fact?' the rancher said.

'Come winter,' Johnny said, 'and you've got no flowers, have you? So my boy and my wife, that's why they go out there in the fall onto the flats off from town and gather what some call weeds, and then they dye them, and you've got flowers all winter.'

'That a fact?' the rancher murmured, and somebody coughed.

'Nor is that all,' Johnny said, and carefully slopped a drink of whiskey into his glass. 'My son has a surgeon's hands, very clever hands. He'll take crepe paper and twist it and make it into artificial flowers and those, sir, are what you find on our dinner table in the winter months. Imagine,' Johnny said, 'a boy twelve studying the drawings of Vesalius and reading very deep material at the age of twelve years! Will you imagine that.'

'And making paper posies, too,' the rancher said.

'Sir?' Johnny looked up and down the bar, from face to face. Now he felt a sudden need to impress them further, and quoted some Greek concerning flowers.

'What's that?' the rancher asked.

Johnny smiled, and glowed. 'Greek, sir. A doctor studies the Greek language, a part of his arduous training.'

'It don't sound like Greek to me,' the rancher said.

'I assure you, sir.'

The rancher laughed. 'You better go back then to your little school, wherever it was. The word in Greek for that sort of flower is πόθος. They put them on graves.'

The laughter was like a shot, and Johnny stood uncertainly, trying to understand and to focus on some face that might comfort him. He didn't find that face. 'Well, sir . . .'

Now the rancher spoke, and the room was quiet again, thick with quiet. 'Did you ever hear this one, doctor?' and the rancher quoted a line from Ovid in Latin, 'What do you think of that one?'

Johnny understood, and blushed the color of blood. 'Why would you say that to me?' he asked.

'Because I believe in telling the truth, doctor. Would you care to tell the fellows here what it means?'

'No, sir, I would not.'

'Then I'll tell them,' the rancher said. 'It means you're a horse's ass. And for that matter, so is your sissy of a son.'

Johnny removed his hat, smoothed his hair, and put his hat back on. He didn't take his eyes from the rancher. 'My son is not a sissy.'

'The boys around here say so.'

'Because he reads. Because he thinks.'

'Because he makes paper posies. Because he don't know a foul ball from a fly.'

Foolish of a small man like Johnny to lunge. Foolish of him to say, 'You can't call my son a sissy!' because the rancher could and the rancher did and did and did.

The rancher held Johnny by the front of his starched white shirt, held him and shook him, and then straightening his arm, flung Johnny like a wet rag so that he smacked the wall opposite and fell in a heap. There Johnny started to rise, but sank back. Then after a little, looking at nobody, he got to his feet and they watched him wander across the road, across the empty space to The Inn. His progress disturbed some magpies who had found a dead gopher and they cried at him.

'My God, what's happened to you?' Rose cried. 'Who tore, who tore your shirt?'

'I got in a fight, Rose.'

'Please, are you hurt?'

'No, Rose. I'm not hurt. I just want to go up to my bed.'

'To bed, John? If you're not hurt, why do you want to go up to the bed?'

'I don't know. But I want the bed.' He got up from the chair. 'Where is the boy, Rose?'

'I don't know where he is.'

'Where do you suppose he is?'

Rose spoke quietly. 'I think he went down to the river.'

'I wouldn't want him to see me fighting.'

'Please, don't worry about that.'

'Rose — Rose?'

'Yes, John.'

'Rose, I wasn't telling the truth. I wasn't worried about him seeing me fighting. Maybe the trouble with me is, I can't stand the truth?'

'I'm not sure I know what you're talking about, John.'

'Second ago, I said I didn't want Peter to see me fighting. I said that.'

'Yes.'

'And it wasn't the truth.'

'Why wasn't it? You wouldn't want him to see you fighting.'

'Yes, I would.'

'Why, why would you?'

Johnny screwed up his face. 'To show him I'm a good fighter.'

'There are better things to be. You know that.'

'If you're a good fighter, you can knock down anybody who tears your shirt and knocks you against the wall and says your son — says your son is a sissy.' Johnny closed his eyes. 'There, I said it.'

'Said what, John?'

'Said all the truth. What I wouldn't want him to see is his father knocked down against the wall, and fellows looking.'

'He didn't see, John.'

'Who can be sure? With so much noise in the place? You know how people hear a voice, and how they gather?'

'I'm certain he was by the river. He has a place there he goes.'

'You see, what a humiliation,' Johnny said, and stared a moment into his wife's eyes. 'What a terrible, terrible humiliation. For a boy.'

'Humiliation?' Rose said. 'For the boy or for you? How can there be humiliation if we're humble, as Christ tells?'

'Christ,' Johnny said. 'Would you fix me a cold towel.'

She fixed the towel, and applied it and watched him until he slept. She expected the usual when he woke, the request for a drink; for the next few days she would carefully portion out just enough so that he could function; he never asked for more than she thought necessary.

But now when he woke he lay there, staring, demanding nothing. Nothing. It was this time that she suggested he take a drink, for he had often told her that whiskey killed pain, and it was pain he had.

'No,' he said.

She brought him soup. It cooled, untouched. He lay with his hands clasped outside the covers; the day lengthened, the light faded, geese flew south. From the saloon across the vacant space came the bright tinkle of the player piano.

39

'Please close the window, Rose.'

It was not Rose who answered him, but Peter. 'I came to bring you something, father.'

Johnny opened his eyes, and smiled. His son stood in the middle of the room. 'To bring me something?'

'Can you see in this light, father?'

'Oh, certainly.'

'I did these things for you. This summer.'

Johnny sat up, and his son propped pillows behind his back, 'That feels good, Peter. The pillows. Now, what have you got there?'

'These drawings, father.'

Father, Johnny thought. My God, what a word, what a responsibility, and he took the drawings. There were ten, all of the root systems of plants from near the river. Johnny closed his eyes and sucked his lip. How they reminded him, in their excellence, of his own poor drawings! 'I'm mighty proud,' Johnny said. 'I never did so well.'

'You taught me,' Peter said. When Peter had gone, Johnny turned his face to the wall. So the boy knew, or had heard, for why else would he bring gifts, but out of pity?

During the next year, he didn't drink. He no longer sang; the flesh fell away from his face and his eyes invited no intimates. He spoke to few, and no one called him Johnny anymore. Late one fall afternoon, the air smelling strong of snow, Johnny returned from a trip out into the hills behind the town. He had delivered a woman of a dead child.

Lucky, lucky child, he thought. One soul who would never fail, would never cower before the inexorable naturalistic principle — that the weak are destroyed by the strong. Traveling up there in his old Ford motorcar to that tar paper shack he had looked down from the crest of the hill and seen the dust disturbed by the buggies and thin old saddle horses of the Indians thrown off the last of their land in the valley — thirty families, off to the reservation, wards of the government now, objects of stingy charity. So do the strong dispossess the weak. Some are singled out.

'I saw those Indians,' he told Rose that night.

'Maybe in some ways they'll be better off?'

'In some ways? But dispossessed, dispossessed. Rose, where is the boy?'

'In the shed out back. He says he has more things to show you.'

'He shouldn't work by lamplight. His eyes.'

'John?'

'Rose?'

'John, are you all right?'

'Yes, of course.'

'You looked funny for a minute.'

'Funny?'

'You had gone away. Left me.'

'I'm fine.' He smiled, then went suddenly to her and he kissed her. 'You're a brave person,' he said. 'Now I'll go see Peter and then I think I'll go upstairs.'

'Do you want anything? Is there anything?'

'No, there's nothing, Rose.'

The shed, over which the windmill whirled, was attached to the inn; a small wood stove made it comfortable, and it smelled of smoke and kerosene. Around the walls Peter had built shelves that sagged a little under the dead black weight of Johnny's medical books. There, too, were the stuffed bodies of gophers and rabbits, the beakers and retorts and such chemical paraphernalia; there Peter escaped the pain of the daily Gethsemane at school, the taunts and jibes; there he lost himself in a private world, the world he never doubted; sitting there at his table, his eyes had an inward

41

gaze, the withdrawn, intent look of the deaf. His pale face was so smooth Johnny wondered if he'd ever have to shave, and nothing betrayed his emotion but the faint throbbing of a vein in his right temple.

'Your mother says you have something new to show,' Johnny said.

'This new slide, father.'

Johnny approached. 'Peter, you seemed to be listening to something.' The boy had fixed a flashlight to a wooden stand that threw the beams exactly under the lens. 'Mmm. That's a rare one.' The slide was of a bacillus that kills rodents. 'And fine drawing, too.' Johnny straightened up slowly, and like an old man he reached around and pressed the small of his back, making a small grimace. 'You have fine hands, Peter. Let me take a look at one of your hands.' He took Peter's hand, and looked into the smooth palm. 'It's so funny, you know.'

'What's funny, father?'

'Oh,' and Johnny smiled, 'I guess it's funny that it's so hard for a father to speak. Maybe my own father found it so. Maybe that's why he never did. But I'm going to say just once what I mean. And what I mean to say, Peter, is that — I love you.'

Peter was silent then, and fixed his enormous eyes, eyes that seemed to reflect the entire room, the entire world, on his father. But the blue vein in his right temple, crooked as a worm, grew a little. Johnny was about to turn away when Peter spoke. 'Father,' he said, 'I love you, too.'

Johnny sucked in his lips, and when he could speak he said, 'So then, all is well. And if I was going to tell you one thing, you know what that would be?'

Above them the windmill turned in the cold, dry wind, that mill turning to no purpose, doing no work, going through the motions only. Johnny hadn't even conquered that, for it turned on him and cut him long before this brilliant son was born.

'I'm not sure, father,' Peter murmured.

'I would tell you, Peter, never to mind what people say. People can never know the heart of another.'

'I'll never mind what people say.'

'And Peter, please don't say it quite like that. Most who don't mind — most of them grow hard, get hard. You must be kind, you must be kind. I think the man you will become could hurt people terribly, because you're strong. Do you understand kindness, Peter?'

'I'm not sure whether I do, father.'

'Well, then. To be kind is to try to remove obstacles in the way of those who love or need you.'

'I understand that.'

Johnny sucked in his lips again. 'I've always been something of an obstacle, Peter. But now I feel good. Thank you for understanding. And so now I'm going to go.' But he stood yet another moment, a small smile on his lips, and then stepped suddenly forward and laid the flat of his hand on Peter's head. 'Good, good boy,' he said. Then he went out and went upstairs to one of the rooms up there.

Up there Peter found him later, having heard a noise.

'Peter?' Rose called. 'Peter? What on earth are you doing up there?'

Peter didn't answer. She called again in a stage whisper from the bottom of the stairs. 'Try not to wake your father. I think he's very tired.'

'I'll be right down.'

When he came down, he stood in the doorway of the kitchen, and he addressed her as 'Mother,' not 'Rose.' The word in his mouth sounded so odd, so formal that she turned from the stove where she boiled water for tea.

43

'Yes, Peter?'

He had apparently just completed combing his yellow hair, for he still bore in his right hand the black pocket comb he always carried, and before she spoke again he dragged his thumb over the teeth, and then again and again. She found the sound chilling. 'Peter, please.'

He stood looking past her, at the opposite wall. She turned to follow his eyes. 'What do you see there?'

Peter stood wondering what words he would use to tell her he had found his father upstairs, and had just cut him down from where he had hanged himself from one of those ropes coiled by the window for escape, in case of fire.

3

Neighbors, of course, and then tourists, having got wind of the suicide, pointed out The Inn as the place where 'it' had happened, and as customers drank in the saloon they gazed across at the whirling windmill and wondered at the courage of the handsome little woman who darted out to remove clothes from the line, touching this and that garment, who stooped to water flowers. Some longed to see her and the boy closer, to discover if in their faces there might yet remain some trace of the tragedy. She was now running the place as an eating house, but thanks to the stories she had but few customers: the room where one was eating might be just below where 'it' had happened, might point up the deaths and disappointments in their own lives.

But then many who had actually known Johnny moved away, for livings in and around Beech were marginal and desperate. As automobiles broke down less often, the man who had turned his barn into a roadside garage closed up and went away, weeds crowded in around the red gas pump. The chicken farm failed. The man who sold strange rocks and petrified wood had never made a go of it. There were new bartenders. The Inn itself was painted red now and renamed the Red Mill. Drummers passing through Beech were too tired to heed the old stigma or arrived too late at night to have been told about it — and anyway the only other choice was a dirty room above a store. The war, too, was distracting, and left people to cope with the curiously unsettling fact that men they'd known, had drunk with or quarreled with or loved or cheated — that such men had died in France, in trenches. How could it be, they thought, watching the sun sink down over the mountains in the west — how could it be that someone they knew could be dead in France?

Then for a time the saloons were closed, and Rose Gordon bought from one of them a two-thousand-dollar player piano for ten dollars! Then the saloons opened again — cautiously — run this time by bootleggers who raced Hudson automobiles down from Canada. Which was the faster, the Hudson or the Cadillac? Well, I'll tell you, the other day Paul McLaughlin, that attorney in Herndon in a Cadillac and Jerry Disnard the bootlegger in a Hudson, they got to going up the new highway, and McLaughlin started to pass Disnard . . .

So with the war and the bootleggers and their night driving down from Canada, the old suicide at the Red Mill drifted off into the misty land of myth and wonder. Some got it wrong and told that Johnny had shot himself. Some said he had taken a poison available to doctors. Some said he had simply disappeared, deserted his wife and child, and in any event the little woman who remained behind was a fine person with a lot of guts to stay there and turn the place into a kind of roadhouse. Folks from Herndon, the tony crowd, war-rich, would roar down the highway in Mercers and Stutzes and stop at the bootleggers' places and then have chicken at the place called the Red Mill. Did something with the batter on the chicken, and let me tell you!

Of course, you could have the steak if you wanted, and

there were stacks of hot biscuits to melt in your mouth and wilted lettuce salad. She made the coffee fresh when you came so it wasn't sitting around in those big urns like at other places, and then afterwards if you wanted to dance, there was a player piano, all the old ones, 'Just Like a Gypsy' and 'Joan of Arc' and the rest of the war tunes but who wants to think about that. 'Tea for Two' and 'By the Light of the Stars.'

The boy? Her boy? Waits tables, but she comes in and asks if all is to your liking, and everything always is.

No, but the boy.

How should I know? Almost through or half through high school, I guess. Oh, it's sort of that he *looks* at you. But doesn't see you, or doesn't want to see you. No, a lot of those bright kids are that way. Too much studying. I don't know. A doctor. Of *course* it costs a lot. Who in hell said it didn't? Why do you suppose she works so hard? No, you ought to drive out there sometime and if I was you, I'd make reservations. And I'd order the chicken, if I was you. And she might play the piano for you. That's what she did, once, played for a living, they say.

It was Peter who fattened the fryers, who mixed a sour-smelling mash of bran and skimmed milk the dryland farmers brought in, and when the fryers were fat, it was he who killed them because Rose couldn't, couldn't even watch, wouldn't watch. When killing time came she went inside and shut the doors and windows and sang and if necessary stopped her ears against the ungodly squawking as Peter quietly cornered first this and then that chicken in the corner of the pen. They knew what was coming, and Rose knew what was coming, so she stopped her ears or sang.

He wrung their heads off as kinder and surer and cleaner than using axe and block. He took a bird suddenly by the neck, twisted his wrist just so; the body twirled around twice and fell headless to the ground where it hopped and flopped and contracted and the discarded head beside it gazed with bright astonished eye at its own jerking body; only when the body faltered and lay quiet did the lid come down over the eye, and all was over, all was over. Never did Peter spatter blood on his clean shirt; he looked on this immaculate proficiency as a preparation for the future. Scalded, plucked and singed, the chickens could now be looked on by Rose as produce, and she could fry them.

All was now prepared for the Burbank outfit; a Burbank had telephoned the saloon and the bartender had come to say the Burbanks expected chicken for supper and beds for twelve; Rose moved out of her room and fixed a cot in the kitchen; Peter moved into the shed with his father's books. All was prepared, even a pencil nicely sharpened and laid beside the register. 'My,' Rose said, 'if the Burbanks will just come every year, and then the other ranches. My!'

Peter seldom smiled at anyone but his mother.

You could see the spirits of the young fellows perk up as they approached Beech; down there the country was a little more settled and the sharp eye could see the roofs of barns and houses on the pint-sized ranches down there; several automobiles plowed slowly through the herd that parted and flowed around the craggy-looking machines like water past a rock; the young cowhands showed off a little for the drivers and passengers in the cars, spurred their saddle horses on the off side so they shied and pranced like real wild stuff. Phil grinned. Damn young fools! But he felt a real affection for them; they might not be of the quality of cowhands of years before, of the quality of men like Bronco Henry, but they were the best there was, these days, and in a way George was right as rain: you had to ride with the times, to accept the automobiles and the signs the drugstores tacked up on fenceposts and plastered against the sides of abandoned barns and sheds; Phil guessed they'd never again have Mrs Lewis pack a lunch big enough to last them for supper in Beech now that woman had started up her place. Fact was, Phil could do with a good chicken dinner himself! Fact was, his stomach was doing a powerful might of growling!

And like as not they'd run into some old-timers at the bar who remembered the country as it used to be, and they could chew the fat and have a shot or two. Phil enjoyed setting up drinks for friends, and he liked how when the Burbank outfit drove in, the town was theirs. The riffraff pretty well kept their distance, stayed away from the bar, the Mexican section hands who couldn't even talk United States, the ignorant dryland farmers and sheepherders from north of town.

If there was anything Phil hated, it was drunkenness; it offended his keen instinct for order and decorum. Now, you take a drunk: he'll get hold of you and chew your ear off with drivel. He'll pretend he's something he's not, too big for his britches. And you can insult them or do any God damned thing to put them in their place and they'll keep right on spouting. Phil remembered a time some years before when he'd been standing there at the bar enjoying the atmosphere and this barfly waltzed in and began to make himself objectionable. Now, Phil didn't mind people taking a drink or two — he took a drink or two himself sometimes. But Jesus H. Christ!

You take when you've been trailing cattle twenty-five miles down the road and you've got your face all fixed for a drink and some loudmouthed scissorbill of a barfly; by

49

rights, the barkeep ought to throw them out, but if they don't, what are you going to do?

Phil had the fellow sized up right off, had from the beginning, soon's the fellow'd come to Beech — oh, when was it? There'd been complaints about the fellow before; just happened Phil had never run up against him. Well, once was enough!

Used to be a drunk of a sheepherder come in — come in with his bitch of a dog and Phil hated animals in the house where humans are. This bitch'd lie sniffing at the sheep-herder's feet, gazing up at him, watching his loose mouth. That bozo would talk your ear off about that dog, how smart she was, how fast, how quick, how trusting, how loyal, and by God how loving.

'That little dog,' the sheepherder said, hanging onto the bar to keep from falling over, 'that little dog is just like my wife.'

'Wouldn't surprise me,' Phil had said dryly. But the sheepherder didn't get it. Just went driveling on. By and by somebody led him out and there was peace and quiet in the joint, and Phil sighed.

You can't win every time and Phil had got caught with this duffer who for God's sakes talked to the company at large about flowers, and to Phil in particular. There was poor Phil there, stuck. Silly duffer in town Phil wouldn't have trusted as far as you could throw a cat by the tail. And then when Phil had tried to make it as plain as the nose on his kisser that his company wasn't desired. So then — well, what the hell.

'I wouldn't a done that,' George told Phil.

'Sure you wouldn't,' Phil said cheerfully. 'You didn't have to listen to him.'

Old George was a great one for feeling sorry for people.

Phil wondered right now how much it had to do with feeling sorry for people that made George make arrangements to eat and sleep at that woman's place. For that half-baked barfly had suicided some years back. Loco.

Phil now rode over beside George. 'Well, Fatso, there it is ahead of you — the metropolis of Beech.'

George nodded. 'There it is all right.'

'Looks pretty quiet in town. Guess they're all under cover. Ought to get the bunch in easy.'

'Seems like.'

Phil frowned. 'What the hell's wrong with you, Fatso?'

'Not a thing, Phil.'

'Seems to me, it hurts you to take two words and hitch them up.'

'I was never much of a one for talk, Phil.'

'You're no Edison talking machine, that's a gut.' Phil rode off at an angle through the herd, and then came up beside one of the young fellows. 'I'm so hungry,' he remarked, 'that my big gut's eating my little gut.' The young fellow laughed at this, but still Phil didn't feel good. Twenty-five years, a kind of silver anniversary, and there'd been something sour about the whole drive. Exactly what, he couldn't tell. Was it age? He was just forty. Had the times got out of hand? Then he laughed. There for a minute, he'd begun to feel sorry for himself!

It was four in the afternoon when the Burbank outfit, tall and proud, rode into Beech; it had seldom been so quiet. The cowhands knew people watched admiring from the windows, and the girls upstairs would be prettying themselves, getting themselves ready. Even the wind seemed quieter. Far across, high on the hill, a few wild horses grazed. Seldom had it been so quiet, yet Phil kept his eyes peeled for any scissorbill wandering out to spook cattle. Nobody did; not a dog barked; the lead steers stood stiff-legged only a moment before the wide gate, heads down, sniffing, then they suddenly bucked on through giving the good swift kick at the gate posts. In fifteen minutes the herd was safe inside, the heavy plank gate closed on them, eighty thousand dollars' worth of steers.

'Never seen it quieter,' Phil said. 'Eh, Fatso? Never saw 'em go in so easy.'

'For a fact,' George said.

'Well, Chatterbox,' Phil said, 'what say we mosey over and rinse the dust off our tongues?'

The young cowhands made happy sounds, and the old cowhand, oldest in the bunkhouse, smiled. Sitting straight, spurs jingling, they rode over to the saloon and tied up at the hitchracks. Inside, Phil grinned. 'Set 'em up for the outfit,' he said, and the barkeep did, except for the two who had already gone around the side and up the outside stairway. Phil had winked at them. They wouldn't be seen for maybe half an hour.

'Well,' George said. 'I'll mosey over to the telegraph office and see if they know anything about the power.' The power. It was a cant term, half slang, half esoteric. As engineers used 'slipstick' for 'slide rule' and realtors 'pass papers' when they transfer property, so did ranchers refer to 'the power' when they meant the locomotive. Without the power, only the cars already spotted at the chutes could be loaded.

'They already phoned it'll be late,' Phil remarked. 'Well, don't get lost in the streets,' and he watched George walk stiff and straight across the sagebrush space toward the depot. Poor George, Phil thought. He made people uncomfortable and he knew it. The young fellows couldn't enjoy their drinks, couldn't whoop it up with George around; they kept their eyes lowered and tried to watch their talk, with George around, and to see the girls they walked around outside and took the back stairs, and the girls never came down later, with George around. Nobody liked to put a nickel in the music box, and any place George graced was a funeral, for sure. Now, he'd go over there to the station and shoot the breeze with the operator and stay out of sight as long as he could. Anyway, it was considerate of him.

That is not to say that Phil himself ever had traffic with whores or told fast stories or jigged around like some men his age; that crap was not for him, not his dish. He was a Burbank, too, and his personal standards were — well. But he was tolerant — life had taught him that — and the men knew it, and he got a kick out of seeing them frolic around, even if they made damned fools of themselves. It embarrassed George.

For instance, as it grew dark (it looked as if the power was going to be even later) Phil went out back behind the saloon to take a quick leak, and there was the youngest of the young fellows sitting on the running board of an automobile, slumped there with his noggin bending low between his knees, already sick. Car must have belonged to some one of his sidekicks come down the highway from Herndon. Phil had to laugh. One of the young fellow's friends was poking the kid, trying to get him to come alive.

'Go way, go way,' the young fellow kept moaning. 'Oh, Jesus, go way.'

And the friend kept insisting. 'Come on now. We got to do it. We got to do it now.'

'Oh, go way, please just go way.' In the white light from the gas lamp inside the poor young kid's face was green. The kid'd remember that a long time, being sick, and hearing the bright music from the music box.

Phil finished his leak, sighed with comfort (his teeth had

been floating) and he buttoned his levis, and walked over to the kid. 'Having fun?'

'Oh, Phil,' the kid said, looking up with eyes like little boiled beets. 'Oh, Phil.'

Phil chuckled. 'You'll maybe be all right after you eat.'

'Oh dear Christ, don't say eat. I'm gonna die.'

'Die, hell,' Phil laughed. 'You got years and years of misery ahead for you.'

When *were* they going to eat, anyway? They all sure required more than the pickled egg, herring and peanuts handed out in the bar. If the power had been there, they'd be loaded by now, filled with grub and in the hay. But it wouldn't be the first time they'd loaded by lantern light.

'Recall one time,' Phil said seriously inside, and told of loading cattle there in the dead of night in the dead of winter, in the days of Bronco Henry. 'Fifty below it was,' he recalled. 'You got to be careful in that weather. This fool greenhorn working for the Ainsworths got all gowed up on booze and was chasing cattle around the pen and breathing deep through his mouth. Frosted his lungs. Dead the next day.' He turned. 'And where in hell you been?' he now asked George, who had appeared out of nowhere.

'Telegraph fellow asked me to his place up over the station for a cup of java. Got a real nice little place up there, nice little wife.'

'What's the story on the power?'

'Won't be in till morning. Stopped over at the eat-joint and said we'd be over pretty quick to eat.'

The woman over there at the eat-joint had pushed three tables together so there was room for the whole bunch. She greeted George and Phil pleasantly enough, so her suicide husband mustn't have tipped his hand about being taken by the scruff of the neck. Well, hell, what man would dare tell a woman a shameful thing like that? She had got out white napkins for each place, quite an experience, Phil thought, for the cowhands who had about as much use for napkins as for finger bowls. La-di-dah. Worth the price of admission to see what the fellows did with them. The place was kind of roadhousey, and Phil guessed that accounted for the candles she had in old wine bottles.

And the paper flowers, the paper flowers.

Phil would have preferred to have had the whole place to himself, just for the Burbank outfit, but over in one corner was a party of six that gawked at them when they entered. Phil always had hated strangers around gawking and whispering and touching their lips with their napkins as if they were ladies and gentlemen. One of the women was smoking a cigarette, bold as brass and twice as cheap, and my wasn't she trying to look elegant touching her lips with her napkin, like real quality, and then smoking that cigarette! It was Phil's opinion that a woman who would smoke in public would do anything. And she was. She was drinking.

Over there, too, were paper flowers on the table, paper flowers in a bottle painted so it wouldn't look like a milk bottle.

'Well, where's the service?' Phil asked aloud. 'If we can't get the power, we ought to get the service, eh, lads.' The young cowhands, cowed by the prissy roadhousey atmosphere and the napkins looked at Phil, admiring his poise.

Then there came through the swing door the woman's son with a white napkin over his arm, just so. He wore pressed dark trousers and white starched shirt, and smiled at them there at the table, at the Burbank outfit, and went right on past to the table in the corner. Phil made a harsh chuckle. 'Hmmmm,' he said aloud. 'I guess we-all must be black.'

Well, there's one thing Phil could tell you: that young kid with a napkin over his arm was a sissy. Phil watched him standing there by the party of six. A little bit too heel-clicky to suit Phil, a little too spruce, funny little arrogance. Must have been the kid's idea of some Frog waiter, something picked up from some moving picture he'd gone to, or maybe some fool story in a magazine.

Yes, the kid was talking to the party of six and yes, the kid had a little lisp just like every sissy Phil had ever heard, and a way of tasting his own words. Now, some people can get along with them, just as some can get along with Jews and shines, and that's their business. But Phil couldn't abide them.

He didn't know why, but they made him uncomfortable, right down to his guts. Why in hell didn't they snap out of it and get human?

And oh, didn't that sissy kid just walk right by them, with that glance of his, and the lips set in a way that made Phil want to smack them!

'Yeah,' and Phil leaned back in his chair so the front legs were off the floor. 'I guess we-all must be black.'

George sat there like the Great Stone Face.

Hmmm! Phil knew how to get the kid's goat, and he chuckled, thinking of it. Imagine having a kid like that! Oh, Phil knew how to get his goat. Phil was sitting at one end of the improvised festive board, George at the other, just as they sat for breakfast at the back dining room table now that the Old Lady and the Old Gent were leading the social life in Brigham Young's paradise, as Phil called Salt Lake City.

Now at that table in the town of Beech in the year 1924 at around eight of a fall evening, he reached across the table and picked the paper flowers out of the painted milk bottle; they did look absurd in his cracked, chapped, long-fingered hands. He had cut himself at noon opening a sardine can, and had neither mentioned the fact nor wiped off the blood. So there the flowers were, helpless in that marvelously clever hand.

'My, oh my,' he said, 'but I wonder what young lady made these pretty posies?' And he leaned to smell them, brought them to his thin, sensitive nose.

It surprised him that the boy didn't color. The pale face remained pale, and Phil noted only the slight throbbing of a blue vein in the boy's temple, a vein that emerged suddenly, like a worm. The boy then turned and marched right over.

'The flowers? I made them, sir. My mother taught me how. She has a way with flowers.'

Phil leaned over and elaborately put the flowers back, and touched them, pretending to arrange them. 'Oh, do pardon me,' and he made a broad wink at the company around.

'Would you care to give your order now, sir?'

Phil leaned back on the hind legs of his chair. His voice was a drawl. 'I thought we had that settled. I thought we'd made previous arrangements.'

Now George spoke, first harrumphing. 'It's the chicken we want, boy.'

The men had decided to ignore the napkins. George did with his what you're supposed to do. Phil then tucked his own under his chin and leaned forward to enjoy his chicken. He was bound to admit it was good, but maybe because of hunger sauce. The party of six had pulled their freight, hightailed it, and the kid fussed over there clearing up and putting out their candles. Phil felt a lot freer with the party of six gone, and he told an amusing story of Bronco Henry who had got himself plastered there in Beech one time years ago after they'd got the cattle loaded, and he woke up next morning in the barn across the road with a halter around his neck, tied up like a horse to the manger. One of his pals had pulled the trick on him. 'And let me tell you,' Phil laughed, 'he looked pretty sheepish.'

'Well,' George said, 'you fellows go on over, and I'll settle up here.'

'Ain't he brought you the tab yet?' Phil asked.

'No, you all go on over to the lights and the music,' George said, pretty fancy talk for him, 'and I'll settle up.'

So they scraped their chairs back and went over. The girls from upstairs had come down and stood at the bar smoking cigarettes and smiling around and cadging drinks and Phil watched the young fellows oblige. He felt strangely remote, even lonely, and sort of wished he wasn't a Burbank, something like that, something. Those kids'd all have big heads in the morning, loading cattle, and maybe pick up the clap or syph, but they were sure kicking up their heels now, and maybe, who knew, maybe it was worth it. They threw their little bit of money around and loved up the ladies, and then they began to sing.

. . . hot time in the old town, tonight.

Most of them didn't know the words, just went la-la-la, but Phil remembered them, and he looked into his empty glass and moved his lips with the true words. How he recalled being a punk kid at the time of the Spanish War, brass bands in those days in every park in every city, fireworks every Fourth; gone, proud, dead days. Wasn't it on such a day he'd first laid eyes on Bronco Henry?

. . . hot time in the old town tonight.

Phil went out to take another leak, and looked off toward the east where the moon was about to rise. He sighed and shivered, buttoned his pants and when he was through, he walked around the saloon, all through with them in there, and across the sagebrush space to the hotel — Red Mill, for a fact. Nobody there at the desk, so he just went to work and picked up the pencil and wrote his name and George's because George had apparently forgot that little nicety.

Upstairs, Phil peeked in first one room and then another, but George wasn't in any of them, so he went into the last one he looked into, took off his shoes and pants and slid into the hay. He'd have to stay awake until he heard George's heavy, familiar footsteps on the stairs, and then call him in there.

The moon was up, the room full and bright with moon. It caught the white pitcher and basin, the tall narrow wardrobe, caught the coil of hempen rope underneath the window; Phil turned this way and that way in bed and then on his back he stared up and thought about how they tell you when you're a punk kid that the moonlight will drive you batty. He got up, tall and thin in his long underwear and walked to the window. The moon was strange on him. Where in hell was George? He suddenly smiled to himself, remembering the Old Lady's words.

Go find George. Go find your brother. Different as they were, they were both brothers. And one thing at least they had in common — a blood tie.

George was probably with the telegraph fellow. Phil walked in his stocking feet to the opposite window. Hey, Georgie boy . . .

The windows in the upper part of the station were dark; in the moonlight the arm of the semaphore was raised to signal the power when it came, and the moonlight quarreled with the pale white eye of the lantern on the switch. Beyond, the moonlight lay like water on the stubble that grew on the hill that rose behind the town, and it picked out the gravestones at the bottom, stones like a handful of dice rolled down.

Had he dozed? Had Phil dozed? For George was standing in profile in the room, simply standing, but Phil felt he had caught George at something. Something, for who would stand still in the middle of a room?

'George?'

'Mmmm.'

Phil felt George's weight sag the bed. Then George leaned over and pulled off his boots, grunting at the effort; then George rose, to loose his belt.

'Where you been?' Phil whispered. 'The others bedded down yet?'

Came a long silence. Then George spoke. 'What you said tonight, Phil, said about her boy, made her cry.'

Her?

Her!

Well, then. So the kid had run to mama, or mama had been eavesdropping at the swinging door. Her! Phil snuffled up an obstruction in his nose and swallowed. However George had been concerned about 'her,' Phil was not concerned that George would blame him. Far as Phil knew, George never blamed anybody, a virtue so remote and inhuman it probably accounted for the discomfort people felt in his presence; his silence they took for disapproval and it allowed them no chink to get at him and quarrel with him. His silence left people guilty and they had no chance to dilute their guilt with anger. Inhuman! But Phil felt no guilt. He always called the cards as they fell, played the cards as they were.

If she was behind the swinging door when he'd spoken — well, she shouldn't have been listening, and if she had, what of it? Wouldn't hurt her to know what people thought of the kid. Maybe she'd get hep to herself and put a bug in his ear, get him straightened out.

But what had kept George down there so long? Had he stood and talked to her? Had she cried on his shoulder? Had he touched and fondled her? The idea of such a thing made Phil wince. As George climbed into bed, Phil licked his lips. Damned if he could imagine George touching and fondling a woman.

Phil spoke into the moonlight. 'Hear anything about the power?'

'Nope,' George said.

She was crying.

She!

4

Phil saw George.

Phil's eyes were day-blue. Expressionless? But some said innocent. But they were sharp, very sharp eyes, and the iris was no less sensitive than the cornea; so the subtlest change in light or shadow alerted Phil. Just as his bare hands sensed the hidden rot at the heart of the wood, the secret weakness, so did his eyes see around and beyond and into. He saw through Nature's pathetic fraud called protective coloring, saw the vague outline of the stock-still doe, camouflaged against dry, thick branches, leaf and earth; smiling, he shot to kill. He knew if a timber wolf was lame, noted the fainter print of the favored paw in dust or snow, saw a quivering in the stubble and watched the grass snake unhinge its jaws and bolt down tiny new mice while the mother leapt in circles, screaming. His eyes followed the ragged flight of magpies seeking carrion, the bloated animal, the leg of beef gone rotten and dragged out behind the woodshed. In the sudden elbow of a stream where the baffled water turned upon itself he watched the trout 'conceal' itself in the shadow of a rock. But he saw more than Nature's creatures. In Nature herself — in the supposedly random and innocent way she disposed and arranged herself — he saw the supernatural. In the outcropping of rocks on the hill that rose up before the ranchhouse, in the tangled growth of sagebrush that scarred the hill's face like acne he saw the astonishing figure of a running dog. The lean hind legs thrust the powerful shoulders forward; the hot snout was lowered in pursuit of some frightened thing — some idea — that fled across the draws and ridges and shadows of the northern hills. But there was no doubt in Phil's mind of the end of that pursuit. The dog would have its prey. Phil had only to raise his eyes to the hill to smell the dog's breath. But vivid as that huge dog was, no one but one other had seen it, George least of all.

'What do you see up there?' George had once asked.

'Nothing.' But Phil's lips were twisted in the faint smile of one who is in close touch with the arcane. So Phil lived — watching, noting, figuring — as the rest of us see and forget.

Now he stood at the forge in the blacksmith shop, gazing out through the wide doorway; one foot up on a block of wood he'd nailed to the side of the forge, he rested an arm along the smooth, worn beam of the bellows; he bent his long body easily at the waist; the bellows expanded, collapsed, a huge leather lung forcing the flames that heated strap iron for a sled runner. He watched the coal smoke drift out and settle low over the dry ryegrass, a dirty gray quilt. He sniffed, and scented certain snow.

It was a Sunday. The night before the young hired men had run off to town with friends who'd come in old used cars, gone off in their cheap suits with a check in their hands they'd cash at one of the saloons in Beech or Herndon — if they got that far. Phil smiled. Before breakfast Monday they'd be back — sick, hollow-eyed, broke, maybe diseased. Phil heard the bright clink of the latch on the bunkhouse door, saw the door open and two of the older men haul out a washtub of water and dump it; he watched them watch the water run and spread, sink into the earth. Age had taught them abstinence, if nothing else. Sundays they used to bathe, to wash clothes, pounding their socks and drawers with a coffee tin tacked onto the end of a shovel handle; they shaved, slapped on bay rum and then sat and rocked. Those who could write wrote letters, squeezing the pencil, squinting and forcing the cranky ABC's between the wide lines of their coarse tablets. Later, they would shoot a few games of horseshoes or take a twenty-two rifle and pop off magpies back in the willows near the secret place where Phil bathed himself. Near there he had once in the late spring found a ramshackle nest — twigs every which way — and four young 'pies just on the verge of flight. The old ones coaxed the young, yammering away calling, encouraging. For the fun of it, Phil captured the young ones, took them back to the barn in a gunnysack — an idle thing to do, and once he got them home, he lost interest in them. They say if you slit their tongues, they'll talk, but Phil had long ago found out that isn't true.

It was a Sunday (like today) and he turned them over to one of the men in the bunkhouse who said he knew right well what to do with them.

'Miserable bastards,' the fellow had growled. For magpies ride about on the backs of horses and cattle and pick at sores they find there and eat the living flesh. They light on the ground in the spring and walk perkily forward, eyes bright, twisting their heads, seeing everything; they mean to pick a newborn calf's eyes out.

The fellow had some dynamite caps, the size of twenty-two cartridges. 'Naw,' the fellow said, 'I used to do some blasting.' Up the anus of each magpie, he shoved a cap, and then a short length of fuse. Everybody gathered out behind the bunkhouse to watch. The sun was warm and promising;

some men were called from the barn where they sunned themselves and chewed on matches.

'What's going on?' Phil asked.

One of the men, a card, chuckled. 'Ass-ass-ination,' he remarked.

'Well, you miserable bastards,' the ass-ass-in said. One by one he tossed the young 'pies into the air. Their strange chance to escape gave them a brief skill and they soared, and leveled off, and then one by one they exploded up there; a few feathers drifted down like ash. Well, it was a quick death, quicker than shooting them or wringing their necks, and not a purposeless death either, like most, for it had afforded a little fun on a Sunday, Phil thought. 'To be perfectly frank,' he nodded to himself, moving his lips. Alone, Phil often talked or laughed to himself, aware that he did so, knowing it was not the speech of madness but merely his way of heightening or giving permanence to some thought as others will take a pencil and write it down. But he wasn't sure he approved of what the fellow had done, and after the first two birds had exploded, he frowned and walked away.

'What are they doing out back there?' George had asked.

'Usual thing,' Phil had said. 'Shooting at targets.'

'Doesn't sound like a rifle,' George had said. Phil had gone into their bedroom and lain down on the bed, angry with himself and somehow angry with George. They had always been close, their lives had so complemented each other's, one thin, one stocky, one clever, one plodding — they were like a single twin, and it irritated Phil when he couldn't be frank; he felt lost and angry.

Now he removed his foot from the block nailed to the forge, chose the proper hammer from the rack beside him, took the length of strap iron to the anvil and began to beat and temper it; he thought George might hear the ringing anvil and mosey out and talk, if he ever finished reading his everlasting *Saturday Evening Post*. George had picked it up after breakfast, gone to his chair in the living room, crossed his legs, and begun to read. Recently he read the livelong day, and it was pulling teeth to get anything out of him. George never read anything worthwhile, as Phil did. Phil saw no point in reading short stories, stories about animals, mystery stories; you learn more about animals from observing them than from reading about them, more about mystery in simply contemplating.

Yes, it did smell of snow, and wasn't it early in the day for the wind to rise? It whined in the rigging of the windlass they used to hoist up a fresh-killed beef; Phil looked off there to the butcher pen. Two magpies had lighted on the cowhide thrown over the fence flesh-side out, and they were rapt, cleaning it of remaining flesh and fat; the sudden wind blew them off balance and Phil smiled; how they scrabbled around before they got their footing and went to stuffing themselves again!

He returned to the forge with the strap iron, and looked out across the ryegrass that shook and shivered in the morning wind — useless stuff. Then Phil saw George.

He saw George walking across the road to the garage, and Phil took his foot down from the block.

What was George up to?

George opened one of the garage doors.

Phil paused, the bellows collapsed and sighed, the fire sank down, Phil watched George.

Something wrong with the old Reo?

Mmmm, Phil said to himself.

When George opened one of the garage doors it meant that he was going to work on the car, take out one of the spark plugs and clean it with his pocketknife, blow through the fuel line, God knew what all.

Phil felt it was good for George to have — and to feel he had — a special skill and function; thus Phil always allowed George to do the actual palavering with the cattle-buyers, merely listening to be sure George didn't make a fool of himself. Recently Phil had gone out there to see what George was up to and found George sitting in the front seat behind the wheel, just sitting there. Phil had joined him. 'What doing there? Dreaming?'

George had looked at him, and then coughed and then leaned forward and reached up under the dashboard, as if something were up under there. 'Fuse,' George murmured.

'I wondered what you were up to.'

'Oh, I'm never up to much, I guess,' George said.

Phil couldn't remember George working on the car on Sunday, and George hadn't said anything about anything being wrong with it, and there'd been plenty of opportunity to say, if there was.

Phil stood in the wide doorway of the shop spraddle-legged, looking with his day-blue eyes across to the garage. He had built it himself there under the hill before the house.

Now George was inside the garage, and Phil was just about to walk over there when the other door opened! Strange, on a Sunday morning, to see both doors open!

George was starting the car. In a moment blue plumes of smoke shot out the exhaust pipe, then turned gray, then white, and George was backing out, the gray day showing pale on the little oval window at the rear of the old Reo. Without looking back, George drove down the road.

Phil watched from the shop until the car was a black speck disappearing over the rise down there, upended the unfinished sled runner against the wall of the shop and walked swiftly to the house. In the bedroom he lay on his back on the bed, his fingers threaded under the back of his head; he lay there awhile and then sat up and took his banjo down from the shelf in the closet, got it out of the case and picked at it a little, head cocked, frowning. A little out of tune?

Cleared his throat, looked straight ahead, and tried 'Red Wing,' and then 'Jolly Coppersmith.' When the notes of that had died away, he cleared his throat and put the banjo away. It was all right, it was in tune. He lay down again.

The triangle at the back door rang for dinner. Phil heard the men clattering in to the back dining room; the outside door slammed behind them and they seemed to be having a good time, laughing and joking. Phil heard the angry voice of Mrs Lewis, maybe crabbing about the men's letting the cold in — sort of an old joke; then Phil got up and stood in the room because Mrs Lewis might now come into the hall to announce dinner and Phil didn't like people to see him lying down, not even on Sunday. When Mrs Lewis lumbered into the front dining room with the big roast, Phil was already at the table, looking out across the gray fields with his day-blue eyes.

'Brother George has gone down the road,' he told Mrs Lewis. 'He ain't back yet. Put a slab of meat on a plate and some spuds in the warming oven for him when he comes.'

'You expect him, then,' Mrs Lewis said.

'Yes, I expect him,' Phil said. When Mrs Lewis had gone into the kitchen and closed the door against the unholy racket of the hired men, Phil went around to George's place where by habit Mrs Lewis had set the roast, cut himself off a chunk, helped himself to braised potatoes and turnips, and took it around to his own place. He looked out the window again, and then set to. Before he had finished, Mrs Lewis brought in the soggy peach cobbler. It had begun to snow.

Dinner over and Mrs Lewis vanished to her quarters out back, Phil lay down again. Animals he and George had killed looked down with eyes that wanted washing — three deer, an elk, a mountain sheep, a mountain goat. The antelope had always been there.

Phil had to smile. When they were kids, and Phil those two years older, kids six and eight, Phil used to spoof George, spoof him and tell him the antelope was alive. Didn't George see it shake its head once in awhile? George's eyes would get big and his mouth would pucker and he'd turn to the wall.

'You can't get away from him,' Phil would say. 'He's looking at you right now, and a-shaking his old mean head.' It'd make George wet the bed in his sleep, and Phil would tease about that, too. The Old Lady had had to get George a rubber sheet. He bet he could make George blush about that sheet right now.

But all the other animals they'd killed themselves. The Old Gent never killed anything, wasn't any kind of hunter, never even a rancher, really, a gentleman rancher, so to speak. Somebody must have given the antelope to the Old Gent, somebody trying to suck up to him.

The animals looked down. It had got so dark Phil had a notion to turn on the light, but he had never done that in daytime, and never would. The snow was coming fast. Suppose it kept on like this, and Georgie boy got stuck in the snow? Did he have his snow chains with him?

Although George was slow to learn, once he learned, he never forgot anything, kept it locked inside him. You could say, George, how many benches of hay did we stack in 1916? and he'd tell you, and you could check with the figures he kept in the roll-top in the office. He never used a bookmark or turned down the page of a book because he could remember the number of the page he stopped on, a curious mechanical knowledge, a mechanical memory that many such people are said to have. Phil thought it was because George's mind was slower than his own that George could remember so. George didn't think about so many things, and riveted his entire brain on those few things.

Thus George never forgot to pull up the weights of the big clock that stood by the front door in the living room. Every Sunday afternoon at exactly four, George rose from his chair, walked to the clock, looked it straight in the face, reached up on top where the key was hidden, inserted the key in the long narrow glass door, turned it, opened the door, reached in with his thick, soft hands, carefully that he might not disturb the heavy brass pendulum that caught a pattern of light, two wedges, their points kissing at the center; then George pulled on first one and then the other chain, hand over hand, as if climbing a rope, slowly, strongly, surely. Having closed the little door and hidden away the little key, George would again look straight into the face of the clock, and then at his accurate pocket watch.

And that was that! But wonderful to watch. It was more than watching a man wind a fool clock. It was watching a man seeing to it that things went on as they had, and always would.

When the Old Lady and the Old Gent had run off to Salt Lake City to live in the fancy hotel in the middle of a winter week after a sort of set-to between them and Phil, the clock was briefly left an orphan, for the Old Gent had always wound it. Phil wondered what would happen when four o'clock came without the Old Gent, and made opportunity to be in the living room at three, and read *Asia* awhile so it wouldn't be obvious he wanted to know what would happen at four. He hated tipping his hand. He had begun reading the same line over and over after the clock struck the three-quarter hour. Suppose at four that George made no move, just sat there with the *Saturday Evening Post*? Should he prompt George, or should he wind the clock himself? No, it was not the sort of responsibility he himself wanted nor thought he should have to shoulder.

There was a little click, tiny gears meshing; then a small interval of time. Then came the chimes announcing the hour.

BONG.

Phil snuffed up an obstruction. The sound died off in the room. Phil could almost smell the death of time. Then George rose. George laid the *Saturday Evening Post* in the seat of his chair without looking at it and walked to the clock.

The whole operation was done by George with the dignity of the Old Gent, and Phil, smiling to himself behind *Asia* magazine, knew that George had been watching the Old Gent for years, preparing himself for this moment of stepping easily into the breach. Phil needn't have worried, but you do wonder sometimes if people are what you think they are, or if you only think that they are and they are what they are and not what you think.

For a moment Phil wanted to rise and congratulate George for not disppointing him, for being what he hoped he was, thought he was, knew he was. But of course that wouldn't do, because there had never been any spoken sentiment between them and never would be. Their relationship was not one based on words. He'd never known anybody yet who talked too much who wasn't a God damned fool.

So there was no reason to wonder whether George had

his snow chains with him, except that he had left so suddenly. The chains were kept stretched between two spikes driven in the wall of the garage so they wouldn't tangle; that was like George, too. But suppose it kept on snowing, and he didn't have his chains?

Phil felt he needed a little fresh ozone anyway, so he picked up his hat from the top of the bookcase where they had always kept their hats and the binoculars, slapped it on his head, got into his old blue denim jumper, and walked through the living room past the clock and out. Snowing pretty hard, all right. He paused and breathed deep, looking into the falling snow. He hacked and spit. Couple of stray cattle hunched up there on the hill against the barbed wire fence.

He stood in the garage out of the snow and wind; the concrete floor was hidden under the clay the Reo had brought in over the years, two humpy ridges of it where it fell out from under the fenders, or whatever you call them.

And no chains on the spikes.

Course not. Phil knew George wouldn't forget. George hadn't forgot to wind the clock, either, for in passing it Phil had noticed the weights had already been pulled up out of sight. George had wound it sometime before he went off down the road — had never intended getting home by four! Serve George right if he got stuck and had to walk the whole damned distance from where he'd got stuck. But when he did get home, damned if Phil was going to make any inquiries, and that was a gut! You bet your little own sweet life, it was a gut! He tramped back to the house and lay on his bed.

Just past midnight an automobile pulled into the side yard.

Ah!

But it was only the young fellows coming home from a spree. Until he heard them talking and singing and then somebody shouting, 'Oh for Christ's sake cut the comedy' — until then Phil thought they might have rescued George and brought him home, but if they'd had George with them, they'd not be singing out there. Phil sat up in bed and then swung his long legs down over the side, thinking maybe he'd ought to go out and see if they'd seen anything of George. But why would they hear? And it would look bad. No need for them to know anything — that George was gone. Phil lay down again and laced his long fingers behind his head.

The clock struck two.

Then George came. Instead of coming right into the bedroom and undressing in the dark and getting right into the hay, he remained for some time in the living room. Sitting in a chair? Standing by the fireplace under the Old Lady's portrait? Smoking? Whatever George was doing, he was quiet about it. Phil waited.

Then by and by George walked down the hall and turned into the room. Phil heard him sit on the bed, heard the squeak. George grunted and pulled off his boots. No, not his boots. His shoes. Sounded like shoes. Then Phil saw George's black shadow rise, and George was unbuckling his belt.

Phil made a sudden groan, a wild-animal sound as if surfacing out of sleep. 'Ahhhh!' he groaned several times. 'Hey — who's there?'

'Pipe down,' George said quietly. 'It's me.'

'What in hell time is it?' Phil wondered if George, for some reason, would lie.

'After two.'

73

'Christ! Wake a man up this hour.'

'Well, go back to sleep.'

'No, guess I'll have me a smoke, long's I been woke.' Phil's hands were never confused by the dark. He reached out, felt for and picked up his book of papers and tobacco. Match flared, and he took a drag and coughed. 'Run into any snow down below?'

'None to speak of,' said George.

'How far down'd you get?' asked Phil.

'Beech. That's where I aimed for.'

'Beech?' And then Phil violated a principle. He pried. But he covered up the violation with a light, light voice and a jaunty lilt. 'What you doing down there, Georgie boy? Maybe a little tom-cattin'?'

Small silence, and the wind under the door. 'I was talking with Mrs Gordon.'

'Yeah. She cried on your shoulder, didn't she.'

'So she did.'

She! She could mean the end of the world, as Phil knew it.

Ever since they were kids some of the Eastern relatives would wander out every few years to be entertained, and with them they'd bring friends, girls usually, and it was pretty obvious by the time he and George could get a hard on what the Old Lady had in mind, and it was pretty obvious what the girls had in mind too. Indigent aristocrats, Phil called them, come out to recoup their fortunes. All of them talked as if they had a pork chop wedged in their teeth. Phil had little use for dudes, male or female, and from the first he simply took to the high timber whenever they were around, and George would get caught with them for the picnics the Old Lady arranged; George would have to take

74

them off to Yellowstone Park. Good Lord! When George first started riding herds of relatives and indigent aristocrats off to Yellowstone Park, they had those old six-horse stages.

All George had to do was look at himself in the mirror to know what the girlies wanted was not him, but his name and money, a good soft berth for the rest of their conniving lives. Oh, they'd get George out for moonlight rides over the years, and it would have served them right if George had knocked them up and sent them packing, but of course the upper crust doesn't often get knocked up. Just the bottom crust.

But George had escaped, and so far as Phil knew never answered the letters, the billets-doux that trickled back from Boston and the better suburbs about what a 'lovely' time they'd had and how 'quaint' the West was, my dear, and wouldn't it be enchanting if in the winter 'season' George — and so on. Phil had to snort to think of Georgie boy dolled up in a soup-and-fish, couldn't think of anything but a penguin tripping the light fantastic with the tomato soup queen. 'The New People,' the Old Lady called them.

'I will never forget the Western moon,' one of the damn fools wrote to George. Well, apparently George forgot the little dolly that remembered.

Then figure, if you will, why George who might have had some of the finest ass on the East coast could get himself mixed up with a floozy with a suicide husband and who used to play, used to tickle the ivories, in some honky-tonk. The Old Lady would croak. Get out those smelling salts of hers. Suppose he had to introduce the woman to relatives? Laugh as he might, Phil respected quality, real quality, and at least if he'd got hooked up with the moonlight girl, George would have taken her out into public without first pulling a sack over his head. Couldn't he see what the woman was up to? Did somebody have to come right out and tell him? If he wanted a piece of ass, if that's what he was so all-fired hot on getting, you can bet your last buck he could get it without a license.

Phil chuckled to himself. Reminded him of a story. Fellow went to the sheriff in a little town for a marriage license and after he'd gone the sheriff discovered he'd given out a hunting license instead of a marriage license so he hightails it over to the hotel where the couple are shacked up and pounds on the door and shouts out, 'If you ain't done it, don't do it. Tain't for it.'

Oh no, you don't need a license.

Or maybe he *had* got her knocked up?

Well, there were ways around that, too, unless your heart was bigger than your head, and sometimes Phil thought that's the way it was with George.

The Old Lady would have a hemorrhage.

The *Saturday Evening Post* went unread, the brown paper tubes that contained it began to pile up on the table like cordwood. Without saying anything to Phil, George drove right down the road after breakfast Sundays and sometimes didn't get back until all hours. One of the hired men happened to pass it on to Phil that George and the woman — her name was Rose — were seen on the streets of Herndon, but Phil turned away and pretended not to hear.

You could tell, maybe, what George really thought of the woman, what he really wanted of her, because he hadn't brought her to the ranch; if George were serious, he'd certainly want her on the ranch, wouldn't he, instead of sneaking around with her on the streets of Herndon after dark?

Phil did a lot of carving and whittling Sundays; and some

braiding. He started working on a new map of the ranch to put up on the wall in the office, a present for George, one to remind him, perhaps, of his responsibilities to the family. Phil whistled a lot and lay on his bed thinking.

Early in December a sudden cold snap followed snow. The sun rose late and tired over the sagebrush hill before the house; right on top of the hill, visible from the front windows and front porch, Phil and George had built a stone cairn of rounds and rounds of flat shale at the very spot where the sun rose on the twenty-first of June — oh, hell, when was it they built it? Aught-one? Around there, anyway. The sun that morning of the cold snap was far south of it, drifting. After breakfast they still needed lights on in the living room; and the pop of the electric light plant echoed against the hill. Phil walked out onto the front porch and stood sniffing. Across the fields he heard a coyote howling — unusual at such a late hour — and then the damned fool dogs began barking. Phil scratched a match with his thumbnail and looked at the thermometer tacked up on one of the thick log pillars that held up the overhanging roof. He whistled, and peered again. Fifty-six below! There was something to tell George, something to start the conversation of the day.

'Well, George,' he said. 'Guess I'll have to get out my gloves today.'

'How's that?'

'Fifty-six below, young fellow! It's like the old days!'

'Phil,' said George.

'What's it you want to know, old-timer?'

'Phil did you write to the Old Lady?'

'Yeah. I shot them a line the other day.'

'You said something about Rose.'

'Rose? Oh, Rose. Well, frankly speaking, old-timer, you

know well as I do what the Old Lady would say if you got mixed up with her. You know what the Old Lady would think, what she'd feel. George, we've always been close, family people, what? Think what the Old Lady would feel.'

'The Old Lady would feel,' said George, 'what one Mrs Burbank would feel for another Mrs Burbank.'

'Come again?' Phil cocked his head, to hear better.

'We were married Sunday,' George said. 'She's got rid of her property down there.'

Phil was so God damned shocked he went outside and stood in the barn. Just the morning for his saddle horse to act up, shying around in the stall as if he'd never seen Phil before, the ignorant bastard, so Phil took the horse out of the stall and tied him up close and then slapped him over the head again and again with the saddle blanket to teach him a thing or two. The dirty God damned fool, and Phil clouted him again. The horse strained at the rope and rolled his eyes so the whites showed.

5

When George had found Rose crying, he knew he was far over his head. He thought he might have dealt with anger, but he had little experience with tears. 'I came,' he said, 'to pay the bill.' She looked at him, and shook her head. 'Then,' he said, 'send it to me?'

She nodded, and turned away. He did a daring thing. He reached out and patted her upper arm, and smiled, and left, to walk down to the river, to think — he who never walked. He who had never walked by that river before, had never before heard the faint sound in the middle of it where the slow water parted around a sandbar. Suppose, he thought, if someone had found him there in the moonlight, sitting on the bank of the river where he had never been before. Well, he thought, suppose somebody did.

She was astounded to see him again a few weeks later.

What she ran was a hotel and restaurant, and people simply walked in. When you deal with the public, say good-bye to privacy.

But George Burbank knocked. He said, 'I thought I would come to see you.'

'Do please come in,' she said. She was apprehensive, for why would George Burbank come to call. She had sent a bill. She had received a check. She imagined that already his car had been observed passing the saloons, and that already her reputation was slipping. 'There's a party coming here at noon,' she said. 'You see, I'm busy in the kitchen.'

'Mrs Gordon, I don't want to be any trouble.'

Then why didn't he go, do you suppose, if he didn't want to be any trouble?

'Would you like to come sit in the kitchen?'

'Yes, thank you,' said George Burbank.

Beside the kitchen window was the deal table where she and Peter ate. 'Would you like to sit down here? I've got to mix the biscuits.'

'You go ahead with the biscuits. I'll just sit here.'

And so he did, and began reading the words on the sauce bottles. Peter had a penchant for sauces and spices. This most wholesome sauce, George read, is excellent with meats, cheese and fish. He traced the flowers on the oilcloth with a finger. 'It has certainly been a dry fall,' he offered. 'The river is low, I notice.'

'Hasn't it been dry, though? Some people in here the other day were saying it's the driest fall they remember.'

'They're right, those people,' George commented. 'Dry fall.'

'I guess you have to expect them,' Rose said.

He liked the look of the flour on her hands. 'Yes, you have got to expect them. You've got to.' He knew no more of love, he told himself, than he did of tears, but he enjoyed sitting there. And he enjoyed the conversation which seemed to him on the verge of taking an even more sprightly turn. In other words, he knew all there was to know about love, that it's the delight of being in the presence of the loved one.

'Peter is over at the school, washing windows.' She paused, thinking he might take her speaking of Peter's absence as somehow provocative.

'I expect you must be proud of him, from what I hear.'

She felt suddenly and fiercely protective of Peter, and the sting of tears was in her eyes. 'From what you hear?'

'Oh, I've heard he's a smart young fellow.'

Two cars drove up out front, the party from Herndon. The door opened and the little bell above gave the warning, and theirs were the voices of those excited by the cold and grateful for the warmth of the open fire. 'I'll go in and seat them,' Rose said. 'Peter should be back in a few minutes.'

It sounded to George as if they were pretty noisy in there. When Rose came back she said, 'They have wine with them. I wish they wouldn't do that. I'm not sure how the new law is on that, but it looks funny, if somebody came.'

George rose slowly. 'Do you want me to go in and speak to them?'

Rose laughed, shocked. 'Oh, no! I'll handle it some other time.' Imagine, she thought, if George Burbank suddenly burst in on them. From the kitchen.

'Just as you say,' said George.

'I don't know what's keeping Peter.'

George sniffed the biscuits. 'I expect he's not through with the windows,' George said.

'And these people are early.' Early and noisy.

'I'd say,' George remarked, 'that they had more in there than wine. Sounds like booze.'

They were early, and getting noisy. Herndon people — the undertaker who looked like Teddy Roosevelt, his delighted grin contemplating your body some years hence. There was a druggist, and two blonde women. The party included the leading dentist of Herndon, a man who had recently made some sort of history by walking down South Pacific Street in a Palm Beach suit sporting a cane, and with him this cold, early fall afternoon was a woman not his wife, a woman named Consuela who handed him instruments in his office; she was a dark beauty much admired in Herndon and the dentist's wife was a woman who thought a great deal about missionaries and the heathen and liked to drive about Herndon with her dentist husband on fine Sunday afternoons in their maroon Cadillac automobile, with the minister in the back seat. The wife was at the moment with a sick friend somewhere out of state. Here now was the new crowd, the new fast crowd from Herndon, people always on the go, always aware of new places that opened up, the Green Lantern, the Red Rooster, dim-lighted roadhouses that opened and closed, shady places, smoky places with little orchestras that played suggestive music. New people with new money, but among them were young ranchers who careened about the dusty roads in big cars, having somehow got hold of the family checkbook. Some of them had been seen returning from all-night parties at sunrise, a pretty young girl sitting on the back seat of a roadster, her feet on the steering wheel! In the rumble seat of the car, a drunken couple cheered her on. Nobody could guess where it would end, people staying up all night getting distant stations on the radio.

'I should never have put that piano in there,' Rose said. 'Just listen!'

As she went from the kitchen through the swinging door George saw past her that they were dancing some sort of wild dance, and they didn't look to be doing too well at it. The whole floor shook, clear into the kitchen.

'Goodness,' Rose said. 'I wish Peter would come back. I've got to get the chicken on, and Peter should be serving their salad. Sometimes if you get the food on the table.' She paused, thinking. 'Mr Burbank, I'm going to run over and get Peter.'

'Oh, you baby doll!' they screamed in there.

'Shake a leg!' someone called out.

George said, 'Mrs Gordon, I'll serve their salad.'

Before she could speak, he had picked up two plates from the counter, and shouldered open the swinging door. Rose saw past him that the dark beauty was kicking high and swinging her long jet beads.

When the swinging door was still behind George, Rose moved over near it, appalled at what George had done.

For a moment the noise and laughter continued, the voices rose higher. Then there was sudden and utter silence; a chord on the piano went unresolved. In the silence she heard George. 'Afternoon,' he said and laughed. 'Looks like I'm the new waiter. How do, Doctor.'

When George came back for more salad, he found Rose leaning against the sink. He went to her at once, leaping to the conclusion that she was weeping, since he had once found her so. She was weeping now, but from laughter. 'You were so perfect,' she whispered. 'They were so shocked. In their wildest dreams . . .' and she doubled over again. 'You were so perfect.'

Well! he thought to himself. He *had* done it rather well. And no one had ever thought him amusing before.

'Mr Burbank,' she told him later over coffee in the kitchen. 'Twice when I've been worried you've been here. And you know, I'm not worried often.'

Had Johnny Gordon told her who'd torn his shirt and tossed him like a knotted rag against the wall, Rose would never have accepted George Burbank. But Johnny hadn't said, feeling when you give a man a name you give him a face as well, and his humiliation was easier if the man was faceless, a force, like Fate. As she came to enjoy George's quiet company — even to look forward to it — she rationalized the incident of the paper flowers. Maybe Mr Phil Burbank had meant nothing. For what grown man would humiliate a boy? Was she too sensitive, too quick to remember old taunts in the schoolyard, to recall them again in the words of a perfectly ordinary conversation? What grown man would humiliate a boy!

George made a grave request. 'May I call you Rose? Will you call me George?'

'Of course, George.'

A Sunday later, another grave request. 'Will you marry me?'

She didn't pretend surprise. 'I want to be fair, George. I loved my husband. I don't know whether a woman can love twice.'

'Of course. How could you know? But if you liked me, and then maybe later? And I could put your boy through school. Any school at all.'

'I could do that alone. It meant so much to John, getting him through school. Maybe the last thing he believed in.'

'You understand I'd put him through school, lend you the money or whatever you liked, whether you marry me or not. You see, when we're together, when we laugh and talk, why, that's worth anything I could ever do for you or the boy.'

'But don't you see, I don't want your money.'

'Isn't it funny,' he said. 'I used to think that's all I had, was money, until we sat here and laughed and talked. Isn't it funny that even when I'm alone now, I feel so good.'

She looked down at his wide feet. His shoes were old, but freshly polished. She raised her eyes to his hands, almost as wide as they were long, and warm, even when he'd just come in from the cold. Suddenly she felt she knew exactly what he'd looked like as a child.

He said, 'Please don't do that.'

She said, 'I'm not going to cry. But I was thinking how lucky I've been, to have known two kind men.'

Driving home in the old Reo he hummed again and again the waltz from *The Pink Lady*. Suppose she was to teach him to dance, suppose that. When he squinted at the stars the light seemed to shoot right down to the ground like spears. And what a Christmas they could have together!

The elder Burbanks were luckier than most retired ranchers; many, at last broken by the long cold winters, the howling wind, the thought of uninhabited space — crippled by rheumatism and arthritis fingers twisted, drawn up into their horny palms like a dead bird's claws, forced to watch the young take over, to watch the young ride and rope and hunt and manage as they'd never do again — many retired into dipsomania, seeking out the bars in Beech or Herndon where they stared at the reflection of their disappointed fierce old faces in the cruel mirrors behind the bar; the self-made among them thus ended drinking with the very men they had spent their lives rising above, seeking similar oblivion, sinking into the same old age. Only a picket fence, they reflected, separated Mountain View Cemetery from Potter's Field.

At home they watched and criticized, quick to take offense, insisted on writing the checks, sulked, certain their sons and daughters wished they were dead before they, too, turned the final corner.

It was not so much that the elder Burbanks were richer than the others, for some half dozen ranchers could put their hands on two hundred thousand cash. Old Tom Bart, say — in spite of the rumors of wild spending and all-night parties in hotel rooms; the Barts and the Burbanks seldom met except perhaps on the streets of Herndon, and it was Tom Bart then who stood modestly aside, he who was known as the life of the party; he would stiffen, smiling and tongue-tied, before the Old Lady's poise and the cut of the Old Gent's clothes. George, of all people, secretly admired Tom Bart. Phil thought him a fool, and referred to him as a Vocal Yokel.

No, it was not that they were richer, but that they were educated and had social contacts; reading and thinking took the place of whiskey; they played Melba and Galli-Curci on the Victrola, lost themselves in the texts of *Town & Country*, *International Studio*, *Mentor* and *Century*, magazines that piled up on the table until someone drove to Beech and dropped them off at the school. Serious discussions on current events took the place of the curious excitement some find in anger and despair — furious discussions during which they sometimes paused and glanced at one another in the sudden silence.

They could not suit Phil, they could not please him, and his glances reminded them of their useless lives. After certain unpleasant episodes, the old people took a corner suite at the best hotel in Salt Lake City, had the hotel furniture (good as it was) removed and installed their own things, made friends with others like themselves, retired ranchers, lumber people, mining people who knew Australia and South Africa quite as well as they knew the American West. They wrote frequent letters back East, read the Boston *Evening Transcript*, walked in the sun or regarded the snow-covered mountains from their big windows on the top floor. But in their sometimes long silences the one of them would look suddenly at the other and smile quickly a brief, encouraging smile, a smile quickly acknowledged, and then the silence again.

The Old Lady's eyebrows flew up when she read that George might marry. On receiving Phil's first letter, the Old Lady wrote several to George, tearing up all but the last. How absurd, she thought, writing to a grown man begging him not to marry until his fiancée had been approved, for Phil's letter said the woman had played music in a bar and that she had a half-grown child. There was no mention of a former husband. In her final letter, she begged George to 'think it over,' a phrase that had long served as a maxim in the family, and in any event to allow them to be present at the wedding. 'It would look funny,' she wrote George, 'if we weren't there.' She showed the letter to the Old Gent, who paused in his pacing of the floor.

He looked the letter over. 'I don't think George minds if things look funny. He's never done anything that looked funny before. Why would one thing matter?'

'Phil cares.'

The Old Gent turned to her. The question he was about to ask had often been on his mind. A hundred times he had phrased the question, opened his lips to speak it. Meeting her eyes, he had until now kept silent, wondering if she might not sense in the question some criticism of herself. 'Do you think . . . ?' Shocked, he suddenly realized the same question had been on her mind. It was she, then, who expressed it.

'Do I think there might be something — something wrong — something wrong with Phil?'

The Old Gent felt hollow in his stomach, but it was a relief to get the thing out in the open. 'If there is, it's not your fault.'

'Nor is it yours,' she said, and looked at her watch. 'What time is it, please, I hate these little watches. I can't see the hands, and they lose time.' They sent off the letter and prepared to follow it, packed their bags and asked the maid to water the geraniums. They wired ahead for George to meet them in Beech.

He was on the platform to meet them, smiling came forward in the darkness in the buffalo coat that made him huge, leaning into the winter wind that swept dry snow across the platform. 'Hello, mother,' he said, leaning to kiss her. 'Hello, father,' and formally shook the Old Gent's hand. 'You see, it's begun to snow.'

'It's good to see you,' the Old Gent said.

'Same here,' George said. 'The car's around the side, don't you know.'

'Just as always?' the old man asked.

The Old Lady thought wildly of speech, some word about the trip, about the meal on the train, something seen from the windows, some anecdote. She could remember only a crying child and a cross mother and the smell of a peeled orange. 'Is anyone with you?' she asked.

'My wife,' George said.

'Well, what did you think of her?' The old Burbanks had been installed in their old room.

'The clock is going again,' the Old Gent said. 'But the windows still rattle.' He walked over and looked out the window.

'Didn't you hear me? I said, What did you think of her?'

'Think of her? I think it's mighty considerate of her to turn this room over to us while we're here. But how much can you tell, driving twenty miles in the dark?'

'It's more than twenty miles. When you were in the office talking to George, she knocked on the door and I went and let her in. She said the oddest thing.'

'What on earth did she say?'

'She said, "Somehow knowing George, I knew I could count on your kindness."'

'Well?'

'It pleased me. That she sees George's kindness.'

The Old Gent turned from the black window that reflected the lamp behind him. 'Will you give her a little of the jewelry or such things?'

The Old Lady coughed lightly and patted her chest and went to the window. On the sill was a dead geranium in a pot. 'I see Miss Jones is dead. I think we'd better wait and see. Too bad there's a child. Loyalties.'

'It was dying before we left, remember? It's not — the child. You know that.' The Old Gent turned sharply, walked across the room, turned sharply and walked straight back. 'I can tell you one thing. I feel sorry for her.'

The Old Lady said, 'I haven't seen you pace like that since you left this house.' They began unpacking. 'Isn't it awfully cold in this room? You forget what cold is.'

He looked up from his suitcase. 'I haven't heard you mention the cold since you left this house.'

Rose, too, had felt the cold, her first time in the house. They had married after Christmas in the rectory in Herndon. George wondered whether they should invite some people? She said she thought because of Peter, it should be private. Did he understand? He seemed to. He said, 'Suit yourself,' but he had smiled.

'But of course your brother,' she said.

'He never goes to anything at a church. He hates to dress.'

Peter did some understanding, too. 'You know I will always love your father. If I thought you'd be hurt if I got married, if I thought you wouldn't understand?' Peter had smiled. 'You do understand?'

Peter gazed out the window over the scrubby sagebrush past the schoolhouse down to the river and to the clump of willows where he used to sit planning and watching the moon. 'I understand.'

The stilted cast of his speech had long perplexed her, his 'of course,' his 'for instance' — and so did his calling her Rose. She would not question his motive, maybe fearing his answer, that it might reveal some inferior sort of love for her. In fact, the name Rose more closely fitted his image of her, more the beloved than the mother, the sole object, after the death of his father, of his strange affection, the single remaining subject of the scrapbook that had served him as guide and Bible for five long years. He felt no jealousy of George Burbank, or, if he did, it was as controlled and as impersonal as his hatred of those who might attempt to destroy his private images. Marriage would simply make possible for her what she deserved long before he himself could ever make it possible, and her getting what she deserved was all that mattered to him. Marriage would remove her forever from the Red Mill where she served those he loathed and scorned, where she must parry the drunken remark and the insinuating smile because she must make a living, secure a future for him who longed only to make a future for her. Sooner than he had dreamed, she would travel dressed in fashions from *Harper's Bazaar*, drive a Lincoln or a Pierce, take a stateroom on an ocean liner, and arrange fresh flowers.

The hours before the wedding his mother remained in a room at the Herndon House and George took him to Green's to buy a suit.

'Fix this young fellow up with whatever he wants,' George told the man, and Peter smiled when he saw George take a quick look at himself in his own new blue serge, and draw in his stomach and take in his new belt a notch. 'Your mother wants us to have our dinner alone,' George said. 'Guess she wants to get all fixed up and surprise us. Goodness, but doesn't she always look so pretty!' They ate at the Sugar Bowl Cafe. 'Now you go ahead and have anything you want. Me, I always have the fried halibut when I go out. It's sort of a little change. But you hop to it and have anything you want.' Never before in his life had Peter had all the chili con carne he wanted. 'Fix the young fellow up with another bowl,' George told the waitress. 'This is a kind of celebration for us.'

Peter was the only guest at the wedding and properly so, he thought, for he was the only other principal involved. He liked the array of roses George had bought and the fussy woman at the florist's had arranged in the brass pots on the altar. He was honestly touched that George had made so sentimental a gesture and scarcely breathed through the marriage service and merely moistened his lips when George took his mother's hand and slipped on the wedding band; but his heart leaped when his mother turned and smiled and touched and arranged and fixed the fold of her dark blue traveling suit, as easy and elegant a gesture as he'd ever seen — heartbreakingly beautiful — the gesture of the charming, the enchanting, the rich Mrs Burbank. She walks in beauty, he quoted from his father's books. She walks in beauty, like the night.

He must have one of those roses later on. A few pressed petals would make a good entry for the last page of the scrapbook.

Rose found a Mrs Mueller in Herndon, a dietitian at the hospital, a clean, starched, ambitious woman who was glad to give Peter room and board for the remainder of the school year.

'I'll try to come to you every weekend,' Rose promised Peter. 'And maybe sometimes you might like to come to the ranch? Won't that be fun?'

He thought it wouldn't, but didn't say so. He smiled his faint smile and took her hand. Thus he was removed from Beech where he had been taunted and avoided as the spawn of suicide. At the school in Herndon there was a real library, courses in chemistry and physics. 'This is a pleasant room,' he said.

'Peter,' she said, 'sometimes I think you don't listen to me. Do you listen to me? I never can tell what you're thinking.'

'I'll pay more attention,' he said. He thought what a relief it was to have to think now only of his own future. 'Say hello to — George.'

'I know,' she said. 'It's hard for you to know what to call him, isn't it? But he wants so much for you.'

Rose remembered the cold the first few moments in the ranch house. George's brother stood in the middle of the room as she and George walked in from the winter afternoon; she had waited on the steps while George drove the old Reo into the garage; the sound of the exhaust of the electric light plant smacked against the hill out front. The ranch dogs, alerted by the mutter of the car and the flash of the headlights had barked and come running around the house and now whined and leaped at George as he trudged back from the garage carrying suitcases. These he set down, and opened the door. Rose went in first, and there was the brother standing in the middle of the room.

'Hello there, Phil,' George said. 'You remember Rose.'

'Oh, hello there,' Phil said.

'Something wrong with the furnace?' George asked.

'Search me,' said Phil.

It was a huge room and sparsely furnished, for the Old Lady and the Old Gent had gone away with chairs that left yawning spaces; there had been no rearrangement of furniture since their departure some years before. They had left behind the Navajo scatter rugs they had introduced from time to time as fitting in a ranch house, but the Indian motif had never been able to clear the air of disappointed elegance. The fire was laid in the fireplace, but unlighted. Over it the portrait of the Old Lady stared down with her Boston look, the eyes level on Rose wherever she moved.

'Well, I'll go down and shake it up,' said George.

'We had such a nice trip,' Rose said.

Phil said, 'George, the Old Gent wrote. Stage brought the letter this morning. There's a deed he wants I can't lay my hand to. Mind looking around for it?'

'I reckon that could go till morning,' said George.

'I been waiting around here for you all day,' said Phil.

'Rose,' George said, kneeling by the fireplace and touching a match to the kindling. 'Come over here and get warm. I'll go below and shake up the furnace.'

'I'm perfectly all right, perfectly warm,' Rose said, but moving over there. She was terrified at being left alone.

'No, I'll just go below,' George said. 'Be a minute.' He watched a moment while the small fire of the kindling lapped weakly at the tough, resistant bark of the green logs, then he turned and walked out through the big dining room with all the heavy, crouching mahogany furniture. Rose heard a door open and close, and steps descending.

She was to know that basement well, that basement that

flooded every spring; the rising water, slick with oil that leaked from the water pump, found out the dwellings of mice who drowned and floated bloated and belly-up in the small light that seeped through the ground-level windows. She heard a frantic rumbling down there, then the excruciating scraping of shovel on concrete that made her flesh crawl, then the clank of an iron door. Smelled coal smoke.

She could not control her trembling, nor forestall the beginnings of an unusual headache. Phil had seated himself close to the fringed lamp on the table in the middle of the room and held a magazine at a painful angle to catch the required light; when Phil read, his lips moved. She felt that the silence was bound to be worse than anything she might say, but her light voice caught in her throat. 'Well, brother Phil,' she began, 'it's good to be here.'

His lips continued to move, reading. Then he looked up from the magazine directly at her and smiled. He smiled as already George's heavy steps ascended the still-unknown stairs, and Phil continued to smile, and then said clearly, 'I'm not your brother.'

George entered. 'I heard you two talking together,' he remarked pleasantly. As he spoke, the kitchen door opened and Mrs Lewis, humming something mournful, lumbered in to set the table for three.

After supper Phil read for a time close by the lamp; then he rose abruptly and marched down the hall to the bedroom, closed the door behind him and got out his banjo and tuned up. He had to smile, had to smile thinking of George coming into that house with this woman, trying to make things smooth. How had he said? You remember Rose? That was it. What kind of a name was Rose! The name of somebody's cook. He had to smile, had to smile thinking of George down on one knee before the unlighted fire — a little disappointed that Phil had not lighted it before their arrival, that the room might be all comfortable and welcoming. Ha–ha–ha. George should have known Phil better than to think he would do something he didn't feel. Phil had to smile thinking of the sidelong glance Rose gave him at the supper table. He knew how he looked, knew it would get her goat. It used to get the Old Lady's goat, the rumpled shirt, the uncombed hair, the stubble of beard, the unwashed hands. She might just as well get smart to the fact that he didn't do things like other people because he wasn't like other people, that he left his napkin pointedly untouched, reached for food rather than asked for it, and if he had to snuffle his nose, he snuffled. If the fancy relatives back East could stomach it, God knew this woman could, and if she was unused to a man's leaving the table without first bowing and scraping and saying 'Excuse me,' she might just as well catch on now. Oh yes (he had to smile) she was in for a few surprises.

He had her figured, had her figured from the first time he sighted her, knowing her as one who doubted herself too much to dare put a wedge between him and George by repeating what he'd said about not being her brother. She'd be pretty careful not to test George, risk his anger, tamper with his feeling for family because George was her meal ticket. And suppose by some chance she did whine, what good would that do her? The house was his as much as George's, the money as much as George's, and the ranch so set up you couldn't split it without causing financial troubles, water rights, grazing lands and so forth. If she looked for trouble, she'd really be in the soup. He could see her now, coming into that house for the first time that late winter evening in a new getup that George had doubtless bought her, scared to death.

Phil made no bones about it that he often laughed and talked to himself — 'keeping hisself company,' as he put it. It amused him to repeat the speech of those who amused him, to savor it. And now in a chillingly accurate female falsetto he imitated Rose. How had she put it? *We had such a nice trip.* Phil could imagine about how nice the trip had been, the wind and snow finding spaces between the side curtains where the grommets had torn out. Feet half frozen, hands too stiff to move, aching with the cold, the weak lights of the old Reo playing out over the frozen ruts. Phil had, furthermore, absolutely no use for people who tried to make conversation, knowing it as a ploy people used to make themselves feel adequate and to ingratiate themselves. She knew she didn't belong there among Burbanks. Question was, how long would it take George to get wise to the fact?

And then George's coming up from downstairs, poking up the furnace and then coming up and saying, 'I heard you two talking,' and being satisfied about it. Oh, George was easily satisfied, all right. And the woman and Phil had been talking, all right.

Phil cleared his throat, smiled and began to pick out 'Red Wing,' looking across the room at the empty bed. Beyond, in the darkness, was the butcher pen. They'd have to butcher pretty soon. Not much more than a hindquarter left in the icehouse.

Suddenly Phil's fingers were still on the frets of the banjo, and the fingers of his right hand were still, arched like a spider over the strings. His eyes darted to the light under the crack of the bathroom door between that room and the Old Folks' room. George or Rosey?

When the Old Folks had the big room on the other side, they had always unlocked the door of Phil's side when they got finished in there, had finished their ablutions, made their ablutions, so if he or George wanted to sashay in there, they were welcome as flowers in May. Of course, Phil never did go in there, somehow uncomfortable with the Old Lady's things, her scents and colognes, her Pears' soap and monogrammed towels; the place had the offensive odor of women, and the Old Gent's shaving mug and set of straight razors couldn't fumigate it; it gave Phil a turn to come upon some filmy garment hung up to dry on a folding rack. You'd have thought the Old Lady would have kept those things cached and out of sight, and to hear her speak her la-di-dah language and to see her walk her proper walk, you'd have thought she'd have kept such stuff to herself. No, Phil used the lavatory down the hall, the stark, functional little room that smelled of functional soap and the damp gray roller towel. It puzzled Phil that George could have bathed in that other place while the Old Lady lived in the house, and now George was going to expose his body before this woman. Would he first douse the lights?

Phil picked up his ears. Someone was locking the door between.

Was it George who turned the key, or the woman? Must be the woman, for after a reasonable length of time the door was not unlocked, as in the old days. Must be her hand that, instead, cautiously tried the knob so the door, so to speak, was locked against him. And you can bet your life that even if it were George who did it, it was the woman who was at the bottom of it. Phil lay there, rigid in the dark, thinking how the woman would go lie down with George and let him work away over her, and maybe get her with child.

6

Phil was two years ahead of George in college, and as a freshman made some kind of college history: half a million was a lot of money then, and by the time Phil was registered and walking to the dormitory in the California sun, the value of the ranch, via the grapevine, had perhaps doubled in the minds of the young men in the fraternity houses. The hick clothes he'd brought with him — the same he'd worn in high school in Salt Lake City — only emphasized that here was a fellow rich enough to ignore fashion, and he was invited to house after house and urged to pledge. Blandishments were heaped upon him, beer urged, cigars offered and the Egyptian Deities that some of the young sports fancied.

And he went everywhere, wondering how far they'd go, sat in their leather chairs, his long legs crossed, poised and taciturn, inwardly amused at their small talk of baseball, motorcars; and he ignored the young ladies they brought over from a women's seminary and paraded before him. 'Like prize beef,' he remarked later. Each group looked on him as a prize and suspected the other of taking some unfair advantage, anxious to pledge this fellow who would make it possible in time to come to add a wing, build a new house, refurnish the living room and — above all — to attract other young bloods of similar wealth, for wealth attracts wealth.

On the final night of what they called Rush Week, when the freshmen made up their minds and wrote their choice on a slip of paper and dropped the slip in a box, Phil made his little bit of history.

Naturally the young men at whose house he dined this last night felt it was their company he chose — why else would he be with them this final night? — and thus he found the president of the fraternity at his left hand, and a professor at his right. Those young men who worked their way through college got on their white jackets and served up the fried chicken and hot biscuits.

The president of the fraternity gave a little speech on the meaning of Fraternity. He said it was a good thing. He said men were not meant to be alone.

Then, to applause, the professor rose, sipped water, and spoke of what it meant to him as an older man to have been a member of that fraternity. Good fellowship had seen him through many straits. He sat, to applause.

Now the candles were lighted, and the lights put out. The brothers stood and sang the fraternity song in practiced harmony; their heads were bowed a little, and at the finish they joined hands.

The candles were snuffed out, the lights turned on. Phil noted with amusement a few unashamed tears. He rose.

'I'd like to say a few words myself,' he remarked, and there was clapping.

'Gentlemen,' he began, and he raked the assemblage with those day-blue eyes of his. 'I know, gentlemen, why you've asked me here. You've asked me here for my money. Why else would you want me, gentlemen? You don't even know if I've a brain in my head. You don't know one blasted thing about me, and yet you've asked me here.'

The attention, he said, that they'd shown him, he supposed

they believed he took as a compliment. Actually, he took it for what it was. An insult.

There wasn't a sound in the room but breathing.

'And with that, gentlemen,' he said, 'I take my leave.'

And he walked out of the dining room, out of the house.

Maybe that was why, two years later, George sat — a freshman now himself — waiting in his room for the fraternity men to call on him. He sat in his room with his feet planted square before him, sat at the study table looking at his square hands, ready to smile at whoever might knock and enter. His face was fixed in greeting. Already up and down the corridor he had heard other knocks and voices, boisterous laughter and then footsteps on the stairs.

Earlier that week he had observed the current fashions and gone at once to a clothing store and, perspiring, he bought clothes, went behind the curtains and changed into them. He emerged transformed.

And now he waited, his broad feet in new shoes planted firmly before him.

'Probably,' Phil told him later, 'probably the trouble was they all remembered what I did. Probably it wasn't your fault at all.'

But George never believed that, and never forgot the waiting in that room, a stocky young man, his wide feet planted before him. When the corridor was at last silent, he put on his new pajamas and got into bed; out the open window he heard voices and singing, and the California night was heavy not with sagebrush but with the odor of unfamiliar flowers.

The February sun was bright on the snow that covered the valley — blinding when it flashed against the flat windshield of the old Reo. George and Rose squinted against it, headed for Herndon and a bank meeting, George in his buffalo coat and gauntlets, earmuffs and his town hat; Rose wore a sealskin cape and hat to match pulled down over her ears, and heavy mittens; around her legs George had tucked a heavy blanket. The old car meandered along in the frozen ruts and when they exceeded twenty miles an hour the Weed chains went ka-bang-ka-bang; George squinted, watching the road and the Moto-Meter that replaced the radiator cap, the red column of alcohol nicely below Danger. People's cars were forever boiling over, radiators freezing and then boiling over. Some said a mixture of honey and water was a good coolant and wouldn't freeze; some used kerosene, but George knew kerosene rotted the hoses and leaked on the engine and you might explode. George had been trying wood alcohol with good results. 'But they ought to make some kind of thing you could put in your radiator that wouldn't boil away,' George remarked. 'Sometimes I think we ought to get a Franklin.' The Franklin was a good car, and air-cooled, but George had heard they had their disadvantages, too. Because they didn't use water, you couldn't fill them with hot water to get them started, and you had to put them in gear and drag them around with a team of horses before they'd start. 'So I don't know,' George admitted. 'In a way it was easier when there weren't cars because you didn't have to have one because you couldn't even if you wanted to.'

Rose laughed out loud.

'What on earth are you laughing at?' George asked.

'At you. You're a very funny person.'

George was pleased, and grinned. 'What I'd really like,' George said, 'is a Pierce.'

'Well, then.'

'I always liked engines.'

'Then get one.'

'I'm afraid it would look sort of funny,' said George.

A little time passed. 'This looks like a good place,' Rose said suddenly.

'Good place? For what?'

'For a picnic.'

George chuckled and looked out across the snow and the brown sides of somebody's far-off haystacks, little dots, and cattle huddled close to one of them, the amorphous shape of the herd shifting and changing as they crowded around. The fresh tracks of a jackrabbit beside the road led nowhere. The sagebrush looked faded and brittle, each twig and leaf stiff with cold.

'No, there's a nice view out there,' Rose said. 'The mountains. Just pull over here and stop.' He looked at her, watched her turn and reach back under a pile of blankets. She brought out a sack and a thermos bottle. 'Hot coffee and sandwiches.'

'Well, I'm dogged,' George said. 'But it's not even noon! I've never eaten a thing except at the proper time in my whole life, don't you know.'

The coffee was good and hot, too. George thought it made a cigarette taste good afterwards. 'I don't suppose,' George remarked, 'that anybody in this whole country ever had a picnic in a car before.' He could hardly wait to get to the bank meeting to tell what they'd done. He could see the look on old Foster's face. 'I used to hate these trips,' he said. 'After the meetings first one fellow and then another would ask me over to his place for supper. They sort of farmed me out, don't you know, and their wives didn't know what to do with me. There's not much place for a loner. I never was good at talking. Phil's the talker. Lots of times, I'd tell them I had something else to do, and either I'd drive home, or go over to the Herndon House and have supper.' He paused. 'Rose?'

'Yes.'

'Oh, nothing.' He had been about to make an appalling confession, was about to tell her when he went for supper at the Herndon House he took a booth and pulled the curtains so no one would see he was alone. 'I was just going to say, how nice it is not to be alone.'

'We'll never be alone again, George.'

'You know, I'd like to ask people up, sometimes, to the ranch for a meal. Only, I don't know who to start with, they've all been so fine and neighborly. I guess sometimes I'd just like to have somebody there, our own friends, you know. We could get a hired girl, like we used to have, and she could wait on table, like when my mother was here. There's a bell somewhere around, and you ring it, and the girl comes in. That's the way it was.'

'Do you really think we need a girl to come in?'

'I don't suppose we need her. But I'd like to have a hired girl, or whatever you want.'

'I guess it would be nice.'

'Then you see, you wouldn't even have to think about the table, and we could come in from the table and talk, and if you didn't mind, why you could play the piano, if we had a piano. My, I certainly do like it, when you play the piano. That's something my mother could never do. We listened to the Victrola.' He paused and looked at her. 'Am I talking too much?'

'I love your talk.'

'I wouldn't want to get in the habit of talking too much, don't you know,' and then he saw the reflection of her quick smile in the windshield; staring straight ahead, he reached out and took her hand, overcome by a shocking tenderness.

For a moment he was struck dumb at a habit of hers he saw now for the first time, how whenever she looked up from whatever she was doing, even unwrapping a sandwich in the front seat of a car, she always looked up smiling. He wondered if anybody had ever noticed it before.

The first you saw of Herndon was the grain elevator, the peaked metal roof flashing in the sun; then the coal chute by the tracks, black and hulking, reminding children of a huge animal. Then came the brick Gothic pile of a teachers college that gave the town a sort of tone, for neat young men and women from all over the state studied there and could be seen in the ice cream parlor sitting on stools with legs of heavy, twisted wire talking of their books, or holding hands. Rose and George drove past the brick hospital and the wind brought them the odor of boiled potatoes and roasting meat and chloroform. Ka-bang ka-bang, went the Weed chains. What Rose felt was common enough among all the ranchers who drove into town — an alien feeling of purpose and excitement heightened by the sight of the store windows, the rough-looking men who stared out the windows of the pool halls, the huge clock over the door of the jeweler's, the snowy expanse beside the depot where dogs cavorted, the concrete fountain, dry now in winter, where in summer the head of a lion in bas-relief squirted water through its lips into a scallop-shaped basin where horses — few these days — might drink.

The automobiles before the Herndon House were parked diagonally, and inside, sitting proud in the big green leather chairs, old retired ranchers stared out as if offended at both automobiles and pedestrians who loped along, shivering in the cold. Well, no wonder, the old ranchers told one another, shifting about in their chairs to rest their old bones. Town folk wore too few clothes. Among these old men there was much grunting and snorting, for they were often angry — angry with the government, with the times, with prices, and with their children and grandchildren, whom they loved. They were angry because their children and grandchildren didn't come often enough with the great-grandchildren, and when they did, you ought to hear the excuses they made for getting away and about their own business, whatever that was! The old men seldom got a chance to ask the questions they wanted to ask, seldom got a chance to play host at dinner because the young people said they had to get right back to the ranch, seldom got a chance to take the children to the moving pictures and to walk the streets with them. Young people had to get right back to the ranch, or so they said. Serve the young people right if they got married again or changed their wills! That would make them sit up! And there were plenty of women in town to jump at the chance!

Ah, but then the young people would be angry, and the old people would be lonelier than ever. They'd never get the chance then to see their great-grandchildren.

In the Herndon House in an alcove off the entrance to the dining room, the public stenographer tapped out her briefs and her wills. The door of the men's room opened and closed, the brass mechanical elbow hissing and sighing, opened and closed, offering the briefest glimpse of the same white tile that covered the floor of the lobby. There were smiles and greetings, and the people who were not used to the excitement of town smiled in an embarrassed way.

Today the Herndon House was even more charged than usual; the lobby buzzed and children deserted their parents and ran and stiffened their legs and slid across the tiles; time and again the clerk at the desk rushed out to stop them but he couldn't so he huffed and glared.

'Quite a crowd around here today,' George remarked, slowing up the old Reo. 'Somebody important around.'

And then they saw. Around the corner, at the side entrance, were two big black limousines, each with a chauffeur. 'Oh yes,' George said. 'That's the Governor's outfit. Some shindig here at the hotel. I forgot about it.'

'What did you forget?'

'I forgot to answer him. I was supposed to be at this shindig and I forgot because I was thinking about you and about getting married and I didn't answer him. Well, anyway, I had this bank meeting.'

'Then you know him?' Rose asked.

'Oh, I met him a couple of times at the capital. The Old Gent knew him well. Sort of sidekicks.'

George got out before the red brick facade of the bank where, inside, the directors met in a room set apart and talked about money; then they all went to the Sugar Bowl Cafe for lunch because that's where they had always gone, and they ordered either the fried halibut or the steak, and then they had the pie. 'I'll meet you at three at the hotel,' George said. 'And say hello to Peter for me, and ask if maybe there's something or other he might like to have.'

Rose slid over behind the wheel. 'I'm going to miss you,' Rose said.

He looked at her. 'Miss me? Will you, Rose?' His face lit up. 'Oh, that's fine.'

She leaned over and kissed him, and he blushed. What a day, what a day it had been! A picnic, mind you, in the middle of winter, and then being kissed by a lovely woman in the middle of town, before a brick bank with assets of fifteen million dollars. What strange, what strange wonderful things could happen to a man if he had but a little patience. 'And please miss me, too,' Rose said.

'I wanted to say something,' he told her, 'all the way driving here. I wanted to say, how proud I am of you, about how happy I am with you.' Then he left her, and entered the bank before he said some unbearably delicate thing.

In the house where Peter roomed and boarded, the roomers wiped their feet, entered quietly and switched off the lights when they left the bathroom, as the neat little sign commanded. Speech was low-pitched and discreet, as in a hospital or mortuary. Not a cheerful house, but the silence and order suited Peter exactly; there he could think.

Rose knocked before she entered and Peter himself, formal as a host, let her in and kissed her. His face was shining from soap and water, his shirt was stiff with starch, his shoes gleamed. He led her up to his room where she felt a stranger. It had obviously been a room set aside for infrequent guests, furnished with pieces too good to throw out and not good enough to live with. It was more a living room than a bedroom. The ornate brass bed might have been the setting for an Edwardian accouchement. In one corner was a table whose base was a bundle of bamboo sticks tied in the middle with a band of rattan and splayed out to support the top that held a painted vase of gilded cattails; the wallpaper was the color of dried blood and two walls displayed pictures, Christ as the Light of the World looking hurt and quizzical. Opposite hung a long narrow plaque, the top of which was a bad print of the Laughing Cavalier; below it was a printed text difficult to reconcile with the subject:

Sleep sweetly in this pleasant room,
Oh thou, who'ere thou art . . .

'Are you very happy here?' Rose asked. It seemed a reasonable question, and she asked it sitting in the straight chair by the table he used for studying. There each pencil was lined up straight, not a paper, not a book was out of line with another. Peter never misplaced anything, never lost anything, never was late, never forgot.

'I couldn't be happier,' he told her. 'And I've got a new friend.'

'Tell me about him.' What a warmth she felt!

'His father teaches at school. He thinks he wants to be a professor. He's taught me chess, and we play a lot. There's no luck to chess, it's all skill.'

'I expect you're good at it.'

'I will be.'

'And school?'

'It's great.'

She wondered if he had ever expressed a stronger emotion.

Each time she had suggested he come for a weekend at the ranch he excused himself — studying to do, reading, had made other plans, plans she did not inquire into. She was certain it was Phil who made him avoid the ranch, but she could not bring Phil's name into the open.

'And are you happy?' he now asked her.

She was not prepared for the question; she spoke stiffly. 'George is very good to me, you know. Oh, we had such fun driving down today — stopped for a picnic, looked out at the mountains. My, but there's a lot of snow. I'd fixed some sandwiches, and we had a thermos of hot coffee, and we talked there, eating. You know, he's the sort of person you can do things with.' But she had not answered the question. She felt Peter's eyes. 'You know, I'd forgot all about gilded cattails!' Her sudden laughter in the room was strange, and she wondered suddenly what she was doing there. What was Peter doing there in that unlikely room? Would he remain there all summer with one excuse and then another until at last the problem of Phil was dragged out into the open? What had that room to do with her and Peter? In only one way was the room a part of them, of her and Peter and John, and that was John's medical books neat in a glass-front sectional bookcase that must once have displayed sets of Dickens and Scott. And the skull.

'Your father's books,' she said. 'Will you bring them with you to the ranch when school's out?'

'All of them. And I'll take the skull.' Only the skull remained of the skeleton Johnny had been proud of, proof that he was a doctor, for only a doctor could get a skeleton, only a doctor had the ghastly privilege. The bones Peter had buried in Beech, in a sack. She had hoped never to know where.

The French doors of the dining room in the Herndon House had already opened and beyond them waitresses whipped around rattling silver and clanging the heavy hotel china, cleaning up the Governor's leavings. One waitress, eyes innocent, plotted the theft of the Governor's plate, something beyond the teaspoon she had already popped into the pocket of her uniform; she would give it to her grandson. It might one day be valuable. She would say that the Governor, pleased at her service, had given it to her.

And out drifted the men, talking, making points with their good cigars; these who had been asked to represent the City of Herndon, to swell the progress, were local Society. They were not bright people; as such, they would not have settled in Herndon, but they were the best Herndon had, the storekeepers, the undertaker, the doctors, the dentists; the more ambitious of them had had at least a brush with the state university and were now hot after their first fifty or one hundred thousand dollars. At the moment — now that greatness walked among them — their purpose was clearer: Except for their money, would they have been summoned to share with the Governor his peas and creamed chicken and the Neapolitan ice? They would not. Indeed, they would not! Their leader, the richest man in town, was president of the bank with many irons in the fire, but like George Burbank, he had had that meeting. Leaderless, the rest hesitated to approach the Governor — could only surround him, awed by tales they'd heard of the Governor's traveling with the richest man in the state by private railroad car to Washington, a car with a bathtub, among other luxuries. En route, terrapin had been served, champagne had flowed; fresh-cut flowers had been taken on at certain stops.

The Governor, lonely in his eminence and sick of the conversation of his aide who could think of nothing and talk of nothing but politics and of a tooth that began to give trouble, was happy at last to be greeted by George Burbank whose surname led the list in a book called *Prominent Men of Our State.*

'Long time no see,' the Governor grinned, and clapped George on his broad back.

'How do, Governor,' said George. They spoke as equals, each from an eminence. The one inquired after the health of the other, and of the health of the other's dear ones. The Governor asked after the severity of the winter, and they compared its blessed mildness with the awful winter of '19, that winter still fresh of mind, when the hay gave out, when cattle starved and froze and wild horses ate pebbles they found under the snow.

'Now where was it,' the Governor wondered, 'that we last talked together?'

'Why, in the senate restaurant,' George said. 'My father and I were having beef stew.'

The Governor chuckled. 'When you get right down to it, George, there's nothing like a good beef stew.'

'Yes, that's the truth,' George said.

'That stew, George, is a specialty of the restaurant. We have got to get together over stew again sometimes.'

'Now that's a capital idea,' George said. 'I'm sure my wife would like that.'

'Your wife you say?' the Governor asked, stepping back. He grinned. He had not been told of this. That was his aide for you. Aide for what? 'Congratulations. I hadn't heard.'

'It wasn't a big wedding. You see, my wife was a widow.'

The Governor nodded and chewed his cigar. He seemed to understand how George's wife being a widow cleared up certain things. 'Not a big wedding, you say.'

'Not big at all. That's what she wanted.'

'Well, George,' the Governor laughed. 'I can see you're getting halter-broke just like the rest of us. You dog, you! I'll tell you, my wife and I want you to dinner with us, and not for stew, George, either. Not for stew!'

But then George got his own idea.

Mountains rimmed Herndon and the sun set clearly. It was thus dark before they finished their errands; the store windows were warm and inviting. George went off to the harness-makers for a new set of collars and to pick up a saddle one of the cowhands had left to be repaired. He dropped Rose off at the grocery store and she bought the cases of canned fruit, for the Burbanks fed their men well, and the men bragged to men on other ranches. She chose pears, much admired in that country, and the flinty peach halves, much fancied, so hard and slick with a thick sweet syrup that one faulty motion with the spoon sent them flying out onto the tablecloth. Having run the Red Mill, she was used to buying in quantity — half a pig, thirty dozen eggs, four hams, four sacks of potatoes, gallons of raspberry jam. But in her days at the Red Mill, she had waited her turn to be waited on. Not so now. Now, as Mrs Burbank, she was embarrassed by the clerks' obsequiousness, by the owner himself who came to serve and ask her pleasure. 'The elder Mrs Burbank,' he told her, 'used to like to stock up on specialties,' and he touched the shelves of canned crab and lobster, the potted meats and cheeses. 'You people have always set a fine table,' and Rose despised herself for ordering half a case of this and of that — exactly why she despised herself she didn't know. Maybe it was — maybe it made Johnny Gordon somehow less, and the Burbanks, who needed nothing, somehow even more. Nobody had ever pointed out the lobster to Johnny Gordon's wife, nor left other customers waiting.

They took their supper in the Sugar Bowl Cafe; above them two huge fans hung motionless from the high ceiling of coffered cream-colored metal, reminders of the distant summer. The big room was empty except for them and two traveling men who joked with the slovenly waitress who hung over them, a new girl in town, for she did not hurry to serve Rose and George.

'Funny thing to think of,' George remarked, 'but a few hours ago I had dinner in here. Lunch, they call it in town.' He laughed. 'And do you know. I'm going to have the halibut again.'

'Again, George?' Her heart went out to him when he made conversation; the making came hard and she suspected he'd been told (as he most certainly had) that he had no gift for talk. How he worked to make himself agreeable!

When they had finished he said, 'You stay in here a minute. It's cold out. I'll hop out and get the curtains up. You go ahead and finish your coffee.'

He had loaded the new collars and the saddle into the back seat, and the side-curtains enclosed the stale odor of horse sweat, reminder of the ranch — that cheerless destination: the dogs would run out and bark, move out of the shadows of the moon where they slept; together she and George would tramp down from the garage, bewitched by the silence of the night; they would open the big front door and enter the silent room; George would go ahead and grope for the light switch; the room would have that astonished look in the sudden light; the light would cause the generator in the cellar to start popping its exhaust, and they would hurry to their room to undress, to put out the light that had caused such commotion. Then in the new silence she would hear Phil's snuffling and coughing, the snuffling and coughing of one who has long been awake and waiting.

As the town slipped behind them and the last lights disappeared behind, she grew a little melancholy, thinking of people, simply people she had seen through a window, sitting down to a meal.

'Well, we're on our way home,' George said. 'Yes, siree!'

'What a nice trip it's been,' she said and drew her cape close about her shoulders and shivered, recalling the still heat in Peter's room, the curious hothouse atmosphere there and the human skull. 'I like the moonlight.'

'You know, Rose, I've been thinking.'

'Thinking what?'

'Remember — we were talking about pianos.'

'I remember.'

'Rose, what is the best piano? I always liked it when you played. Mighty cheerful, don't you know?'

'Of course I'd like to have a piano, but I don't play well enough to have the best.'

'Of course you do! You're capital. My goodness, my mother liked to listen to music on the Victrola, but she couldn't play a thing, Rose. I told her you played, and she said how she wished she could. She said I was lucky to find a gifted wife. That's the word she said. Gifted.'

'You didn't paint me a little colorfully?'

'How could a man do that? And do you know who you're going to play for?'

'For you.'

'Me, of course. But you'll be playing for the Governor. And the Governor's wife.'

'Oh my good Lord, George!' and her throat closed.

'He's coming first of the month. I thought you'd like to meet him. He's capital.' They drove for a time in silence, and he spoke again. 'Right back there we passed the place we had our picnic. The winter picnic, Rose.'

'Was it just back there?' With a chill, she felt there was much more than the picnic spot they had passed, and she prepared herself once again to approach the ranch house that would loom in the moonlight, all the bulk and logs; she'd hear again the barking dogs — it was as if she and George were strangers or gypsies. They would enter the house, and then she would hear Phil coughing and snuffling.

The Mason & Hamlin piano arrived in Beech from Salt Lake City and remained on one of those express trucks shrouded with a gray tarpaulin against possible snow until the station agent could follow instructions and get a truck down from Herndon to haul it to the ranch. He said he judged it weighed a ton. The station agent made several calls to Herndon and called George to report that the trucking company was all tied up and that one of the men who was sometimes available to lift and haul things had got married and was gone for a few days' honeymoon like a man would, he said, but that the company was trying to find somebody else to help the driver, who said it was impossible to come out alone because you needed more help with a piano than he would likely find around a place like Beech. George remembered the driver as a tall man who looked over people's heads.

Then the trucking company called the station agent, said they'd got hold of a young fellow to help the driver, a stout young Swede, clumsy and willing, but when he got down to Beech with the driver in the solid-tired chain-driven truck, he lifted the wrong way and damaged his back before they even got the piano off the express truck. He collapsed in pain on the station platform, his face ashen, the sweat beading his forehead. Was his back broken? By a happy coincidence, the sheriff of the county was standing at one of the bars in Beech with his usual and thus was available to drive the young Swede to the hospital in Herndon. They got several other men out of the bar, and between them and the driver and the station agent they got the piano on the truck, but the driver later told George frankly that piano hauling was a specialized business and it's a wonder the lot of them didn't break their backs. He said that somewhere between Beech and the ranch the chain drive on the truck broke, and the driver was caught there in zero weather until he improvised a pin to fix the son of a bitch.

Rose was alone to receive the piano. The driver refused the coffee she offered. 'It's bad for the kidneys,' he explained. His father had never drunk the stuff, either. 'Last time I'll ever contract to haul a piano.'

'I can't tell you,' Rose said abashed, 'how sick I am it's caused such trouble.'

'When do you figure your menfolks will get back here?' the driver asked, taking out his Ingersol.

'Surely by noon.'

'A wonder he didn't break his back,' the driver said. 'He's got three little children.'

It had begun to snow when they started to unload the piano. The hired men got two-by-fours and ropes from out back and they constructed a ramp to the ground from the truck, and the driver directed them, looking over their heads. 'For the love of God,' he said, 'don't do it like that. That's how the Swede cracked his back.'

George worked along with the hired men, and at last they dragged the piano up the front steps, uncrated it, and inched it inside and got the legs screwed in. Phil remained in his bedroom. 'Your fellow at the station in Beech didn't say what you had there was a piano,' the driver remarked. 'Lots of places they get, oh, ten dollars an hour. I expect because of how you are likely to break your back.'

Hired girls, like whores, were recruited from the families of small farmers or ranchers to the south where the land was bad, alkali land, dusty land, land of tumbleweed and thistle. Unhappy, sullen, stupid girls, they loathed their lot, their fathers, the knowing they were the extra mouth to feed; and so forth.

They came with pasteboard suitcases, with their hair tightly curled — as they believed the world required — washed dishes, scrubbed floors, made beds, waited table and giggled with the hired men who had their own immediate plans. Few remained long anywhere. They soon glimpsed the aridness of their situation: they could not marry a hired man, for there is no place on a ranch for a married man; like married priests, they can't keep their mind on their work, always running off to where the wife is. Some girls got pregnant, and disappeared; others returned to where they came from and once again wept and quarreled with parents. Some found the Dixie Rooms, where they got two dollars a trick, and ten for all night — an interesting bit of economics.

Lola, who answered George's advertisement in the *Recorder,* arrived with a nightgown in her suitcase and a treasure of old movie magazines she read and read again in her small room upstairs. Many movie stars had also come from nothing, and now they rode about in limousines, took countless baths, and wore the skins of precious animals. She was a quick, frightened girl, pigeon-toed and willing. She seldom spoke above a whisper, should her voice offend. She feared Mrs Lewis who quoted gloomy axioms and spoke of pretty young girls found trussed up in trunks in California and such places; she feared the hired men who winked and suggested that she ride out with them Sundays on horseback.

Her presence left Rose idle except to plan meals and to practice the piano that had caused a fine young Swede with three children to hurt his back. Thank God, the back was not broken. The piano was black and gleaming and worthy of more than the sheet music she placed on the rack; her repertoire was pitiful, a few Strauss waltzes, a military march, sugary accompaniments to songs like 'The Rosary' and 'Just Like a Gypsy,' a piece that George liked and one he would certainly request when the Governor arrived. The pride George took in her small talent frightened her; he never noticed when she missed a note. She began to practice diligently that what she played she might play well, that he might be proud.

Phil left the room when she played; so pointed was his

leaving she could no longer practice at all until she knew he was out of the house or in his bedroom with the door shut; she suspected his taste was far better than George's, and that he silently laughed at her, knowing she practiced to impress the Governor.

Doors, doors, doors, doors; five outside doors in the house, and she knew the sound of the opening and closing of each one. The back door Phil used let the prevailing wind billow the hall carpet so it writhed like a snake. She knew one afternoon that Phil entered the house: he walked with a quick, light, high-arched step on his rather small feet; she heard his bedroom door close behind him. Protected from his thoughts and emanations by that closed door, she sat down and began to play; but as she listened critically to her own playing, she heard another sound, that of Phil's banjo, and knew suddenly that when she practiced, he played, too. She paused, staring at the keys. The plunk-plunk of the banjo stopped, too. Cautiously, she began again. The banjo again. She paused, banjo paused. Now she knew a crawling sensation up the back of her neck: he was playing precisely what she was playing — and better.

Phil could not read a note nor did he have to; he played by ear, could play anything, having heard it once, quickly recognized the composer's intent and pattern. Just so he recognized the logic behind Mozart's music, music he had often heard escaping from the louvers of the Victrola; those old records caught orchestras playing Mozart arrangements for brass and woodwinds alone because wax wouldn't catch strings in those days. He scorned what Rose played, neither one thing nor the other — the stuff she must have played in the honky-tonk or whatever; and he knew well why she practiced as she did.

Old George had let the cat out of the bag.

'His Nibs will be here for dinner,' George said.

'Well, sir, ain't we going up into Sassiety,' Phil remarked. 'Out with the finger bowls?' And Phil laughed. So this was Georgie boy's way of introducing his piano-tinkling wife to Sassiety! He got a kick out of hearing her play at the new pananno, making one howler after another, dropping notes like crumbs, and then when she'd finished, he'd play the thing correctly.

It was days before she savvied what he was doing, and then she stopped playing unless he was out. Time and again he'd hear her stop when he opened the back door, and that was almost as good as aping her. Easy to get her goat. How her hands shook, pouring the coffee! Phil had no use for people who felt sorry for themselves.

Poor thing had apparently got into her noggin she ought to dress for supper, with a thing around her head somebody must have said looked pretty, practicing maybe for His Nibs. (His Nibs was a hick lawyer until some slick politicians got hold of him and married him off to a woman with a little class.) Even old George, since his marriage, dolled up in a clean shirt, and Phil had caught a pained look from George and the little lady herself when he came to the table exactly as he always had and always would. They were living on a ranch not on some fool dude resort, as the little doll seemed to think.

Phil was surprised when George spoke to him in the blacksmith shop. Phil was standing at the forge, one foot propped up comfortably on that wood block, his long arm comfortable on the arm of the bellows; he pumped away, bending easily at the waist, chewing tobacco in time to the pumping. In the fiery nest of coals was yet more fancy ironwork. The shop was littered with pokers, andirons and pieces with no practical use but simply expressions of Phil's remarkable brain through his hands. He worked barehanded with hammer and tongs that no leather or cloth might blur the sharp image his brain conceived. Waiting for the metal to heat to the proper cherry red, he stared out at the snowy hill, watched the rich coal smoke drift out the big door and settle slowly to the ground. He did not speak when George walked in, looked around, and settled himself on a sawhorse. George always sat quite a spell before he spoke, for he was a slow thinker. But Phil knew he was troubled and small wonder. Maybe now Georgie boy had come to see that marriage wasn't all it was cracked up to be. Almost every weekend he had to drive wifey to Herndon to see the precious child who needed his dear mommy. Why couldn't she drive to Herndon herself and leave George to his *Saturday Evening Post*? She was scared of the winter roads. One of these days somebody would give her something to be scared about!

What had driven George from the house? The plunking on the pananno? The little lady would get started on one of her renditions, make a mistake, start again — and make the same mistake. Set your teeth on edge. Poor old George would sit there waiting for the mistake.

Or was it George was cogitating about the summer when the kid would come slinking in and out of the house, a constant reminder that Georgie boy wasn't the first one to put the blocks to her? He had a hunch George hated sissies as much as he did, and now there would be one such right there in the house, messing around, listening. Phil hated how they walked and how they talked.

Wouldn't have surprised Phil if George had begun to worry about the dinner with His Nibs. Just how had she worked that, *anyhoo*? Well, if a man's crazy enough to want a woman that bad, there are things she can hold back unless he invites governors for dinner and so forth. Phil had read *Lysistrata*. What a laugh it would be, that dinner. Phil would have to carry the whole God damned conversation himself, and then our little Miss Honky-Tonk would hammer out her little pieces with the old mistakes. Well, all right. Teach George a lesson. Phil was no snob, but you can't marry outside your class. And what would His Nibs' wife have to say?

George sat there on the sawhorse. There was stuff on his mind, all right, something he hated to say. And he'd better speak pretty quick if he wanted to speak privately, because pretty quick one or another of the hired men would come out of the bunkhouse. Although on Sundays when the men had finished feeding cattle, the rest of the afternoon was free — free to oil their leather goods, to wash their duds, to write letters (if they could write), to swamp out the bunk-house or read the cowboy stories in the magazines they laughed at and secretly believed — still they weren't comfortable in the bunkhouse if George was abroad; he had a queer authority without even knowing it, an ability to upset you, maybe because he so seldom opened his talker and his silence made you look in upon yourself, on the guilt you always knew was there. In a few minutes the men would be out, walking to the barn to look busy. Phil smiled.

No sense for George to suffer any longer, so Phil helped him out with the balm of human speech — prime the old pumperoo, so to speak. 'Well, pard, what's in the old noodle?'

George raised his eyes to Phil's. 'Well, Phil,' he began.

'Go ahead, old-timer. Spit it out?' And Phil shifted his cud far back in his cheek so he could talk plainer.

Phil enjoyed George's little confessions. One early morning in 1917 the cattle-buyers were coming around, sucking around trying to get your cattle for their own price.

Now, Phil read widely and closely. 'You just hold off,' Phil advised George. 'That knothead of a professor from Princeton is going to get us into war pronto, and when he does, we're going to make a bundle of the old do-re-mi.'

But George, whom you couldn't always push, got his back up, and sold. And sure enough, in April, Mr Veelson got us into the shooting war. George dropped five thousand bucks they could have had, and it did Phil good to hear George eat crow.

And back in college. Phil was getting straight A's, and the dean himself called Phil to congratulate him. The dean was interested in ranching, and so forth. 'But by the way, Burbank,' the dean said suddenly, and walked over to lower the shade against the harsh California sun. 'What's wrong with your brother? In English, especially.'

'You mean what's eating him?'

'He's failing.'

'Failing?' asks Phil, seeming surprised.

'He can't seem to get the English. Maybe you could help him a little?'

'I'm not so sure he has the equipment.'

But he spoke to George. 'I don't mind telling you, old-timer, it was pretty embarrassing for me. Dean wanted to know how one fellow out of the same family could cop himself an A and the other went flunky-dunk. What's up with you, brother mine?'

George got red as a herring. 'I'm sorry, Phil,' he said.

'What the hell good does sorry do? You're going to have to set to and use the old yankee-noodle, or they're going to sack you and you're going to have to face the music with the Old Gent. You know damn well what the Old Gent thinks of failures.'

'I know,' says George.

'Matter of fact,' Phil says, 'if I was you, I'd drop out the end of the year. You better face up to the fact you ain't got the equipment for this so-called higher education. No good battering your bean against a stone wall, kid.'

Struggle as George might the remainder of the year, he got sacked in the end. Phil remembered how George stood looking at himself in the mirror. Phil was graduated with honors. George would have saved what was left of his pride if he'd followed Phil's advice.

George, sitting now on the sawhorse in the blacksmith shop didn't look as if he had much confidence now, either, and Phil watched him reach down with a gloved hand and pick up a handful of fragrant shavings Phil had earlier planed off a two-by-four. George looked at the clean shavings that were tangled like a mouse nest in his hand. 'Sort of a hard thing to say,' George murmured, 'what I'm going to say.'

'You go right ahead and spit it out.'

'It's about His Nibs, the Governor,' George said.

So that was it. So Phil was right. 'About His Nibs, you say?'

'Not so much about His Nibs, but about His Nibs' wife.'

'Go on.' The corners of Phil's mouth tensed a bit in a smile, and he began to chew.

'I was thinking, His Nibs wouldn't mind so much, but his missus might.'

'Mind what, for dear Christ's sake?'

'Mind if you come in to eat without sprucing up a little.'

Phil scarcely lost the rhythm of his pumping. He just kept looking at George until George dropped the rat's nest of shavings and walked out into the cold, gray afternoon.

At first it wasn't clear to Rose why her thoughts turned more and more to the past — to her father who was proud of his house and everything in it, the umbrella stand in the hall and the telephone he approached gravely and spoke to courteously, saying always, 'Wilson residence . . .' with a rising inflection, to her mother's anxiety over the health of house plants. Her mother dressed more carefully on the day the postman delivered the *Ladies Home Journal,* as for a holiday; and thanked the postman, as for a gift. Then suddenly, thinking of the postman who brought the *Journal* and of the house plants, she would recall the curious quiet of certain Sunday afternoons and the sound of the piano next door, the muffled scales and exercises of her closest friend who played duets with her and sometimes brought over a book on the meaning of dreams. Upstairs they would interpret dreams, stifling giggles.

Her mother's voice: 'What are you girls up to? I heard you way outside. Hattie Brundage called on the telephone and says she has all the Eastern Stars coming to her house tomorrow, God help her, and will you do the flowers. If people were strangers, I'd think you ought to charge. I swear. I think later on you ought to work in a flower shop. What on earth am I going to give your father for his supper? And he hates leftovers.'

Then high school and the exchange of class pictures and the final passing around of the autograph books and Graduation Day and the smell of cut grass and a few of the girls close to tears, Miss Kirkpatrick of the English staff moving imperiously among them straightening this flounce and that hair ribbon. 'Now we must everyone look his or her best.' Miss Kirkpatrick was alert, should some girl cheat and wear rouge. 'Rose, the flowers are stunning this year.' Outside in the hall, the boys trooped past carrying slatted folding chairs and the janitor scolded.

She was neither valedictorian nor salutatorian nor even close. She sat at rigid attention in geometry class and drew neat triangles and trapezoids and labeled them in her small, assertive script, but she couldn't understand the subject. Yet her name, too, appeared on the program, apart.

Flower Arrangements: Miss Rose Wilson

For the past four years, it was she who had arranged the flowers donated by the Elks and the Eagles and the Woodmen.

'Now, I'm sure all of you here know me,' the principal began his address. 'Some of you only too well . . .'

Nice laughter all around, for some of the young men knew the principal all too well, knew his office, the varnished woodwork, the hissing steam radiator, the bust of Lincoln and dusty American flag. The principal was an old man who believed in things and now talked of Brightness Through Obscurity.

Thus — graduation. 'That looks stunning on you, Mummy,' she said. 'Daddy, you look just like a young man.'

'Yes, doesn't he,' her mother murmured. 'Do you honestly like this hat? I think it's simply terrible how they're using bird feathers on millinery now.'

Her father had laughed. 'Well, we've all got to go sometime. I expect there's many a man my age who looks a deal younger than me.'

'I,' her mother murmured. 'Than I. Your father wants to know if you can get more of the programs? With your name? He says he's willing to pay for them, but I said they wouldn't charge for them, would they.'

'Why, I'm sure I can get extra ones. And it isn't really very much, to arrange the flowers.'

Her father said, 'Bushwah! Why do they put you there on the program, then? I can't think of a nicer thing for a young woman to do. Plenty of them these days can't even sew a button on a shirt.'

'It might be nice to show your own little girl someday,' her mother said.

'Now, I'll tell you what we're going to do,' her father announced. 'We're all three going to go down to McFadden's, and we're going to sit ourselves down and we're going to order us up any concoction we want. What do you say to that, my ladies?'

'Pete,' her mother said, 'I think that's just splendid.'

Proud as royalty they sat at McFadden's on chairs of twisted wire. 'McFadden has a fine establishment here, in my humble opinion.'

'When was any opinion of yours ever humble?' her mother smiled.

'I see,' her father said, 'he's even got a shaker of nutmeg here on the table.'

'That's what the young people are putting in their malted milks,' her mother said.

'I should imagine,' her father said, 'a man would put on a lot of weight if he ate like this very often. He wouldn't keep very young looking.'

'I shouldn't imagine,' her mother said, and nodded and arched her brows and her lips distinctly formed the words Good Evening toward some people they knew who then came over. 'So here's the girl who arranged those lovely flowers.'

'For four years,' her father said. 'She has a way with flowers.'

The flowers, the flowers, the voices and the flowers. She wondered if others concerned themselves with such fragile recollections, searched among such shadows and dusty voices — and for what? For herself?

For recently it seemed she had lost her identity, and it was precisely to find it that she constructed a flower arrangement of materials bizarre enough to challenge her considerable skill, materials first seen through the binoculars George used to look at the mountains. She saw them against the woven-wire fence that enclosed the horse pasture below the house, nothing in themselves. But what was art (she defended herself) if not the arrangement of trivia? What was Cezanne but line and color, Chopin but sound, perfume but calculated odors, crackle of linen but flax? The arrangement, like her piano playing, her careful dressing for dinner each night and the foolish picnic beside the road, was meant to please George. She meant to surprise him. And she did.

He had never seen such a thing in his life, and he grew a little red in the face, and spoke gravely, choosing words. 'Why, that's quite a thing! Why, I — think it's right pretty.'

'Pretty? I'm not sure of that, but I hoped you'd like it. I used to do other things like this.'

'You did? I guess there are all sort of things people used to do. Yes, I certainly do like it, and I think my mother couldn't have done such a thing. She was more a reader, always reading and bringing up various things, don't you know.' To himself he thought, My wife weighs scarcely a hundred pounds. I love to see the side of her face. He thought, The thing is made of weeds, and he anticipated Phil's reaction to such a thing and it struck him as intolerable that this innocent bit of handiwork would certainly bring down on her Phil's hooting laughter — if not to her face, then in the bunkhouse, the sort of tearing, hooting laughter Phil had turned on him one Christmas not so long ago when he, to please his mother, had put on over his clothes a dressing gown of blue silk and funny slippers to match — her Christmas gift to him.

Phil had appeared suddenly.

And later, there was that hooting laughter in the bunkhouse, like echoes out of a barrel. Christmas *had* been an embarrassment since he could remember. The Old Folks expected him to choose the tree which he selected carefully from some spot where the tree had got the sun all around and the branches were nice and even and he brought it down from the mountains in a sleigh, and carried it into the house, and set it in the proper corner and the Old Lady always said, 'I do love Christmas!' and began the decorating and the Old Gent reached up high where she couldn't reach with the shiny glass balls that caught and distorted the image of the room, left it reeling around the reflections of the window that faced the sagebrush hill. The day of Christmas Eve was always long and terrible and had a special smell, or maybe it was how dark the house was, or maybe how strange, because of the furniture that was moved to make room for the tree, and the hours of that day always led to the same thing, the Old Lady bringing out gifts and piling them under the tree. 'How good the tree smells!' In her eyes, in her smile he saw a reflection of what she must once have been but — like the room in the shiny balls — distorted. Then the boxes from Back East were opened and the gifts taken out and put under, and then supper, and the men in the back dining room laughing and exclaiming over the gifts of neckties and the checks the Old Lady always distributed out there and George still did (but not wrapped, of course) and then Phil rising from the table and going into the bedroom and closing the door while the presents were opened, and the Old Lady pretending. She had never learned — *they* had never learned — to accept Phil as he was and to hell with it. She wanted to think — *they* wanted to think — that the Burbanks at least on that one night were like anybody else. And they were not. Phil saw them as stumbling, fumbling dabblers and wishers and dreamers and except for Phil, that's what they were. How does one man, how does one man get the power to make the rest see in themselves what he sees in them? Where does he get the authority? But from somewhere he does get it. It wouldn't have hurt Phil to come in that one night and pretend, even if Christmas did embarrass him, even if he had no more use for the gold watches or hunting knives or the stuff from what he called Abbie, Dabbie and Bitch than George himself did for the blue silk dressing gown and the queer slippers with just a place for the front of your foot. Mules, she called them. Mules!

What had possessed the Old Lady to buy him such a thing? When would he wear such a thing? Was there a place in the world where such things were worn? Did men, the relatives, the friends Back East dare to cinch themselves into such an outfit and walk without shame through a room?

'Of course I like it,' he told her. 'I like it fine.' Then, feeling her eyes, he put it on over his clothes because she was his mother and by God, he wasn't afraid of love. Then there was Phil in the doorway.

'Well, get a load of the Big Mogul.' And the ripping laughter.

Well, George thought now, I've lost a lot of weight since then.

The Old Gent had said, 'Phil, there are other worlds besides this one. I have a dressing gown like that myself.'

Phil's eyes were lazy on the Old Gent. 'Sure you have. But this is the world we live in. It was you who left the other world. I never figured out why.' Phil paused. 'Did *you*?'

The Old Lady smiled, her mask against everything. When Phil had gone back down the hall she said, 'I think now it might be nice if you put on the Schumann-Heink. It hardly seems Christmas, without.'

That record on the Victrola really shot the works, because the idea of angels, shepherds and the Holy Virgin and the Son of Man in that room was just plain crazy.

He would buy Rose flowers, flowers and more flowers — real ones, dozens of them. He would buy flowers to make them sit up and take notice, buy every flower in the place! Flowers to take the sting out of the laughter he was sure would come because she tried to make flowers out of something that was not flowers. He *half* liked what she had done! Proud, even! But, oh, there wasn't a chance in the world that Phil wouldn't notice the thing. Not a chance.

And George was right. Phil gave it the old once-over; Phil never missed a trick. Alone in the room, Phil stood over it, his feet wide apart, head cocked. He sniffed, as for an odor. Before him on a flat shingle of shale she had picked up, he looked at a dried tumbleweed twice the size of the human head; the outer tendrils cupped up to describe a perfect sphere and enclosing the network of lesser branches inside. On these, and not at random, the woman had fixed flaming red wings of a material that at first confused him, but then his sharp eye saw beneath the deceit to the shape and color of the original — a dirty, blood-colored plant with flat, sharp leaves that thrived along the fence of the horse pasture and dried in the winter to an even darker color. She must have soaked them in water to lighten their color. He'd heard or read that the Indians used them to make a crimson dye. In drying again, the sharp leaves curled smartly. Pulled apart, they now perched on each branch of tumbleweed alert as scarlet hummingbirds. By God, he thought. The woman might be dangerous after all! He stood back, and squinted. His was a nimble imagination. Often in the rolling clouds he saw smiles and frowns, sometimes the face of terror, and for him the wind hummed tunes. Precisely, it was his gift to arrange the facts of Nature into patterns that would stir the senses; it was this gift that let him see that thing his heart called The Hound on the Hill.

'By God,' he murmured, and looked at the thing the woman had made. She must be pretty all-fired proud of herself, he thought, to have made so much out of so little. Why, the thing looked alive. He squinted again. What was it? Caged birds? Was it a puff of smoke, enclosing flames? So much out of so little; and he said to himself something about a silk purse, and a sow's ear.

8

Over the years the old Burbanks — perhaps out of *noblesse oblige* and perhaps out of loneliness — had given a series of dinner parties, and not one had been successful. It was not merely that the Burbanks had little in common with the other ranchers; it was that men and women in that country had only in common what could not be mentioned at dinner parties. From the earliest days, when the guests arrived by buggy and team — elegant matched pairs of Hambletonians or Standardbreds — to the present when a man with great dignity behind the wheel of his Maxwell or Hudson Super Six drove his wife into the yard, the sexes separated, husbands and wives parted and remained as though they had never met and did not ever wish to. The hours before dinner were strained, the women lined up on one side of the room and the men on the other, the air in the spaces between them charged, hostile and embarrassed.

The women feared their gowns were not adequate, nor their hair nor their hands and fingernails. They took refuge in sitting straight and tense as they imagined ladies did, fearing to open their mouths should some ugliness pop out like a toad and mock them. They could respond to old Mrs Burbank's chatter of books and articles come upon in her use of the newspapers with but the stiffest smiles, for they had neither read books nor papers. Until this moment, caught in this room, there had seemed no reason to.

On his side of the room, the Old Gent was no more successful in getting the men to respond to his talk of politics, the war with Spain, then the Boer War, then the trouble in the Balkans. They knew nothing of Spain, nor of the Boers, certainly nothing of the Balkans, and they, too, found refuge in sitting straight, sweating. They touched their neckties and collars and looked at their feet, strange in new shoes. The Burbank music, played on the Victrola, could not weld the sexes — selections from *Aïda,* from operettas of the day, *The Runaway Girl, Mademoiselle Modiste, The Red Mill.* They had the rugs rolled up and called on the group to dance, but the Burbanks had no reels and schottisches, and the ranchers and their wives hobbled about only briefly in the waltz and two-step and longed for the dear walls of their own establishments.

Uneducated people, they felt talk risky, for if they spoke of what they knew, of ranching and the breeding of cattle and horses, the talk might treacherously veer to the facts of breeding, to the purchase and worth of bulls and studs, delicately called gentleman-cows and he-horses, but suggesting all the same that there was more to life, more to marriage, than merely living in the same house together, and that every couple in that room was guilty of it — however far they now sat apart with wooden faces, however unresponsive. The world must suspect their guilt. Topics that were at once safe and required little imagination or education were few. Recent deaths among their numbers were dwelt on, the duration and nature of the final suffering, the last words, the final scene, the last food taken, and the bereavement of the survivors.

The weather offered a variety of aspects fit for talk, and the subject when broached was leapt on with almost hysterical enthusiasm, that each guest might express and relieve himself before the subject was left lifeless and limp, on the extremes of temperature, of humidity, rain, snow, sleet, the velocity of the wind, winds past and winds yet to be. The weather exhausted, the company might sit dumb until dinner was announced by the chimes struck at the door of the dining room by the hired girl.

The elder Burbanks learned early not to embarrass guests by finger bowls and butter plates; they kept silverware to a minimum. Group eating was scarcely less embarrassing than bodily functions, and guests watched carefully to see how the Burbanks did it.

To eat and to talk at once was especially difficult, but George remembered one dinner party that had been intruded on by the Episcopal minister in unexpected parish call, perhaps not realizing that the Burbanks had no particular need of God and — when they did — they would come to Him. It was the minister himself who had brought up the subject of cabbage (his wife, of German extraction, fancied cabbage) and he was both astounded and flattered by the avidity with which the company took it up, the women expressing either affection or dislike for the vegetable, the men using it as a springboard to memories of their mothers' preparation of sauerkraut, of the primitive gardens in the country, and of the dear past long gone. Recipes for the preparation and preservation and the enhancing of cabbage were exchanged and each woman vowed, with a nod of the head, that she would soon attempt the recipe of the other. Phil referred to that as the Cabbage Dinner, and it was one of the last parties that the old Burbanks ever attempted. But there had been others — the Mud-Hole Dinner and the Grizzly Bear Dinner.

Dinner over, guests were free to make, shifty-eyed, their

lame excuses and to depart, leaving the Old Gent squatting before the Victrola, filing away his records and rising to stare at the green felt cover of the turntable before closing over it the coffinlike lid, leaving the Old Lady to remove her jewelry before her dressing table, staring sober-eyed at her face in the mirror. The guests, now some miles away in their cold cars, drove in silence, ashamed of each other's wooden performance, wondering what was wrong with them that they couldn't talk, couldn't waltz, couldn't rise to an occasion. Why had they married? Why labored to acquire property and money when the end was sitting in chairs in the Herndon House, watching the townspeople go about their legitimate, mysterious errands?

The day of the Governor's visit stalked ever closer.

'Whom should I ask?' Rose asked George, who greatly admired her English. 'You'll have to give me a list. And of course they'll all come. You can't refuse a dinner given for a governor. Oh, George!'

Mrs Lewis was cooperative; she had never seen a governor, and fancied the opportunity.

'Why of course you can meet him,' Rose said.

'Thank you, no,' Mrs Lewis said. She wished only to look on him from the window when he drove up, and departed. She would make popovers and prepare chickens as her dead mother had prepared them. 'For a time it looked as if she would take the recipe to her grave,' Mrs Lewis said. She would have one of the men bring ice from the icehouse, and make maple mousse.

'Well, I'll tell you, Rose,' George said, recalling the Cabbage Dinner. 'If you don't mind, we won't ask anybody. Just you and me and Phil. Phil's a crackerjack talker, and after dinner you can liven things up at the piano. It never worked out to have a lot of people.' He explained the Cabbage Dinner. 'My mother's face got pale, and it was years before she could laugh about it.'

'Whatever you want, George.' She had so counted on the safety in numbers (the table would seat twenty-four), had so counted on dazzling the Governor with numbers, wanted to hide in the presence of numbers. 'I just thought it might be easier.'

'No, it wouldn't be easier,' said George. 'It would be harder. I almost wish sometimes we hadn't got ourselves into this.'

'Don't worry, George,' she said.

'Oh, I'm not worrying,' said George.

The table was set for five, and there were finger bowls and butter plates that April day that opened threatening snow, the clouds lowering over the mountains, the smoke from the bunkhouse settling down. From upstairs there seeped like a wraith the odor of singeing hair, for Lola the hired girl had been busy with lamp and curling tongs. By two in the afternoon all hope was dashed that the Governor and his lady would not arrive because of some gubernatorial business, some pardoning of a criminal, some presiding at solemn ceremony, for he telephoned from Herndon that they were indeed on their way. 'He sounds in capital spirits,' George told Rose, and they stared at each other a moment. 'He says he's looking forward to a drink, and his wife likes one, too. Don't be surprised when she smokes.'

The doors on either side of the buffet were locked on such whiskeys and gins as nobody else in the valley ever drank, and the key hung hidden inside the china closet. Until the Old Gent went to Salt Lake City, only he used the key or touched the bottles, and George had felt curiously emancipated when first he opened the doors and looked on the array of bottles, Holland gin, Booths, House of Lords, Chivas Regal. The Old Gent had long been opposed to women's drinking just as he, like Phil, was opposed to women's cutting off their hair and generally acting up, but the swell of the times had forced him into offering females a cocktail called an Orange Blossom, and the recipe was included in the *Bartender's Manual of 101 Drinks*, also locked behind the little door.

'I'll make the cocktails when they come,' George said, 'while you talk to them,' and his eyes escaped hers. Behind him she touched the napkins on the table. He lifted out gin and bitters and set the bottles on a silver tray, reached for the silver cocktail shaker with the monogram, the sort that people like the Burbanks gave each other. 'You haven't seen Phil, have you?'

'Why, no,' she murmured. 'Why?'

'He's probably in the shop,' George said, 'or in the bunkhouse.'

'Did you look in his room?'

'Oh, yes, I looked in his room. He isn't there.'

'Then I imagine he's outside.' George could not know, she thought, how it disturbed her to speak of Phil. Was he unaware that Phil had not spoken directly to her more than twice? And both times only at the table when he wanted and couldn't reach something with his long arms and then, in her direction, he mentioned its name — the salt, the bread? Or did George take it for granted that Phil would not speak to her, their having nothing in common, the one a man, the other a woman? Or was he aware of the strain and only able to bear it by ignoring it? When she spoke of Phil her mouth grew dry, her tongue thickened. The thought of him scattered all pleasant and coherent thought and reduced her emotions to a child's. Almost with relief she saw the speck appear far down the road, at the top of the rise, and the sun picked out some glass or metal on the Governor's automobile.

'There they come,' she said, her heart beating.

'So they do,' and George's hand went to his necktie. She had never seen him dressed in a suit except on town occasions, and she felt as if they were about to attend a funeral.

With smiles fixed, they walked down the porch steps and stood at the gate meant to keep wandering livestock from trampling over the feeble lawn. The Governor's automobile pulled into the driveway, and halted. Then George and Rose in her new satin slippers with the cut-steel buckles crossed the gravel patch.

The Governor alighted, and opened the door for his lady. Then he turned. 'Long time no see!' he shouted, and under cover of his cheery voice his lady unfolded herself and arranged her little fur about her and got down to the troublesome gravel. She was a handsome, gray-haired woman with a stiff, nervous carriage and a quick smile. 'So good of you to let us come,' she cried. 'Not really breathed all winter. The air out here!' and she laughed delightfully. 'But in this state, you never know whether to carry an umbrella or wear snowshoes. My word!'

'We couldn't be happier to see you,' Rose said.

'My!' the lady breathed. 'The air!' She turned easily to George. 'I should think your parents would miss it here. There is such a promise about the spring.' She moved easily around the puddle of water.

George smiled. 'I'm afraid the old people began to mind the cold, some years back.'

'I suppose they would,' the Governor agreed.

'I suppose as we grow older, we do mind the cold,' his

lady said. 'But don't they find it cold in Salt Lake? I can remember being cold there.'

'It is pretty cold there,' George admitted.

'I believe I read it was thirty below, this past winter. And they have such dampness. The lake.'

'They're in this hotel down there,' George said. 'They have goldfish in the lobby and they keep it warm.'

'Oh, I love Salt Lake and I love the Hotel Utah.'

Rose grew a little desperate. 'I have never been in Salt Lake,' she admitted.

The Governor's lady took her hand. 'Don't you worry. We'll meet there one day for dinner. We'll plan something enchanting.'

They could not seem to get started, could not seem to get to the house; and to appear busy, George frowned at the front tire of the Governor's automobile and kicked it speculatively, and raised his eyes to the Governor. 'See you've got on the new balloon tires!'

'Well, sir, I have at that,' the Governor said thoughtfully, 'and believe me, it makes a difference in the ride!'

'I imagine it would,' George said. 'Great big tires.'

'What are you driving now?' the Governor asked.

'I'm afraid it's a Reo.'

'Now, George. The Reo is a good machine.'

In spite of the sun the air was chilly with a small wind that whispered of snowdrifts not far off in the mountains, and the two women, their arms folded, looked at the men. Why could they not move to the house? Rose glanced at the Governor's lady, noting the veiled look of boredom, fatigue and discomfort. She had driven two hundred miles to stand here watching men kick tires.

'Well,' Rose smiled, 'why don't we just go in?'

'Capital idea!' the Governor roared. 'Capital idea from a

capital little lady!' and across the gravel patch they went, women first, men behind, George admitting that he had once considered buying a Pierce-Arrow.

'Mmm,' the Governor said. 'That's quite a machine.'

George deposited the Governor's coat in the office off the living room; the Governor threw back his shoulders and looked around. The two women disappeared into the bedroom, and in the center of it, the Governor's lady stopped and took a breath. 'You'd never guess you were on a ranch, would you? Never, never know you were in the country, in a western state.'

It was an enormous room, rose-carpeted. On the shell-white walls big prints of Fragonard in silver frames — pretty sylvan scenes — caught the cold north light; the big windows were framed in lavish white lace caught by satin bows, and similar bows were poised like enormous butterflies on the lacy shades of the lamps, one beside a chaise longue. The canopy bed had an alcove to itself, and was flanked by highboys; the mirror over the dressing table was as large as a pier glass, casually reflecting an array of heavy silver objects and crystal decanters worth surely several thousand dollars: the number and disarray and the fact that old Mrs Burbank had not bothered to take them along with her to the hotel in Salt Lake struck the Governor's lady as an insulting attitude toward luxury. How strange that she who had been born for such things had them now only on loan, only so long as her husband remained in office! Then away would go the official cars, the mansion, the cook, the gardener and the maid and again they'd repair to a fair-to-middling house, her husband to his fair-to-middling law practice, awaiting a change of heart in The People. And this small woman beside her had been born to nothing. She had inquired of her husband as to who Mrs Burbank was, and he had inquired, and found she had run some kind of rooming house. Rooming house or not, it was she who now possessed these treasures, her husband who could talk of maybe or maybe not buying a Pierce, depending on his whim — or rather on *hers*. But suppose this little woman in black beside her failed at living up to it all? She must constantly feel herself on trial, playing a role, wearing a mask that might someday slip. The Governor's lady could not but feel a little jealous of her who pretended to be born into this room. 'Imagine finding such elegance — on a ranch!' She had paused to admire the two Dresden figures that flanked the dressing table — Love, and Love Blinded. Into the ear of the first, a fat cherub whispered nothing. A similar cherub fixed a band of flowers about the eyes of the second whose hands were raised in dainty protest. 'Such elegance.'

'I'm afraid it is,' Rose smiled. The Governor's lady felt herself stiffen, for here was a casual acceptance of wealth equal to that disarray of the silver pieces. But then she smiled to herself. For wasn't the little lady perhaps deliberately casual, that the loss of these things would be tolerable, should she fail . . .? 'Well, now,' she said. 'I'm sure the men must wonder what's happened to us!'

The men were smoking cigars. Both rose at once. George said, 'My brother will be here soon. We might just as well go ahead and have our cocktails. Something must have held him up.'

And it was then that Rose knew Phil would not appear.

Until then she had wondered if perhaps it was better that he didn't, for how could she or George explain — if explanations were even possible — the clothes he wore, his hair, his hands raw with the weather and only casually washed? Now she began to pray silently that he would appear, for when she spoke — and her voice was so frightened it came from the very top of her throat — when she spoke she spoke the very commonplaces George had said made all those other dinners dull, dinners attended by no more important people than other ranchers. The duller the conversation, the more would depend on her piano playing. Without Phil, everything depended on the piano playing.

'The weather has been awfully changeable,' she began, and the Governor and his lady agreed, while George clinked glass against glass in the buffet in the dining room, and made Orange Blossoms as he'd seen his father make them.

'Female weather,' the Governor laughed. 'Can't seem to make up its mind.'

'Well, sir!' his lady said, pretending to be offended, but there was George with the cocktails. 'Why, what lovely cocktails!' she cried out. 'Orange Blossoms, I do believe.'

'Yes, indeed,' George said, 'That's what they are.'

'Now, I tell you!' the Governor boomed.

'I'm afraid they're something of a ladies' drink,' George remarked with a certain shyness.

'And whyever not?' the lady asked. 'Ladies are here present!'

They all smiled at this simple truth, but when the silence fell, Rose found herself staring at the place at the table Phil was to have occupied, just occupy, and she looked away, and her eyes met George's, and his were miserable. He coughed, and rose. 'I'll just take a quick look-see out back for my brother.'

'Why, of course,' the lady murmured, and sipped her drink, eyes pleasant over the rim of her glass. The Governor half rose, and subsided. 'The funniest thing happened recently,' his lady began. She told a story of how a pack rat had got into the Governor's mansion, took spoons marked with the official crest from the State Dining Room and carried them up to the bedroom closet where it had built a nest to hide treasure. 'I went in there one night,' she recalled, 'and there was this rat up on its hind legs, defying me, showing its teeth!' She rose, and showed how the rat had looked, 'Well, let me tell you, I didn't laugh — then! I called my husband, here, and he came running in his pajamas! I think the rat would have attacked him — no respecter of persons — but our son had stored his skis there, and my husband took the skis and defended himself beautifully, and eventually killed the thing. Don't you call them varmints in this country? I have been eternally grateful for winter sports . . .!' Rose felt the story was worth more than a smile, that more than a smile was expected, but she could bring no warmth to her laugh; she listened for the sound that would mean George had lifted the steel latch of the bunkhouse door, had entered, had inquired, and left, lifting the latch again. George had had time, now, to do all that, had time enough to walk to the barn, into the long, dark barn where Phil sometimes sat thinking and doing things with his hands. And time now to walk back, and Rose raised her chin, listening for the opening of the back door. It opened, and as always a cold draft fled before George's footsteps.

George cleared his throat. 'I'm afraid there's something my brother had to do. Rose — maybe you'd tell Mrs Lewis we can eat in a few minutes.'

'Oh, that's a shame!' the Governor's lady said. 'I don't mean the eating. I mean your brother. Nothing could have happened to him could it? I've heard so much about him. Isn't he said to be brilliant?'

'Oh, now,' George said, 'I expect there was just something he had to do.'

With what dignity remained to her, Rose walked through the dining room to the kitchen.

At the table, the Governor's lady began again. 'I was just telling your wife, when you were out back, Mr Burbank, about the oddest thing that happened. This rat . . .'

'Yes, they'll do that,' George said seriously. 'My mother lost several rings and a thimble. No respecter of persons, and I don't suppose there's any small animal that's got such defiance.'

Now Lola brought in the coffee in the silver pot, and set it with the cups before Rose. Dear God, prayed Rose, don't let my hands shake.

'It's a shame for your brother to have missed this good meal,' the Governor said.

'Well, on a ranch, you never know,' George said. 'Things are always coming up.'

'Yes, I suppose that's true. Not like other businesses, other professions.'

'No,' the Governor said, 'on a ranch there couldn't be any working hours, regular ones. And I dread the day when the ranch hands get mixed up with unions.'

'Do you think it's coming to *that*?' the lady asked.

'Well, you can't tell,' said the Governor. 'These wobblies sit right up and defy you, like that rat.'

'I'm sorry,' Rose said. 'You said you didn't want sugar.'

'Now, now, now, now, that's perfectly all right. I like good coffee like this any old way.'

Her hands did not shake much until they had taken their second cup of coffee to the living room. Lola had not been told to remove Phil's place, and from where Rose sat she could see it. Suppose something had happened to him? Suppose his scorn of her had driven him off to his death? Like air into a vacuum, tales crowded into her head, a horse stumbling into a badger hole, the rider's neck broken, a rock slide covering a man with tons of crushing smothering shale; maybe Phil had crossed a creek and the ice, rotten with April, had given way, and he'd been sucked under the swift, silent water — all deaths common enough in that country, and the subject of more than one song sung by the men in the bunkhouse. Because of the ticking of cup against saucer, she set both aside and folded her hands, twisted her ring.

The Governor's lady glanced quickly around the room, hoping to find some object that might spark speech, and fixed at last on the portrait over the mantel, the full bosom, the eyes, the pearls. 'That's your mother, Mr Burbank?'

'Painted some years ago,' George admitted.

'I'd say she has the face of a woman of many accomplishments,' said the lady, thinking privately that a woman with such pearls need not be much concerned with accomplishments.

'She reads a lot,' George said, 'and she writes a lot of letters.'

'Letter writing is a great art,' the Governor said.

'Or it *can* be,' said his lady, modifying the remark.

'There's a book called the World's Greatest Letters,' the Governor revealed. 'Very instructive.'

His lady laughed. 'You've used it more than once,' she said roguishly, 'in your speeches.'

'State secrets!' he laughed, and waved a hand at her.

George was about to remark that single-handed, his mother had raised the entire sum for the hospital in Herndon, but thought better of it just as the lady spoke again.

'Did she also play the piano?'

'No, no,' George said. 'Not a note! I imagine I've heard her say a thousand times how she wished she could.'

'Just you, then, Mrs Burbank?'

'You can scarcely call it playing,' Rose said, her lips stiff. 'Before my first marriage, I played the piano in a pit in a moving picture house.' She smiled. 'And I'm terribly out of practice.'

'Why, Rose,' George objected. 'You've been playing a lot. You know you have.'

'I expect you're much too modest,' the lady said. 'Do play something.'

'Indeed a pleasure,' urged the Governor, seeing in the piano a reasonable end to an uncomfortable evening, knowing that when the last note sounded they could rise and make their excuses. Often, he had found, it was a last cup of coffee, sometimes the last trick taken at whist, sometimes the insistent ring of a telephone.

Rose glanced at George, but he was smiling with pride, and she rose and walked to the piano that had, perhaps, broken a young man's back, whose chords had provoked Phil's vicious mimicry. Placed as the dining table was, bare except for Phil's setting, she looked directly at it, and felt with temporary madness that Phil had arranged things just so, and was smiling wherever he was. His implacable malice pursued and confused her. Her palms were wet, her throat dry. 'Very well. I'll try,' and she smiled.

Somehow she got through an easy Strauss waltz, not daring to do more than play it mechanically as a child might repeat ABC's, mindlessly.

The three behind her clapped, and waited.

George spoke. 'Play that one I like, won't you, Rose?'

'What one is that?' she asked, to gain time, time to think, time to will away the strange creeping numbness that now started in her shoulders and crept into her hands and fingers.

'Why, the gypsy one. The one about the gypsy.'

'Oh, yes. "Just Like a Gypsy."' She blushed, knowing

146

he knew she knew what he meant. It was a simple enough piece, but sentimental, and after each phrase she had always made a little coda, a little cascade of notes that lifted the piece somewhat above the notes written on the sheet. It was a thoughtful little tune and sent one's spirit singing and winging away into an ephemeral land of sweet longing. It was curious that George, George the prosaic, George the tongue-tied, had seen in it perhaps what she had, and it might have been that his affection for the tune had been the beginning of her affection for him in those first days, when she played for him at the inn, on the old mechanical piano.

In professional fashion she rubbed her hands a few moments, took a breath, touched the keys, appalled that her fingers had no feeling whatever, no knowledge. She folded her hands in her lap, and looked at them. Behind her the clock whirred, fixing to strike, and she sat waiting for the chime that might somehow release her from this dark spell. But the clock struck, and her mind was as blank as before, her fingers as dead. She turned on the bench, and smiled. 'I'm sorry,' she said, 'but I can't remember it.'

George parted his lips, amazed, but he kept silent. It was the first time she'd seen disappointment in his face, and his first disappointment with her she could not repair.

'Oh, my,' the Governor said. 'Don't worry about it.'

'Goodness,' the Governor's lady said. 'Time and again, I forget things.'

'Speeches,' the Governor said in a tone that rose almost to a laugh. 'I've forgotten speeches.'

'Once in boarding school,' his lady said, 'I was in a play, and I opened my mouth, and nothing came out, nothing at all.'

'I'm terribly sorry,' Rose said. 'But everything is just gone.'

'It doesn't matter at all,' the Governor said, 'it really doesn't.'

'And we should be going,' the lady said. 'I had no idea it was so late. It gets dark so early, you lose track of time. But summer, the long, long summer is close upon us!'

They stood again beside the Governor's automobile; the sun, gone down behind the mountains, had dragged spring down with it. Webs of ice already spanned the puddle of water beside the car.

'Lovely, it was just lovely,' the lady said. 'We must see you again sometime.'

The men shook hands. George held the door for the Governor's lady.

'Please do come again,' Rose said.

'Why, we certainly shall,' the Governor said, with a great grin.

George was staring at one of the new balloon tires. He smiled at the Governor, and kicked the tire. 'Good luck with your tires,' he said. 'And it's been a fine day.'

'Thanks, George, thanks,' said the Governor, and got in. Everybody waved.

'I'll be right in,' Rose told George as he started for the bedroom. She waited a few minutes after the door had closed behind him, gave him time to remove his shirt and shoes — without them she knew he'd never venture back into the living room — and then she swiftly removed Phil's plate, glass and cutlery, swiftly but silently, taking care not to let china tick as she replaced the plates in the cupboard, careful lest silver ring — not so much to hide from George what she was doing, should he be listening, but because the sound of Phil's unused utensils would lend them a further dimension. She could not have faced them in the morning.

When she finished, George was already in bed, he had not turned off the light. 'I'm sorry,' she said. 'I'm sorry I played so poorly.'

'Ah,' he said, 'that's all right. I expect anybody might get stage fright, if you'd never met a governor before. Maybe you felt the cocktails a little too much?'

She started to speak. It hadn't been stage fright at all. Playing before a governor no more exposed oneself to criticism than playing before an audience in the pit of a motion picture palace or for a group of diners. Would he think it queer that she had simply been paralyzed by the eating utensils of someone not present? She thought of the skull Peter kept on his desk in Herndon. She had always hated the thing.

In the bathroom she undressed and lingered drinking a glass of water. Her head was splitting with pain; she could find no aspirin.

He was silent when she got into bed, and in a few minutes he turned away and began to breathe evenly. She began to breathe evenly as if she, too, were asleep. The whole shambles of a day swam in her mind, isolated and sharpened by the darkness. Why had she told the Governor's lady that her piano-playing days had been at an upright in a pit in a motion picture palace — why, since she had wanted that woman to think George had married someone of worth? Certainly it had something to do with Johnny. What an age-old dilemma it was, that of the twice-married, such a dilemma that theologians, to soothe the conscience, insisted there were no marriages in heaven.

George cleared his throat, and she knew he was not asleep. She reached out and took his hand. One of the dogs out back began to bark, a sudden, hopeless barking; another dog joined in. She heard the latch of the bunkhouse clink, and one of the men shouted 'Shut up!' The dogs were abruptly silent, and she imagined them crawling back under the house.

George's hand grew rigid.

In a moment she heard, too: hoof beats, distant hoof beats measured and deliberate as a dead march over the frozen earth; closer and closer, crescendo as they approached the house, diminuendo as they moved toward the barn, and ceased.

Now the dogs again. Another voice shouted an obscenity. Phil.

She winced.

George coughed.

So much time to lead a horse into the dark of the barn, so much to loose the latigo and let the cinch swing free, so much to remove the saddle and blanket and hang up the saddle, so much to let the horse out to the hay pen.

They heard Phil let himself in the back door, and close it as firmly as if it had been noon. They heard his quick step. At the opening of the door the wind whipped down the hall and whistled under the farther door.

Phil's door closed. Then through the locked door of the bathroom came the coughing and snuffling.

Then George rolled out from under the covers and sat on the edge of the bed.

'What's wrong . . .?'

'I'd better go in and talk to him.'

'Talk?'

'I don't know. Maybe I was too rough on him.'

'Rough?'

'Rose, you know — he hasn't got very much. And he's my brother.'

'He is. You must. I know.'

So George dressed and let himself into Phil's bedroom, and stood there. After a while his eyes picked out the dull gleamings of the brass bed. 'Phil?'

Phil's voice was like daytime. 'Yes?'

'I thought I'd come in and . . .'

'All right. You're in. What you got to say?'

'Phil? Hey? I shouldn't have said what I did.' He heard the small hiss of a cigarette paper. A match flared, died, dark.

When Phil drew on the cigarette the glow briefly flooded his face. He said, 'You two can keep your apologies to yourself.'

Now the Governor and his lady approached Herndon where they had reservations at the hotel for the night. For some miles, the Governor was silent, considering the remarkable failure of people to enjoy each other, or even to communicate. He'd found it hard going — but to admit it, even to his lady, was to expose his own belief, that most people gathered only out of boredom, or for gain. To have your table graced by a Governor was no small thing, and he knew it. Was his visit supposed to launch the new Mrs Burbank? But he had his angle, too, wanting to insure the several thousand dollars that had always been the Burbank contribution to the campaign. And now — what did he feel? Defensiveness about Burbank's wife. 'Imagine George Burbank marrying such a pretty woman.'

'Can you light this cigarette for me?' his lady asked. 'She's not all that handsome. There's such a lot of wind in the car. No, I suppose she is, but she's frightened, and pretending she was used to cocktails. They affected her, too.'

'I didn't notice that.'

'A woman would have to fall headlong. You didn't want to notice.'

'And speaking of noticing, did you notice that flower arrangement on the corner table?'

'If you can call it that.'

'Well, what did you think of it?'

'I thought it was — clever. It cried out for some sort of comment.'

'Well, you didn't comment.'

'*You* were supposed to. No woman wants to have another woman say she's clever. You might as well say she's predatory.'

'I don't think she meant to be clever at all.'

'Don't you now.'

They fell silent. Sometimes to the right or left they saw the lonely lights of ranches. Just as they pulled into Herndon, his lady said exactly what the Governor was afraid she would say. The painful thought he'd been entertaining she voiced. '. . . last very long,' she was saying. An automobile that suddenly slowed in front gave him a chance to apply the brakes, to occupy himself and thus to pretend he hadn't heard her. But there was no refuge in that, for he knew she knew he always listened and always heard. 'What was that you said then?'

'I said, I think she's probably failed already.'

'You're always quick to see failure, aren't you.'

'And then just before we got into the machine, she said the oddest thing. Said, "You've been very kind."'

'Well, what the devil's wrong in saying that?'

She turned and smiled at him. 'Don't be so edgy. And I'd like another cigarette.'

A dog ran out from the shadows and the Governor came close to hitting it. 'God damn it,' he said softly. 'You smoke too much.'

9

Mild were the days, the sun moving ever north; few calves froze before they could get to their feet and nurse; few were born crooked that year, spines frozen into the letter S or hoofs so turned they walked on the sides of them; that spring few calves were born dead — slim pickings for the magpies who bright-eyed watched each birth with heads cocked to one side. Slim pickings, too, for the gaunt coyotes who prowled the fringe of the willows that blushed with spring.

The snow began retreating above the timberline, bluebells grew out of their velvet foliage among the sagebrush, small birds skimmed the ground searching out nesting places. Now branding began — three thousand calves. Phil had castrated fifteen hundred head, marveling that this knife he held in his hands, the castrating edge worn down from a hundred keenings, had desexed fifteen thousand bull calves. And there had been a knife before that and one before that. As the last calf struggled to its feet and loped, shocked and spraddle-legged with pain, to join the herd, Phil looked across at the sun that sank fast in the west; there was so much bawling in the corral a man couldn't hear himself think, so much dust a man choked. Who wouldn't be tired after a week of branding? He wiped the little blood off the blade on his pants leg and then snapped the blade back in. Somehow he nicked his thumb, and a little blood began to flow. He reached around to his pocket for his bandanna.

Son of a bitch! he said. Castrate fifteen hundred head and then nick your thumb when you're finished! But he healed easily, and he grinned. 'Well, Fatso, I guess we're finished.' And got to his feet and kicked dirt over the dying fire.

George finished coiling up his rope and walked over and tied it to the pommel of his saddle. 'Guess you're right,' he said. Outside the corral the dogs lay with their noses between their paws, resting but watching, no longer interested in testicles. Two young cowboys who had wrestled calves shrugged their sweaty bodies back into their blue chambray shirts.

'Yup,' Phil said. 'Finished.'

On the day that Peter came to the ranch from Herndon, the men were trailing cattle to the forest, cows and calves whose new brands were already beginning to peel; the fresh leaves of the sagebrush, bruised by the hoofs of the trailing cattle, gave off a heavy odor. Ahead, the mountains were vast and cool.

Much of the flat across which they now trailed cattle had been taken up by dryland farmers, and rusty barbed wire fences blocked the original trail to the mountains; here and there the herd had to zigzag to get around; the fact always angered Phil. The drylanders were foreigners, for the most part, Finns and Swedes and such, and he had not much use for foreigners, and none at all for farmers. The shacks of log or clapboard covered with tar paper, their futile attempts to grow shade trees in the cranky, alkali soil, the clothes they wore — the big overalls and broken shoes — the wives who planted and hoed beside them, all reminded Phil of the changing times.

'The bastards can't even talk United States,' Phil told the young cowboy who rode beside him. Phil was a burning patriot. 'Twenty years ago there wasn't a bastard of a barbed wire fence in the whole country. Not like them days I was telling about, back when Bronco Henry was alive and kicking.' Again the herd had to change direction before starting straight for the forest reserve again. Many of the dryland farmers had failed — most of them — for sufficient rain never came, prayers were not answered, and the ranchers owned the water in the streams. It did Phil good to see the shacks deserted, refuges for bats and mice; after the doors sagged and collapsed on dry leather hinges, wild horses pushed in out of the sun; even so, rusty barbed wire fencing remained to divert your course until you got so God damned sick of it and tired of it you tore it down, rolled it up and tossed it into the brush.

'Them must a been good days,' the young cowboy said.

'You bet your whistle,' Phil grunted.

Just ahead, a cow in heat climbed up on the back of another cow to show her need, and then the broad back of a bull crowding through the herd to her. As she slid off the cow the bull reached and sniffed her. Coy, she ran ahead, but he followed swiftly and mounted her, harpooned her and then hunched away; she staggered under his enormous weight until, sated, he let her crawl out from under him and trot humpbacked ahead.

Sometimes Phil chose to ignore these things. Sometimes not. Now he watched the young man beside him, whose lips were parted. 'Don't worry,' Phil said, 'won't be long before you get to town.'

The young man blushed.

Phil grinned to himself. He judged that was about all they thought about, and what did it get them? Took their money, gave them a disease, or they ended up hitched to some little floozy in Herndon who cheated on them when they were out of the house, and that was the end. It beat him how people could destroy themselves over a piece of tail, themselves and the lives of everybody else. The fact was, George was no wiser than this young squirt beside him. Got himself hitched, and now there would be a stepson on the ranch. 'No,' Phil said to the young fellow. 'Those were the great days.' He felt like smashing something.

Rose left for Herndon in the Reo shortly after the men started trailing the cattle to the mountains, and began to worry at once. At her age, she couldn't accept Phil's silence, his dislike, as simply another curious aspect of life. Doubtless in many families some didn't speak to others. But you had to live to know it, get old enough not to expect much, old enough to accept the unpleasant, to add things up and see the balance.

But was Peter equipped to endure? How would he weather the scorn and the silence? Should she prepare him to expect them? What mother does not want her son to see her respected? What mother not want to spare the young the chaos adults have learned to manage?

Just before noon she arrived in Herndon; the steering wheel of the old Reo was of an awkward height and pitch for her; it was hard to decide whether she wished to be seen — as Mrs Burbank — straining to see over it or crouched to see through it. Already a hundred sprinklers played on a hundred lawns, the mist catching rainbows; the flag hung limp on top of the pole before the courthouse; at the base a dog sniffed; on the steps of the building a group of men talked, their faces to the sun, but as she passed they turned to stare. The sun's reflection bounced off the plate glass windows of the Ford garage where men stood around a new car. In the windows of a grocery store a clerk built pyramids of oranges. There she was catered to; but even there she felt an imposter, a child playing grown-up, playing Mrs Burbank.

Peter was ready and waiting. The water he had used to fix his hair had already dried. His shoes were polished, he wore a tie.

'You haven't been eating enough,' she told him.

'I eat enough,' he smiled.

'Why, your hips are so thin I don't see how you keep your trousers up. I don't, really.'

'Now, don't you worry,' he said. 'I look like I always did.'

His father's books. As she followed him upstairs to the room that looked as if it had never been lived in, she was seized with a dread she couldn't describe, nor could she guess the source. The un-lived-in quality of the room? Surely the boy must cause some disorder! Was it his father's books? They were a painful reminder of Johnny, and of Johnny's conviction that he was a failure.

Rose had taken pride in Peter's neatness; now she saw it as a threat to him; she was sickeningly aware of his slight lisp. That and the neatness would draw Phil's scorn at once, and she now saw the possibility that the boy might be so unhappy he would want to return to that dead room in Herndon. 'And you're taller, too,' she said. 'You could stand a lot more weight.'

If he eventually returned to Herndon, there would be talk in town, of course. They would smell the beginning of the end. How people did like to see the beginning of the end! But she knew there was no good in being aware of talk; and if he was happier in that dead room with the chessboard, the books and that skull — well.

. . . if he was happier in that room until such time

— until such time as what? Her inability to see into the future left her with the dregs of the same sensation she'd had when the men on the courthouse steps turned to stare at her: she didn't know who she was or where she was going. 'Have you thought,' she said, 'of just leaving your books here for the summer?'

'Leave them here?' Peter asked. 'Why leave them here?'

'There are such a lot of them.' And indeed there were. The Britannica. A complete medical encyclopedia, huge, heavy, musty old black books Johnny had got secondhand. Books on flesh and books on bone.

'I thought about it,' Peter murmured. 'But you understand, don't you? Do you understand?'

'Oh, I thought — well, of course I understand.'

'And when we get started for the ranch,' he said, 'you tell me about the dinner you had for the Governor. You didn't say much about it.'

Opposite each of the two brass beds in Phil's room was a similar glass-fronted bookcase, one Phil's and the other George's, they had always been there. George's had not been opened for years, since it contained nothing but stacked copies of *St Nicholas Magazine* and *American Boy* — had not been opened since George took up the *Saturday Evening Post*. Phil often thought that the bookcase was a microcosm of Geoge's life. George's life was largely what he read. He had but few opinions of his own.

Phil's bookcase contained neither books nor magazines, but was used as a display case for objects that caught Phil's interest over the years. Behind the glass were arrowheads he'd found, mounted on a board first carefully covered with green felt; the mounting itself was masterly, each arrowhead having a nice balance in size and material with the one on

the other side, a fan pattern. One of the finest he had fitted
into the shaft of an arrow, exactly as the Indians had. Here,
too, were fossils of trilobites and ferns pressed into sandstone,
relics of the days that country was under ancient waters.
Here was the skull of a wolf, a stone marten he had trapped,
killed, skinned, stuffed, and mounted realistically, its sinuous
body alert on a small log. Each object reflected some facet
of his gifts and talents, his stunning ability to grasp what
others missed, his monumental patience. One shelf supported
rocks, water-crystal, agate — and a fist of gold-bearing
quartz.

Phil often smiled, thinking of the quartz. A friend of the
Old Gent's, a mining engineer, came up for a few days some
years back from Salt Lake; this fellow had held the quartz
in his hands, eyes fairly popping. 'Where on earth did you
pick that up?' he asked Phil.

'Out back,' Phil told him. 'Up in the hills.'

'Did you have this piece here assayed?'

'Why, no,' Phil said. 'Why should I?' Why should he,
indeed? He knew the worth of it.

'Did you look for the vein, where this piece came from?'
the fellow asked. Phil was amused, watching the fellow try
to control his excitement.

'Oh,' Phil said, 'a few years after I spotted it, I tried to
find the place again. I never did.'

'Out back, you say?'

'All I remember,' Phil said innocently, 'is that it was up
Black Tail Creek, not far from a spring that runs into a
creek. Look valuable to you?' and Phil raised his day-blue
eyes.

'Well,' the visitor said. 'Now that I look it over, I guess
not especially.'

So Phil waited. He was good at waiting. He wasn't

surprised the next summer when a pack outfit headed up Black Tail Creek. He got the field glasses off the top of the bookcase and watched from the window while the Old Gent's so-called friend and some of his dude cronies blistered their pretty hands on picks and shovels, looking for something that wasn't there. Phil knew where the vein was, all right. It was a good twenty miles from where the Old Gent's friend snooped around. How he despised people who humiliated themselves for money.

Just before the fellow and his outfit gave up and pulled up stakes, Phil caught up his sorrel and rode up there; did him good to hear the fellow try to explain himself, face red as a beet. 'Thought maybe if I could find some of that quartz,' he said, 'It'd look good in the museum down there.'

'Well,' Phil said, 'enjoy yourself. Going to stop down and see the Old Gent?' The God damned fools.

Now, imagine Phil's coming into his room one June afternoon and stopping short. For something was wrong. Something had been moved, and sure enough, it was George's bookcase. Not only moved, but gone. The furry gray dust of years lay on the floor right there from where the case had been lifted, and in the thick feltlike dust were two marbles of the kind boys used to call chinks. Seeing them, he made his hand into kind of a fist, as if he were playing marbles again. He'd been an expert.

Well! Phil marched himself down the hall into the living room and spoke two of the few words he'd ever speak to George's missus. 'Seen George?'

She touched her throat. 'Why — I think he's in the garage.'

George had the hood of the old Reo raised, poking around, leaning over the fender; without straightening up, he turned his head at the sound of Phil's steps. 'What's up?'

Phil said, 'What became of the bookcase?'

'Bookcase?'

'You know. Your bookcase.'

'Oh,' George said. 'I couldn't think for a minute. I told Rose's boy to take it. He wants it for his father's books.'

His father's books! 'I thought,' Phil said, 'that I'd go to work and make a guncase of it.'

'I imagine it's put to pretty good use this way,' George said, and leaned back over the fender of the old Reo.

His father's books! Phil stood in the middle of his room and looked at the marbles, and reached down and picked them up and put them in his pocket. It's a wonder Miss Nancy didn't take them, too!

For it was as Miss Nancy that Phil spoke of Peter to the men in the bunkhouse, and they had a good laugh, and among themselves they called him the same thing, watched the boy wander up alone along the face of the sagebrush hill, exploring, accustoming himself to the long, long summer. Why wouldn't they laugh at him? He looked like no ranch boy; he was prissy clean, and lisped. At breakfast, the men winked at one another.

Phil knew if you cut off any old willow branch and stuck it into the ground where it's moist, you get the start of another willow; they take root right off and spread. When he and George were just young squirts they'd snitched pieces of lumber and built a secret shack out back where they could smoke and get away from the old folks and everybody; it was so small you had to sort of crouch. They'd stuck willows around it. Then when they got out of the swimming hole in the bend of the creek where the water circled slowly, the surface so still it reflected a perfect sky — when they got out and dried off in the sun that fell through the opening in the willows they could duck into the shack and sit there and smoke or chew and read the magazines the Old Lady would have had heart failure about, some of it pretty hot stuff. They must have been about twelve and fourteen, then. After the first year George lost interest (he lost interest easily) and only Phil went there to swim, sometimes strangely moved by his own naked reflection.

Long, long since the willows they'd planted had crept up to the shack and embraced it, hidden it, moved in, barred the door, latticed the windows and then finally poked right up through the floor and out places in the roof so that pretty soon you couldn't tell what was willows and what was shack, for the wood gradually rotted and fed the willows that twisted and grew thick; no one in the world but he and George — and once one other — knew about the shack, and even right up close you had to strain to see in the dark shape what remained of roof and wall; it was a last proof of childhood, like those marbles found in the dust — a secret shrine.

The opening itself had, in fact, become a sacred grove, the swimming hole a place of ablutions; only there would he expose and bathe his body. The spot was precious, and must never be profaned by another human presence. Luckily, that spot could only be approached through a single passage in the willows, so grown over that you had to stoop and crawl. In all the world, only this spot was Phil's alone. Not much to ask, was it? Even now as a grown man, he never failed to leave it without a sense of innocence and purity; the brief communion there with himself made his step lighter and his whistle as gay as a boy's.

Imagine then, his outrage when that summer he stood naked beside the creek preparing to wade in and wash himself when he heard a rustling that was not a magpie, not a cottontail, and turned, and saw Miss Nancy. The boy was poised as delicately as a deer, and the eyes as huge, and as Phil turned, he ran as a deer might run, leaping back into the sheltering bush. Phil had just time to stoop, grab his shirt and cover his nakedness. Thus standing, he stared at the spot where the boy had stood, at the ragged hole in the atmosphere, the ugly void. His shock turned to anger, and his voice burst clear across the stream. 'Get out of here,' he cried. 'Get out of here, you little son of a bitch.'

10

When the last of the Indians were herded off their lands and sent packing to the reservation, the government no longer even pretended to believe in treaties. Land was now too valuable for bargains, and there was no reason now to fear violence from the Indians and every reason to fear the wrath of the white voters. Those last Indians in the valley that went straggling off in their broken buggies, riding sway-backed old ponies, were those Johnny Gordon saw from the high seat of his old Model-T motorcar, and his thoughts had gone with them to the sunbaked flats of southern Idaho, where in winter the wind howled and the ground cracked with the frost. Few trees grew in so arid, so sour a soil, and the drinking water in shallow wells stank of sulfur.

The Indian agent lived in a neat, white-painted frame house and was scrupulous about raising and lowering the American flag at the proper times. It pleased him to let his two clean, bright-eyed children assist him, and they had learned never to let the flag fly in a storm nor to allow it to touch the ground.

The agent was not a bad fellow, but against the arrival of the men from the Department of the Interior, he thought it expedient to sometimes enforce the rules of the reservation.

No liquor sold or consumed. All the world knows Indians do not drink so well as white people.

No leaving the reservation without a permit. The whites could not be bothered with wandering Indians. Permits were granted only for some pressing reason. As the Indians had no place to go and no friends to shelter them, the question seldom came up.

No firearms. There was no need for firearms. Once the Indians lived on the reservation, all meat was doled out to them at the government store.

But Edward Nappo had a gun, a twenty-two rifle that had belonged to his father and the last thing his father owned that had not been burned, as is the custom, at his father's death. The small rifle leaned in a corner of the shed where the cow slept; not much of a gun, but it was an accurate little piece, and his father's. His father, the chief.

Now Edward would have been chief, had they not come to the reservation, and even so, he sometimes thought of himself as chief, when he got to dreaming, and dreaming he told his son of the land he knew as a child, the land the boy had never seen, for Jennie, the mother, had been pregnant in the buggy as they straggled south.

She was a sensible woman, a tanner of the deer hides the white hunters left at the store, a maker of gloves and moccasins. When Edward told stories to the little boy, she would sometimes rise and leave them and go to the shed where the horse and the cow lived. 'Why tell those tales?' she'd ask angrily. 'Why make him sad?'

But Edward knew the boy's need for stories, food to grow on, thread for dreams, and sometimes Jennie herself listened, and didn't go to the shed with the cow.

He told the little boy the truth, as his father had told him, that thunder was the pounding of buffalo hoofs in the sky and the lightning was the flash of their eyes.

'Buffalo?'

'You don't remember, but your grandfather remembered. He *knew*, and I remember.'

'I remember,' the little boy said, eyes wide. Sometimes you don't have to know, to remember.

'Wild crazy stories,' Jennie said.

'But see how he sleeps, afterwards,' Edward Nappo pointed out.

'Sleep,' Jennie whispered. 'And dreams.'

When the boy was twelve the winter was long and terrible; blizzards bearing sharp dry snow swept down from the north and sometimes it was forty below. Some old Indians died who had been strong enough in the fall, and the nights were lurid with funeral fires, loud with the muffled dirges of chanting women; snow drifted against the tarpaper shack.

Then, alas, the cow got sick. Jennie made her a coat from an old blanket, and during the cow's illness Edward and the boy tended a fire in the corner of the shed, their eyes weeping from the smoke that escaped little by little through a hole. As they waited and hoped and prayed, Edward told more stories of the land to the north, the land of summertime, the fields thick with purple lupine that waved and billowed in the breeze like water; he told of the watery cry of killdeers at twilight, of the dark gray thunderheads that reared high over the mountains and lumbered like grizzlies across the sky, heavy with water.

'It was the Indians' land then, and your grandfather was the chief.'

The boy rubbed the magic ring his father had given him, made of a horseshoe nail. 'We could run away.'

Edward Nappo smiled, thinking of what Jennie would say to running away, that practical woman. You can't run very fast or very far with a sick cow, she'd say. 'That land, not the Indians', now.'

'We could look at it. They'd be good to the son of the chief.'

Edward put another stick of cottonwood on the fire. Turning, he said, 'You'd think they'd be, wouldn't you.' He came back from the fire and squatted again, his shadow was large against the wall. 'I'll tell you,' he said. 'If the cow lives . . .'

And the cow lived.

'Crazy,' Jennie said. 'That land is gone.'

'But the boy could see it. See where his grandfather was chief, see his grave.'

Jennie kept working the deerskins, kneaded them in her strong hands, made them pliable for gloves and moccasins. Her eyes were failing from the fussy work of sewing beads on buckskin; they smarted from the smoke, and the metal-rimmed glasses she'd got at the store didn't help much. Oh, maybe some. 'You're crazy, and the boy is crazy.'

But when summer came, he pointed out again the bargain he had made with himself and the boy if the cow lived, and she put up food for them, canned beans and canned corned beef from Argentina and big hard soda crackers to soak up the juice. As the son of the chief, Edward Nappo did not feel bound to report his plans to the Indian agent; anyway, the man might have made trouble; therefore, they left one morning before daybreak. They heard a nighthawk zoom in the darkness; a thin dog barked heartlessly.

Because the horse was old, they walked unless dust in the distance said an automobile approached; then Edward thought it fitting to ride in the cart, no matter how crazy the wheels on the worn axles. The boy tossed the shoes he wore at school into the box of the cart; his bib overalls were bleached from many hard washings and hung loose from his thin frame and his big cap, though cleverly padded inside with newspaper, slid down over his eyes.

Edward was grand in his checked shirt; he wore his black cowboy hat, uncreased so the crown rode high.

The country, as they approached the north, looked strange, but Edward thought maybe he'd never looked closely at it before. On the way down, he hadn't cared to look at it. When the boy had been silent for a long time, he said, 'Don't worry about your mother. She'll be busy, and she's got the cow to care for.'

The boy trudged along, his eyes straight ahead. 'I wasn't thinking about her,' the boy said. 'I was thinking about the mountains.'

Edward was thinking about them, too, those he had described for so long, the black timber crawling up the sides, then timberline and snow that remained all summer; he had told of cloud shadows that drifted over, drowning the rocks and ravines in shade, and of the springs that leaped out of rocks. The boy loved to hear that the water was sweet, all fit to drink. Edward told of the silence in the pine trees, and the saucy cries of the camp-robbers, known only in those blessed mountains.

And he was thinking. Suppose the Indian agent got somebody after them? But he hoped to get far enough so they'd see the mountains. Each night they made camp off the road — in draws, in hollows, in parks in the willows near a stream. They chose grassy places where the horse could eat. If just once they saw those mountains! Saw them together!

Once they used the rifle. Edward was proud when the boy brought down a woodchuck, and they feasted on stew flavored with onions. 'We can't waste shells,' Edward warned. They had only a box, and the canned meat was getting low.

How that boy ate! They had a little cash in a Bull Durham sack, and at the last minute Jennie had brought out a shoebox with five pairs of gloves she had made. Edward had smiled at her. He saw through her. She intended to justify the trip as a business venture.

'Three bucks for the gloves,' she said sternly. 'Five bucks for the ones with beads and gauntlets.' He had never before known what she got for the gloves. It sounded like a good deal of money to him, and it crossed his mind that she must be putting money aside for the boy. She was a strangely ambitious woman.

He doubted that he'd have the courage to offer the gloves for sale. He had never sold anything, the thought of selling brought blood like a hot hand to his face. It was women, who have little pride and no need of it, who sell and profit.

But give her credit. The gloves in the box were a kind of security, and made it possible for a man to sit straight when automobiles swept by.

In the Indian School they had taught the boy to address his father as Papa. 'Papa,' the boy said. 'The sagebrush smells different.'

'Of course. There's water under the ground, and it can drink.' The gray alkali flats of the reservation had given way to green fields where white men's white-faced cattle grazed, tame as the cow at home, but a good deal fatter. 'But wait,' he said, smiling as he looked into the distance, 'wait till you smell the sagebrush near the mountains.' And he spoke the Shoshone word for beautiful.

'Papa, what's ahead there?'

'Ahead?' They were walking to spare the horse, and when you walk your eyes are so often on the ground. 'Why, those are clouds.'

'They haven't moved, Papa.'

'No wind, because there's no wind.' A shape lay on the horizon, shimmering through the waves of heat that rose like flame from the dusty road; it might have been a thunderhead of the very kind he had described to the boy, those that towered up and toppled of their weight.

It was his eyes, of course. His eyes, like Jennie's, had been damaged by the smoke that filled their shack in winter. And after his first twinge of disappointment that the boy had seen the mountains first, he was glad. How fitting that a boy should have seen that fresh beauty first, he'd always known it was the young who saw things, and the old who did all the talking. Edward smiled. No, the Indian agent had not caught up with them, and since he hadn't it was not likely he would. Doubtless Jennie had some plausible story to explain their absence. She was good at that. It was astounding the stories she could weave, scarcely looking up from her work, and people believed them. Her old woman had been good at the same thing. In her way, that old woman was a good old woman.

Feeling safe, he made plans.

And once they got into the mountains, the Indian agent couldn't find them, anyway.

He would use the money in the Bull Durham sack for fishing tackle and barbs to make spears; it was now the salmon ran in the river. They would fish, and cure the fish with the smoke from sweet green willows. He might take back a gift of smoked fish to the agent; smoked fish was one of the few things the Indians liked that the whites liked, too.

'Maybe three days to the mountains, now,' he said, and spoke to the horse.

Three days exactly! And the boy complimented him!

But they came to a gate that he couldn't remember.

★

Phil had no romantic ideas about Indians. He left that stuff to professors and dudes from back East with their fancy cameras. Children of nature, my foot. That crap. Actually, the Indians were lazy and thieving. They had tried hiring Indians to work in the fields during haying, but as far as machinery went, they didn't have sense enough to pound sand in a rathole. And poor hands with horses. When they'd tried to bunk the Indians in with the other men, in the canvas tents pitched down in the fields, the men complained about the smell, and it was either them or the Indians. The Indians stole — everything from livestock to a pie right off the kitchen table. The Indians that used to camp outside of Herndon broke into the saloons at night and smashed things. No wonder the government finally got onto itself and sent the whole shebang off to the flats.

Phil had to laugh. When the dudes used to come out with those cameras and tried to get the Indians to pose, the Indians got coy, pretending they believed that each picture weakened them, or that the photograph was their own ghost. But believe you me, show them a little old cash money, and they posed.

Look at their handicraft, the dudes said. Handicraft! Handicraft, hell. Phil knew more about their handicraft than the professors did. His collection of arrow-and spearheads was as good as you could put your hand to, and for years they'd been trying to get ahold of it for the museum in the capitol, and one day he'd probably let them have it. When he was finished with a thing, he was finished with it. But that same collection contained 'heads he'd made himself, using the very tools the Indians used, with agate and flint he'd found himself, and they were superior in craft to what the Indians did. You can look at their handicraft all you want! Children of nature!

They always had their hand out, and when the Old Lady was on the ranch she used to collect old clothes and bedding and hand it out, but then all their relatives and friends started coming around with their hot hands out, and the Old Lady had to put her foot down. No telling what would have happened if the government hadn't packed them off. They weren't ranchers. Not farmers, and didn't know corn from oats. The worst of it, they couldn't face the fact that their day was over, over and done.

Phil had ridden up into the foothills to the cow camp, a neat cabin near a spring, pretty little place, fine little corral. They were trying out a new cowboy there, fellow to ride the range, and Phil had timed his arrival about mid-morning to see if the young fellow was out of his bedroll and off on the job, keeping the cattle from wandering over the state line. You take a lot of these young fellows, they get off where you can't watch 'em and they get to reading magazines and lazing around and maybe having their buddies up with a bottle of booze, and first thing you know, you've got cows all over hell.

Phil rode up stealthily, out of sight of the cabin window, tied his horse in the timber, and then walked softly. No snapping twigs! He entered the cabin suddenly.

Calendar on the wall with a prettied-up girl on it, showing September of last fall. The rains had dripped down and stained the thing.

Hmmm.

Phil walked over and felt the cookstove. Wasn't even warm. Cold. The dishes were all done up and put away, graniteware coffeepot washed and turned upside down on the back of the stove.

Hmmm.

Table cleared except for a pad of cheap paper, the cover

turned back under it and a letter begun in dark pencil on the top sheet in the crabbed, uncertain writing of a child or moron, hard to say which.

Dere Ma,
I got me a lantarn here to rite this. I tell you, Ma, it shur is grate been a cowboy.

About the only word he could spell was what he was, a cowboy. You see, there it was. They didn't look on 'been a cowboy' as a job anymore, a man's job, like in the days of Bronco Henry. It was all playacting, like they saw in the moving pictures, and that accounted for the silver-mounted spurs and headstalls that kept them broke, for the records of cowboy songs they bought from Monkey Ward and played on their phonographs. They didn't know what the hell they were anymore, didn't know what was dream and what was life, and no wonder a man had to ride out and check up on them because once in the middle of the morning he'd come on one of these so-called cowboys up there in the cabin mooning and listening to phonograph records, and cattle all over hell. Maybe it was his sudden shadow across the sun behind him that had made the kid look up from his mooning about being a cowboy; for a few seconds the nasal voice out of the horn of the phonograph went moaning on about being a rolling stone or some such crap, and then the kid reached out a hand and shut the thing off.

He was sort of loose-lipped. 'I was riding all night.' They always had some excuse. If there's one thing you can bank on, everybody's got some sort of excuse.

'Well, I'll tell you,' Phil said softly. 'You get your duds, and you pack them in your little old grip, and you get started down the road.'

September of last year.
Now here was another year.

I tell you, Ma, it shur is grate been a cowboy . . .

Phil would see about that. But the kid was off and about, the stove cold, and maybe this kid just needed a little time, because for Christ sake, *everybody* today couldn't be trashy! Phil stretched and stood framed in the low doorway and gazed off across the valley, and listened to the spring play a merry tune on the rocks. Then he moved up into the timber to catch up his saddle horse, swung up and rode down to the new line-fence that separated state land from the forest. Farrest, as Phil called it. 'The Farrest . . .'

He swung down to open the gate, a government gate, the end post set on a block of concrete, the whole shebang so heavy it'd take a four-horse team to budge it, more damn gate than you ever saw in your life, but that was the government for you, and it was you, chum, who was paying for it. A gate like that set in the opening of a simple barbed wire fence! He wondered how much paperwork some punk bureaucrat had gone through before they finally got out a requisition for the design of that gate, how much some two-bit engineer had wasted in time, money and materials before emerging with that monstrosity, that stockade! The gate was fastened by a more than adequate length of log chain, another government extravagance — small in itself, but multiplied a thousand times it played right into the sweaty hands of the Bolshies and wobblies and those nuts. And by God, do you know, Phil pinched his finger in that chain, but not enough to draw blood. Just a blood blister.

He turned alerted at a sound. Some strangeness. Saw far down the draw some sort of single-horse outfit, some sort of cart. He could make out a black hat, and so far as he knew, nobody wore black hats but Indians.

'Sit nice and straight,' Edward told the boy, but no need to say. He sat straight as you might expect of the grandson of a chief about to hold speech with a white man. The little boy's spine was rigid. He pushed his cap up off his forehead. Edward knocked the dust off his black hat and stroked it with his palm, sort of polished it.

They'd been walking. When they saw the man standing by the big gate, they got up into the cart. They were under the stranger's eyes for a good twenty minutes.

'Why does he rest there?' the little boy asked.

'Well, maybe he wants to see who we are.'

'You tell him about your father?'

'Yes, I can tell him that.'

'So he'd have to let us go on by.'

Edward no longer cared, for himself. When they take you off to a reservation and sell you moldy bread and you can't keep a gun there's not much more you can do. Now he hoped only to keep the boy believing that in this country their name was honored, a magic name to open gates. Or was Jennie right in cautioning him about telling stories?

In all truth there were some in that old land, some whites who championed the Indians, took Indians' troubles as their own to the capital of the United States of America, far to the East, where no Indians that Edward had even known had been. There had been whites at his father's funeral, whites in honored places watching the burning of his father's blankets, moccasins, headdress, hackamore, wickiup.

Was this man one of those?

Edward drew up the old horse, smartly, as you might halt

a Hambletonian. 'How,' he said, and grinned. He handed the boy the reins, and clambered stiffly down.

Phil said nothing.

Edward looked around at the country. 'No rain yet,' he said, and walked to the big gate.

Phil cleared his throat.

Edward got his hands on the log chain.

Phil spoke softly, 'Where in hell you think you're going?'

Phil now stepped between Edward and the gate.

Edward turned toward the little boy who sat stiff and straight, chin up, as much to keep his cap from sliding down as from pride. 'My boy and I would camp out a little while. That's my boy, there.'

Phil didn't bother to look at the boy. He brought out a sack of tobacco and — as he always put it — 'manufactured' himself a cigarette with one hand.

'. . . my boy,' Edward finished.

The boy's voice was high and clear. 'My grandfather was the chief.'

Phil lighted his smoke, blew out the match, broke it in two, and pinched the charred end cool with his fingers. He inhaled smoke.

'He's right about that,' Edward said.

Phil still stood between Edward and the gate. 'Right? Right about what?'

'My father,' Edward Nappo said, 'was the chief.'

'Is that right?' Phil asked. 'Well let me tell you. I don't care who in hell he was. You, now. You get yourself back in that contraption of yours, and you and your kid hightail it out of here as fast as that old nag can go.'

Edward's face was so fixed in a smile he couldn't change it. 'We'd only stay a coupla days,' he said. 'Long enough for the horse, for the horse to rest. It's a real old horse.'

'Nothing doing,' Phil said.

So Edward turned, then, and went back to the cart, afraid of the boy's eyes. The boy watched Edward reach down under the seat and then he looked away. But then, what could the father do, but shoot the man? Then they would go into the mountains and live forever, the two, the two hunted ones. But free, free as never before!

Edward turned on the man with the thing he'd brought out from under the seat, but it wasn't the gun. He offered the box with the gloves. The man facing Edward was poorly dressed, and he had no gloves. Edward smiled, removed the cover of the box, and held out the box.

'Just one or two days?' What he would tell Jennie, he couldn't imagine. Maybe thirty dollars' worth of gloves. Edward lifted out the gauntlet gloves rich with beadwork. 'One or two days, mister.'

'Hey,' Phil said. 'Those are pretty slick-looking gloves.'

'Worth five bucks,' Edward said. 'Two or three days.'

Strange how the man made no move to touch the gloves, and no move, either, away from the gate. 'You get your contraption turned around,' he said. 'I don't take bribes, and I don't wear gloves. You picked the wrong customer, old-timer.'

So Edward climbed back up into the seat with the box of gloves. He turned the old horse around, and they started back for the reservation, two hundred miles away. Edward wondered if the horse could make it. If the horse died, what about the cart? He couldn't look at the boy but he said, 'Anyway, we saw the mountains. We saw my father's mountains.'

The boy's cap had slipped down over his forehead.

'I couldn't do nothing,' Edward said. 'You saw, I couldn't do nothing.'

Phil watched. In a way, he felt for the poor devils, and he untied his jacket from behind his saddle and took out the lunch wrapped in it. Mrs Lewis had thrown together a lunch of an apple and two thick roast beef sandwiches. Good, but Phil got so thirsty he thought he'd ride back to the spring and wet his whistle.

The Burbank ranch house was of huge logs; seen from a distance, it resembled one of those story-and-a-half bungalows that sprang up in California around the First World War; but it was a bungalow gone wild. The sensitive viewer paused, looking at it. One's distance from the place could not make so small a house as a bungalow look so large. In fact, the 'half-story' contained a bathroom and six vast bedrooms off which ran closets with gradually sloping ceilings where Burbank junk collected. The roof sheltered a vast porch, and Peter often stood in the dormer windows of his room and looked over the roof at the blank face of the sagebrush hill where sometimes there was barely perceptible movement — the dart of a gray bird or the hop of a cottontail. Sharp-eyed hawks glided overhead, alert to the dead, the dying or the stupid. The hill was so high the sun was late striking the windows of the house, so steep that all sounds echoed against it. Peter heard the latch of the bunkhouse door, the cursing of a hired man, barking dogs, bawling cows, the pop of the exhaust of the electric light plant, and on Sundays the pistol shots in target practice, the bright sound of horseshoes ringing on steel.

Thunderheads reared up over the mountains to the west; their shapes changed but gradually in the faint breeze — the shapes of England, of animals, rabbits.

'Will it rain, George?' Peter heard his mother ask, her

light voice floating up with embarrassing clarity from the porch below.

'Smells like it,' George's voice. 'But search me.' Peter smiled. When George used that little phrase he'd shove his hands into his pants pockets and look at his feet.

'I want to get those trees in,' his mother was saying. 'And more grass. Isn't it funny your people didn't do more about the yard.'

'My mother tried. The soil's so poor. Oh, she talked of the trees in New England. You'd think it was a country of trees. She had some little elm trees sent out. They came in sacks, but they died. She used to talk about something called bayberry, and how the fog looked on it, and the sound of the ocean. When she talked, you could hear the ocean. I used to wish, sometimes.'

'Wish.'

'Oh, to see it all.'

'I never heard you talk like this.'

'Why, I don't suppose I ever did. Rose, there wasn't anybody to listen.' Peter imagined George's smile.

Before the house, sick unto death, two cottonwoods languished, their thin leaves edged in a sort of soot, their little remaining strength sucked out by ravenous aphids; beyond them a patch of grass turned brown, and could be watered by diverting the ditch that ran beside the house; but if allowed to run long, the water found secret holes and flooded the cellar — drowning the mice down there, or a batch of new kittens.

'Wouldn't fertilizer help?' Rose asked.

'Might, at that. Rose, is Peter happy?'

'Peter?'

'A few days ago, I saw him watering the trees. I was thinking of him.'

'I think he's happy. He certainly likes his room, and it was good of you to give him that bookcase.'

'I don't forget I'm a stepfather. I imagine a stepfather's got to try a little harder than a father. I'd imagine there's no reason for a boy to like a stepfather unless a fellow tries. I know how I'd feel.'

'And he's always liked to explore. He explores around.'

Peter listened, expressionless. He had been exploring when he came upon Phil, naked. He still saw the white, hairless body. He said nothing of the incident to his mother — naturally — and he had a hunch Phil hadn't mentioned it, either. In a way, he and Phil had a kind of bond — a bond of hatred, maybe, but Peter felt that one kind of bond could be just as useful as another. Peter had walked with his mother out on the hill, and they had found bluebells in the cool of sage, bitterroots and waxy cactus flowers with the baffling sheen of pearl. 'Why, I walk out here a lot,' his mother had said.

'You didn't walk much in Beech,' he said, glancing at her.

'I forget. Didn't I walk much there?'

'It's the brother, isn't it. He makes you nervous.'

She paused and stooped to pick up a small stone. Everyone he knew winced at the truth. 'Makes me nervous?'

'He doesn't speak when he comes into the room. He brings in the cold.'

'Oh, Peter, he doesn't speak to anybody.'

Now George was saying down on the porch, '. . . came here, I never had a nice afternoon like this, just loafing.'

'Why shouldn't you enjoy an afternoon? I shouldn't call it loafing, bringing in those little trees from out back. Maybe we need a little fertilizer.'

'Well, let me think.'

Peter thought, George is a good man. Then he went

down and joined them on the porch. He surprised them, he came so quietly. Doors opened and closed softly for him. He thought of telling them how clear their voices were, and then tucked the information into a corner of his mind. His world required secrets, and he stored them away.

'Peter, you walk so quietly. Is it those tennis shoes? Look at those little trees George brought. Would you help plant them? I think we might need a little fertilizer.'

'Blood,' Peter said. 'Blood's the best fertilizer.'

'Why, how awful! Rose said.

'I've heard he's right,' George said. 'Think of those tall weeds out by the butcher pen. They're as tall as a man.'

'If you don't mind, sir, I could take the wheelbarrow and bring soil in from the butcher pen. It must be mostly blood.'

'Why, you just hop right to it. And thanks.'

They watched Peter move around the side of the house, his clean trousers and white shirt a strange outfit for loading up blood-drenched dirt, some of it not quite dry and heavy with the stench of recent death. Clouds drifted over the sun, moist and cool as water. 'I wish sometimes he wouldn't call me sir,' George said.

'It was his father's habit,' Rose said.

'Blamed if I ever ran up against such a neat boy,' George said. 'Beats me he doesn't mind going out to the pen and digging up — digging up fertilizer. Isn't it a funny thing, to know about blood.'

'Maybe not, if you only want to be a doctor. He's . . .'

'He's what?'

'Well, it's a kind of coldness. You see, I love him, but I don't know *how* to love him. I want love to do something for him, but he doesn't seem to *need* anything. I think his father would have been more successful if he'd had more of that coldness.' They watched the clouds sweep over.

'Would you hand me my sweater? Thank you. I don't suppose what I mean is coldness. Detachment? I don't mean any criticism. Nor of John either. He was a good person.'

'I've heard that said,' George remarked. 'I've heard he wouldn't get after people about their bills. What a fine way to be.'

Now came a distant rumble of thunder. 'Maybe rain, now,' George said.

'. . . when the lightning strikes close. You can even smell it, Rose said. The thunder came again, and before the rolling echo died, Rose said, 'There's that Indian cart again.'

'. . . cart? What Indian cart?'

'Why, this morning. It was so funny — I saw them up the road coming around the point of rocks, and George, they were talking, and leading the old horse. I watched, and they stopped, and got up into the cart, and drove by, not looking one way or another, and then at the top of the rise out there — see? — they got out and led the horse again.'

'Some sort of pride, I'd say,' George remarked.

'But where do you suppose they were going — going this morning, I mean? Wherever, it seems they didn't stay long. And where did they come from?'

'I expect they came from the reservation. Wait till I get the binoculars.' He got them.

'That must be two hundred miles away.'

'Anyway, I expect they wanted to camp up in the mountains. You know, they're not supposed to be off the reservation.'

'Whyever not?'

'They'd get — oh, to bothering. If some of them got to coming back and bothering, they'd all get to coming back, and bothering.'

George kept watching them. The wind whispered in the

hopvines that grew up the side of the porch. They sat, and George kept watching, and then he handed the glasses to Rose. 'I didn't realize one of them was a little boy,' Rose whispered.

'No? Eleven or twelve, I'd say. He wouldn't have been born when the Indians lived around here. He wouldn't remember what the country looked like.'

'Then, the one in the black hat is the father? You think the father brought the boy back here to show him?'

'I expect so.'

'And they stayed so short a time in the mountains.'

'They wouldn't have got to the mountains at all, I expect.' He coughed.

'Why not? Because of the old horse?' The Indians had passed the house now, and in a few minutes would disappear around the point of rocks.

'Phil went out of here this morning to check on one of the riders. I expect he turned them back.'

'Turned them back? After two hundred miles? Why would he do that?'

'Well, like I say, if they get started coming back. And Phil never cottoned to Indians, no matter who they were.'

'How do you mean, who they were?'

'Unless I miss my guess — hand me the glasses — that old Indian is the son of the chief.'

'The son of the chief!'

'He died up there a little time before they sent the Indians away. They buried him up there under the slide rock. We could see the grave sometime. Go up with a picnic.'

'I suppose they meant to see the grave.' Rose stood up suddenly. 'George, can't you imagine how that little boy feels?'

'Feels, Rose?'

'A white man able to turn back his father, the son of the chief. Imagine that. He'll never forget that all his life.'

'Well, I expect you're right. But strictly . . .'

Strictly what, she never heard, for she was hurrying down the steps. One of the hired hands, riding in from out back, saw her running as if she'd lost her mind, and calling out something.

Her shoes were not walking shoes. Stumbling in her high heels, running and pitching, she cried out to the Indians. 'Stop, please stop.' She was breathless when she caught them, and leaned for support against the side of the cart. She smiled up at the old Indian, and at last she had breath to speak. 'I saw you this morning,' she said. The old Indian removed his hat, but the boy sat looking through the old nag's ears. 'I would have come out to see you,' she said. 'I didn't know you were the son of the chief.'

Edward Nappo spoke. 'Did you know my father?'

'My husband did. You see, we would be proud if you would camp with us. My, but that would make us proud.'

Edward Nappo looked down at her, a tiny, lovely little woman who could not have been much help to a man with a cow, or for cooking, or for making gloves. You might have said, looking into her face, that she wouldn't last many winters, if the winters were hard at all. 'Thank you,' Edward said. 'My son and I, we will be proud to camp with you.' And as Edward turned the old horse around, the little boy looked at his father with haughty pride, and he fixed his cap.

When a horse trots, his legs move in diagonal pairs — the left front and right hind leg go forward at the same time, and so forth. It's a rough gait, and you have to post, have to rise in your stirrups and take the jolt in the flex of your knees, and no matter how you do it, it's bobbing up and down like a fool jack-in-the-box.

But when a horse paces, his legs move laterally in pairs — the right front and right hind legs move forward at once, an easy gait, a swift, rolling gait you can sit out in the saddle by letting your body twist easily with the movements of your horse. Any damned horse can trot: few can pace. Phil's sorrel was a fine, smooth pacer, with a controlled power behind each thrust of leg that reminded Phil of pistons. He rode swiftly down the canyon, tall and straight in the saddle, occasionally relaxing by standing in the stirrups and sniffing the odor of approaching evening, the cooling off of rock and soil. It had showered in the mountains; the tail end of the small downpour had caught Phil, but he fancied getting a little wet, and the damp caught and held the odor of the new sagebrush and the wild roses that bloomed beside the road. Phil had always enjoyed certain odors. Beside the road the creek splashed over the rocks; wild chokecherry had flowered in white and a deer bounded back up into the timber and cowered, foolishly believing it had hid itself.

The young fellow at the cow camp had not come back while Phil waited there after quenching his thirst at the spring, so maybe the young geezer was going to pan out, after all. Phil had been careful not to touch anything in the cabin that might reveal he had been there, and the path leading up to the cabin was so packed and hard you couldn't see a fresh footprint. Phil would check again soon, perhaps uselessly. But the letter the punk had started there hinted that he might take his work lightly, look on it as a lark.

Phil felt good; he took the shortcut to the ranch — from the rear, through the horse pasture, and it meant getting off his horse four times to open the crude 'Mormon' gates constructed of barbed wire that drylanders had strung up obstructing the wagon road that was old when Phil was a child, but so little used — now that four gates blocked it — it was growing up in bunchgrass. Sometimes Phil left the gates open, to show what he thought of them and the nuts who had fallen for the pamphlets the railroads had broadcast, promising big things to Swedes and Finns and God knew who. Take up land! Grow wheat! Well, plenty had took the bait. They took up a section or half-section from the government, bought their seed, plowed, planted and waited for rains that seldom came. Few remained now. They had crawled back to the mines and factories they'd come from. All over that country you saw their shacks, open to the winds, a bed rusting where once a man and woman had slept and loved. The print on the newspapers they'd used for wallpaper had faded. You'd see a kid's doll pitched into the corner. It honestly made you think. In a way, you had to feel sorry for the poor devils, they were human beings, too. But what Phil, for one, couldn't forgive, is that they hadn't used their noodles in the first place, and looked into things.

He scratched the back of his hand a bit on the last gate, barely enough to draw blood, but it warned him to expect some other small unpleasantness; he had noticed in his life that one such thing led to another. And it came. Crouching low over the pommel of his saddle to avoid some willows that arched over his head, one slapped him smartly across the bridge of his nose. He seized it and broke it.

Now he rode through the willows in the horse pasture, not a hundred yards from where he went to bathe. In the open again, where the timothy and redtop was growing good and thick, he suddenly pulled up the sorrel.

He couldn't believe his eyes.

Alone, apart from the rest of the bunch of horses, was a

186

strange Cayuse. Well, if Phil didn't see red! Every muscle in his long body stiffened. He sniffed. He turned his head, and there in a bend in the line of willows near the creek he saw where the Indians had pitched their tent, had built a fire. The thin smoke drifted over the willows in wisps.

Well, Phil rode there pronto. From up there on his horse he looked down. The young Indian was nowhere in sight, maybe inside the tent or snooping in the brush. The old buck had his back to Phil, and he didn't turn at once, although he must have heard Phil's approach. The old buck was maybe putting off the inevitable until the last minute, as some do. The old buck was leaning over the new fire. On either side of the mounting flames the old buck had pushed in a forked willow; these sticks supported a third, a crossbar, and from the bar hung a battered pail of the kind you buy axle grease in. In the pail was what looked and smelled to Phil like fresh meat, fresh beef.

Well, the old buck looked pretty sheepish.

Phil spoke. 'I thought I told you to get on your way.'

'But the lady,' the old buck said.

'But the lady what?' asked Phil.

'The lady to the big house. Said, camp here.'

Phil had to snort. 'So that's what the lady to the big house said, is it? Well, you start folding your tent.'

Phil wheeled his sorrel around and paced to the back door of the barn.

It was a long log barn, huge doors at either end, and damp. The cool, sudden gloom blinded Phil a moment as he led the sorrel up to the stall. He unsaddled, hung the saddle from a peg; as he started to lead the sorrel to the back door, the horse hung back before obeying the reins, and Phil had to jerk him. The sorrel loose and rolling in the dust behind the barn, Phil marched himself right back through the dark barn and, still a little blind in the gloom, almost collided with George.

George was a dedicated user of binoculars. A good pair of Bausch & Lomb, properly in their case, had since memory began rested on top of the bookcase in the living room. Pair after pair of the same make had disappeared — perhaps into the cardboard suitcases of departing hired girls or cooks, for field glasses are both valuable and portable. But still the glasses remained in plain sight up there on the bookcase, for to hide them was to suspect someone of a crime incomprehensible to George, and rather than entertain the painful thought, it was easier to buy new glasses. He would sometimes spend an hour at the window watching the movement of cattle or horses, judging the far retreat of snowdrifts, watching for forest fires. He had this day watched Phil's rapid progress from an upstairs window, and once Phil had stopped to parley with the Indians, George had come right downstairs, picked up his hat and gloves, and gone to the barn where he waited beside Phil's stall. Phil, when angry, would speak his mind no matter who was present, hired men, cooks, family, guests, friends, and in a way George supposed Phil was right — speaking up and not bottling up everything. But the lack of reticence gave Phil a towering advantage, for people thought twice before crossing him, dreading the fireworks and the terrible truths he spoke — even to the Old Gent and the Old Lady.

So if there was to be an explosion over the Indians it had better spend itself in the dark of the barn.

'What in the good holy hell,' Phil began, colliding with George. As always when disturbed or angry, Phil chose bad grammar. 'What in the good holy hell are them Indians doing out back?'

'Take it a little easy,' George said quietly. 'I told them,' he said, 'they could camp here a few days.'

'You told them?' Phil took a step back from George and looked him up and down. 'Boy — are you out of your fugging mind?'

'They won't do harm,' George said. 'I expect in nineteen twenty-five we can hold our own against the Indians.'

'Got a real tongue, haven't you, Georgie boy? A real tongue for humor or sarcasm, what? But just start using your noodle.'

'That's all right, Phil. Take it a little easy. You got to think how people feel.'

'People feel? Who feels? Just exactly who feels?'

'How the Indians feel, for one. The young Indian.'

Phil measured George again with his day-blue eyes that missed nothing, and his lips curled in a smile. 'What's all this sudden love for Indians? That gives me a good fat laugh.' And Phil laughed. 'Sometimes it honestly gets my goat how blind a man can be, Georgie boy.'

George leaned against the stall. 'Just what do you mean by that, Phil?'

Phil ducked his head as he finished laughing, a ripping, tearing, dry laugh, laughter not only at George but at the woman in the house who was going to have to go. 'Take a good look at yourself sometime. Go take a look at yourself in the mirror, take a good hard gander at your fiz. Then you take and ask yourself why your missus married you.'

George blinked once, but he kept his eyes on Phil. 'Think what you like, Phil,' he said. 'But the Indians stay.' And George turned and left the barn. But oh, how Phil knew how to touch the sore place. Lord, how he knew how to lift a scab.

11

Long, long before Mrs Lewis cooked for the Burbanks, a tree fell on Mr Lewis in the woods and killed him in his 'prime.' Mrs Lewis hoped to be one with him again in what she called their eternal home, but the suspended relationship left her with a mixed bag of acid sayings, bitter observations and chilly maxims.

'Eaten fruit is soon forgot,' she would suddenly remark, looking up from her work, from pummeling bread dough and slamming it down without mercy on the scarred face of the zinc-topped table. 'If we could only see before us,' she often remarked, 'the deepest river wouldn't be too deep.'

Rose had made a light, uncertain laugh. 'Things can't be that bad, Mrs Lewis.'

'Do you really believe that, Mrs Burbank?' Mrs Lewis asked.

'It's a small world,' she once remarked, and moved heavily to the cook-stove. Her heavy black shoes were slit to relieve bunions got from years of treading floors of strangers. She dropped the letter into the coals and watched it curl and disappear. 'A friend of Mr Lewis,' she remarked. 'He drank with Mr Lewis. It's a small world.'

She frightened Lola with stories of 'bad' girls who ended up in trunks left forgotten in sheds and railway stations and with tales of people remembered, friends and enemies. She told of a woman with a tapeworm that moved up into the woman's throat at mealtime, to remind her. Mrs Lewis, finishing a story, would blink slowly, like a tortoise.

The removal of a graveyard that blocked a projected federal highway required the digging up of coffins, among them that of a friend of Mrs Lewis; a clumsy tractor driver had split open the coffin with the tractor blade and it was found that the woman's hair had continued to grow after death.

'The whole coffin,' Mrs Lewis marveled, 'just stuffed with her lovely golden hair, except for a few feet from the end, where it was gray.'

When Lola came to work for the Burbanks she used money from her first paycheck for a subscription to *True Romance*, a magazine her father had forbidden her to read; once when he found her reading a copy borrowed from another girl, he had made her stand before him and rip it up, page by page. She was grateful he had not whipped her.

Two women alone so much in the front of the house, she and Rose became friends, a friendship that perhaps began when Lola asked if what they said about the movie stars was true. Like the men in the bunkhouse, she believed that if a thing was printed, it was true. She believed that people could be put in jail if what they printed wasn't true.

'What special thing was it you had in mind?' Rose asked.

'Well, there's this big star,' Lola said. 'Darlene O'Hare.'

'Yes, I think I've heard of her.'

'Well, it says —' And Lola flushed. 'It says she takes baths in milk.'

'Then I'm sure she does. I can't see why they'd say it unless she did.'

'My father would certainly never hold with anything like that,' Lola said.

'I believe your father is right,' Rose said. 'A person could get into no end of trouble, starting with that. One thing would lead to another.'

'You bet your life it would,' Lola said with sudden passion. 'My father is very strict.'

She talked a good deal of her father. He went down to Beech to church, she said. Once the dog was lost in a wild snowstorm and her father went out to find the dog in the middle of a night. It was caught in a trap. One time, Lola said, there were some sick Swedes who had no money, and her father took some meat they had and gave it to the Swedes because he said that God would pervide.

'And do you know what happened?' Lola asked. 'A deer came right down into the yard. It came right into the yard and stood there and looked right into my father's eyes, asking to be shot.'

Each week she wrote her father, and Rose worried because her father never answered, and at last she asked, 'Do you often hear from your father?'

'Oh, no,' Lola said. 'My father never learned to write. He can't read much, either. The kids have to read the letters to him. But my mother was a wonderful reader and a writer.'

'She taught you, then?'

'Oh, my yes. Before I went to school, even. And she's been dead many a year, Mrs Burbank. And do you know what my father said?'

'What did he say?'

Lola stood with a limp dustcloth in her hand, and as she spoke she stared out at the face of the sagebrush hills. 'He said my mother needn't've died.'

'What did he mean by that?'

'The doctor wouldn't come to him. He knew we didn't have money. Oh, we never had money. My father said if the old doctor was still there, my mother wouldn't of died.'

The clock beside the door whirred and prepared to strike the hour before noon. 'What was the other doctor's name?'

'His name? What was his name?' The clock began to strike and all but drowned Lola's voice. Rose looked out the window up the road. A few hours before she had stood on the porch watching the old Reo disappear over the rise; earlier, she had come on a curious scene. George hadn't heard her come into the bedroom and she saw him at the bathroom mirror, looking at himself. He had finished shaving, and simply stood there, looking. Quietly she left the room. Then he came out dressed for town. He made no mention of her driving with him. She couldn't understand it.

'Was his name,' Rose asked, 'Dr Gordon — the old doctor?'

Lola looked at her astonished. 'Yes. That was it. So you knew him, too.' Lola marveled at the coincidence, the sort of coincidence that gave credence to the awful stories of Mrs Lewis. 'Dr John Gordon.'

Rose parted her lips. It was almost as if she had heard her own name on the lips of a ghost. 'John.'

'It's a small world,' Lola remarked.

Yes, Rose thought. Much too small.

Now over the rise up the road came Phil on his pacing sorrel horse. This was the day, with George gone, that she must speak to Phil, and already she felt the terror that preceded her recent sickening headaches.

Did she have a headache at the moment? the doctor had wanted to know.

No, she said. At the moment she didn't.

Would she describe the headaches.

She said they were directly behind her eyes, and that pressure seemed to force her eyes out of her head.

Ah, then. Did she do a great deal of reading?

Not recently. True, she had once read a great deal. She had read often to her husband, and to her son. 'My first husband,' she explained.

The doctor sent her across the hall to the optometrist. 'My brother-in-law,' the doctor pointed out.

The small, puzzled optometrist made her read the big letters and the small ones. He drew the shades and flashed lights into her eyes. Then he sent her back to the doctor, with a note.

'Your eating habits, Mrs Burbank?'

She could think of nothing odd, except that she seldom ate breakfast, and then — well, she'd almost never eaten breakfast.

Ah, then! Hunger can cause headaches. Did she notice that often before the noon meal she had headaches?

. . . Yes, she did. Often she had them just before noon.

'You just start with a good hearty breakfast, Mrs Burbank. Why, breakfast is the most important meal! And I can pretty well assure you . . .'

Breakfast for the men was at six, and George and Phil joined them in the back dining room for oatmeal, pancakes, ham and eggs and coffee, and while they sat smoking for ten minutes and picking their teeth, George would give the orders for the day. Then the men would file out to the bunkhouse, smoking, still picking their teeth, bringing gifts of cold pancakes to the dogs who jumped and whined.

In the days when the Old Gent and the Old Lady ate a breakfast in the front dining room at eight, they sat opposite each other across the white expanse, spoke to each other in well-bred syllables and ate omelettes, perhaps creamed chipped beef on points of toast, salt mackerel and boiled potatoes. They might eat strawberries or grapefruit, delicacies hardly known in that country, and shipped at great cost and the risk of freezing from Salt Lake City. Finished, they touched their mouths with napkins, touched the surface of the water in their finger bowls, wiped their fingers, folded the napkins, rolled them and poked them into silver rings. These little ceremonies took a bit of the curse off the hopeless view from the front windows, the sagebrush hill, off the bitter winter weather and the sometimes appalling knowledge that Boston was over three thousand miles away. Their doubts about the nature of their lives they never dared communicate to each other, each depending on the conviction of the other that what they had done with their years was reasonable if not rewarding. Each morning, breakfast done, the table cleared, the one or the other spoke as the sun crawled up from behind the hill.

'Looks as if it's going to be a good day.'

Or, 'Looks as if it's going to storm.'

Or, 'Well, the storm must be over before long, don't you think.'

Then the Old Gent, hands clasped behind his back, began to pace in stiff, straight, military fashion across the carpet.

Step, step, step. Smart turn. Step, step, step. Watching his feet, watching his feet make the step, make the turn.

The Old Lady escaped to her pink room, there to lie a bit on the chaise longue, if the room was warm; to regard the distant mountains, to fuss with a little needlework. She wrote voluminous letters back East. It had often puzzled people why these two had come West, these two who scarcely knew a Hereford from a Shorthorn, who neither rode nor hunted, who could only nurse their little ceremonies.

She decided against telling George the doctor's orders about breakfast; he might suggest her eating at the table, as his mother had; but servants embarrassed her. She had often felt Phil's eyes as Lola offered peas or beets, aware that her straight back and rigidity was embarrassment and not the poise Lola might take it for. So she went each morning to the kitchen for a bowl of oatmeal.

The doctor might be right.

She was poised, safe for the moment on a tightwire, and no net below.

Then the headaches struck again, swiftly, and the pain pushed tears to her eyes. About one thing the doctor was right. The pain seized her shortly before meals. Aspirin again, and the Bromo-Seltzer. She pressed her fingers hard against her temples, seeking to block the nerves.

Toward the end of Johnny Gordon's life, when he had vowed never to drink again, she had found him pouring himself a drink. He was startled, and his eyes looked naked; when he spoke, he stammered. His stammering surprised her, for she had never judged him. 'I have a bad tooth,' he explained. 'The pain is about to kill me.'

He told the truth. The tooth was pulled.

Now, driven to the same distraction, she went to the liquor cabinet in the buffet, first picking from off its hook the key hidden in the china cupboard. She stooped before the small door, amazed at her pounding heart. Lola's step on the stairs. She rose from a crouching position, and stood until Lola passed into the kitchen. Then she stooped again, and hurried with whiskey to the bathroom, shielding it in the crook of her arm. She locked herself in the bathroom, poured it down. The effort left her gasping. She held the ends of her fingers so tight against her temples that white flames flickered in the dark of her brain.

And it worked. Quite calmly she regarded herself in the mirror over the washbowl. The only other comparable pain was childbirth. Of that agony, she remembered little; surely not sharper, never so lasting as these headaches.

The noon meal was pleasant.

'My, but you seem happy today,' George smiled, and stood awhile in the living room. He glanced in the direction of the dining room, and hearing and seeing no one, he leaned and kissed her.

'I am very happy,' she murmured, and George left, whistling.

When Lola had cleared the table, Rose replaced the bottle and turned the key thinking that deadening of pain was hardly worth the shame she felt. Or so she thought then, for when she thought it, she had no pain. She would not go to the bottle again.

The next attack tested her resolve, and she began then those pointless walks over the face of the sagebrush hill, thinking to find relief in the fresh air, in physical exertion; and the walks did help, at first, and it was on a walk, Peter just ahead of her finding a random path through the high sagebrush, that she understood her trouble. For Peter had said, the brother makes you nervous.

Perhaps in his father's books he had read that nervousness could split your head in two; she was silent, for why burden Peter, who wished to believe that she was happy and respected? But each morning she worried about the noon meal, and each afternoon about the night meal, sick at the thought of sitting with Phil, butt of his silences, his crudities, his scratching himself and snuffling, his talking past her to George. How he pulled his chair out and stepped over it had become an obsession, how he referred to beef as 'a piece of cow.' If this caused the shocking headaches, where was the end of it? Why, there *was* no end of it, to the thrilling pain that would send her again to the buffet, wondering how to replace the whiskey it was so difficult to come by. How long could she go on watering first one and then another bottle before George noticed when sometime he offered a drink to a passing friend?

Where was the end of it? What would she do when the pain struck again, blinding her, when a walk with Peter was no solace — and she knew certain relief lurked behind a small locked door?

How unnatural that she and George live in the same house with the brother! It never worked out; you read that everywhere, and everywhere saw the results. But how challenge George's affection for his brother, his family? If Phil would but understand, and build a place of his own. Near, if necessary, and a place much better suited to his needs. She understood why Phil would be no happier with her than she with him — but it was absurd to think of her and George's building a place on some other part of the ranch and leaving Phil in a house of sixteen rooms. No, no, there was no possibility of Phil's moving and there was no possibility of their moving. Somehow, she had got to speak to Phil, to offer again her friendship, make him understand. After all, the man was a human being. Wasn't he a human being?

But *what* must she make him understand? That he was rude and filthy and insulting? Suppose that after the 'talk' with him he was to report to his brother that she had called him rude, filthy and insulting? Would George forgive her? God knew, blood was thicker than water, and a wife was no blood kin to her husband.

In following days it struck her that she might be a little mad, that another woman might have known Phil and been unmoved. It was not Phil she was married to. She began a score of imaginary speeches that she heard in her mind as quiet-voiced and reasonable, and in each she began by saying, 'Phil, why don't you like me?'

To which he replied, in her mind, 'Not like you? I don't understand . . .'

George himself had said that Phil's strange silences were just Phil's 'way.'

Then, in imagination, Phil would stare out the window — the conversations were in the living room — and Phil would at last smile, and offer his hand in friendship, and there it was. With his friendship, she would welcome overlooking the uncombed hair, the curious odors he exuded, his yanking that chair out from the table and stepping over it, his curious mocking when she played the piano — and above all — his unwashed hands. Those hands! They *were* Phil! He had every right to play his banjo! It was nervousness had made her not quite sane. The headaches in themselves . . .

But when she found herself alone in the living room, the setting precisely so, George gone somewhere, Peter working up in his room — each time she lost heart, teetered on a precipice. Walking that tightwire with no net below, marveling that she'd had the audacity even to consider approaching him.

He's only a man, she would insist to herself, only another with secret problems; but teetering on the precipice, walking that tightwire, she knew he was a great deal more than a human being, or a great deal less; no human speech would move him.

Safe in the pink room, she regained a tiny confidence and reviewed the conversations. It was the sight and sound of him that drained her courage and left her sick and empty — his glance, his eyes, his power when he closed a door, broke open a book; she feared he might break into the cold, derisive laughter she'd heard burst from the bunkhouse when he visited the help, a laughter as jagged and sharp as glass, as keen as lightning; was it directed at her or at her son? And now she had crossed him because of the Indians.

But my God, what could she have done about the Indians? A little grass for an old horse, a few potatoes, a little beef that would spoil anyway. There was an appalling spoilage of meat in the summertime: an entire quarter regularly spoiled and was thrown out as a feast for magpies, dogs, and cats gone wild. It was that, on the one hand; on the other it was a child's humiliation, a little boy's. She'd have been craven indeed not to have spoken up; and to tell the truth, Phil's attitude toward her was the same as before the Indian question.

She had but one chance of speaking with Phil, and that was if she had the courage. And the courage was behind the same locked door. Not quite that: the last time she had removed a bottle, she wrapped it in a towel and hid it in the clothes hamper in the bathroom, reckoning George would not miss a single bottle. And taking the bottle was safer than the dangerous expedient of watering it. And she would replace it.

When she had spoken to Phil (she told herself) she would never again deceive. Once she had spoken, she would confess her curious little theft to George.

George's absence at the table always pointed up an awkwardness; present or not, his place was set and the meat of the day placed there. Since the departure of the Old Gent, George carved. There was an unvarying pattern of meat, a rigid sequence of meat at the table, and the alert knew exactly how long since a cow was butchered — a cow, yes, for steers were never butchered; steers were more valuable on the market, and no better eating than cows.

The one meat, they said out there, that you could keep on eating and eating was beef.

Right after butchering, maybe that very night, the liver appeared sliced, fried so the edges curled, and served up with onions and bacon. Next came the heart, stuffed with bread, and baked. The ribs lasted many days, boiled or braised, sunk in molten suet. Then a week of roasts — some weighing thirty pounds. Last came the steaks — fried heartlessly in suet and drowned in catsup. Little of the front quarters came to the table, for when the hindquarters were used the flies had had their way in spite of the white shrouds that covered the meat, out the front quarters went, eager maggots and all, to animals and birds.

In that log house human speech was repugnant, the chattering of nincompoops and the babble of fools. Small wonder the timid talked of cabbages and speed of the wind.

Rose could no longer even talk to Peter, but reasoned that the trouble might be that he was sixteen, and a male; she could not understand his dedication to a doubtful future, and the activities such dedication required. Two gophers he had drowned out from their holes he had put in little boxes covered with screen; she couldn't imagine them as pets; he seemed to like them, and took them to his room. They startled Lola, gone to make Peter's bed; she reported the gophers healthy — 'cute little buggers.' Later, attracted by a 'funny smell' she found both gophers dead, their bodies skinned, on a newspaper lying with their paws to heaven.

'You shouldn't do it in the house,' Rose told Peter. 'No, I mean it.'

He had smiled and put his arm around her. 'Where would a man get, if he always listened to his mother?'

How he's grown up, she thought, and looked at her hands.

Could she inquire into the fate of the rabbit he had whisked upstairs?

Not only was human speech repugnant in that house, but any sudden sound; the bright clatter of the triangle beside the door of the back dining room made Rose's pulse race; now it rang a few hours after George's departure for the bank meeting.

The hired hands burst into the back dining room and she heard their muffled laughter soaring above the insistent voice of a man Lola reported as crazy, who sometimes lingered in the back dining room and told her pretty things. 'I like to've died,' Lola reported to Rose. 'Oh, he's really crazy.' His craziness drove her to more meticulous care of her hair and the lamp burned long under the curling tongs, the singed smell drifted down the stairs. By the light of the moon the young man said how he saved his money. He would go to Chicago, Lola reported; at a school in the magazines he would repair radios, and make big money.

Lola opened the door to the front dining room bearing a roast she set at George's vacant place; the laughter from the back dining room followed her. 'Everything ready,' she called, and played the chimes beside the door.

This last time, this very last time, Rose had had a drink for courage — well, three drinks over the course of the morning, while she made up her mind. She had masked the odor with a mint. But when Peter came down she kept her distance. His hair was wet from the water he used for grooming. She felt deliciously calm. 'What have you been doing up there?'

'Working on a rabbit,' he said.

'Phil hasn't yet come,' and she had to decide again whether she and Peter should go in and sit down, or wait for Phil — whether it was to her advantage to be sitting at the table with her son beside her, or whether she should wait out of courtesy or protocol. She killed a sharp little resentment that George hadn't asked her to go with him, for having left her to make a ridiculous decision. What did it matter whether she did go in or didn't go in? But the world hung on it. What was her life and George's and Peter's that such trivia should loom as crucial? Living was so narrow that she brooded nights about what dress to wear the next day; she looked forward each day to the passing of the stage, watching for the dust; she dreaded Sundays when it didn't run, and there was nothing to look for, nothing to stop her from thinking of Phil in his room, silent but *there*, his door closed. She felt choked, and tears suddenly stung her eyes.

When the triangle out back was still and the men had settled to their food, she rose, glanced at Peter who leafed through a magazine. He looked at her strangely.

Why would he look at her so? What had she done? She spoke sharply, to test her authority. 'Peter, I told you I didn't want you — doing that to rabbits. Not in the house. It's not much to ask.' Then she knew the rabbit business was no more important than the stage business, that what-dress-to-wear business. 'Let's go to the table.'

Thus, Phil found them at the table.

He gave them a glance. He pulled back George's chair. He stepped between it and the table, carved meat, and handed it to Peter who handed it to his mother. Phil pushed a plate to Peter, pulled out his chair, stepped over it and sat. No word was spoken. As Phil chewed, he gazed with day-blue eyes across to mountains twelve thousand feet high. All at that table had been watchers of that mountain; most, embarrassed by the silence and longing for the lilt of human speech, talked of the advance or retreat of the snow above the timberline. Rose parted her lips to speak but in sudden revolt refused to pay the mountain homage. Instead, she looked up, having found the clatter of silver painful. 'Tomorrow,' she offered, 'is the longest day.'

'That's right,' Peter said. 'The longest day in the year.'

'I like the longer days,' Rose said.

'I'd like a little more meat,' Peter said. 'Would you like a little more meat, Rose?'

'More meat?' She looked at Peter with astonishment; never before had she heard guests or family demand more meat; George, as a good host, saw to it that he offered meat before a desire for it could be expressed. Not only had Peter defied protocol by expressing his wish for meat before it was offered, but in *inquiring* whether she wished more meat had suddenly assumed the authority of one able to offer it.

Whether Phil would have risen and gone to George's place and sliced more meat, Rose never knew; for when Peter spoke, he rose, went to George's place and carved off two pieces. Before Rose could pass her plate, Phil turned a long, reptilian look on Peter, and then on her. He blinked once, pushed back his chair, rose and left the table. She had never heard him excuse himself from the table. Phil made no excuses. But neither had she seen him leave a meal before dessert. Pulse racing, she watched him choose a magazine from the table in the living room and sit, and read.

She looked across the expanse of white cloth at Peter and smiled, uncertain what her smile might mean; she rang the silver bell.

Dessert was a curious concoction known as ambrosia — sliced oranges sprinkled with boxed coconut. She touched her spoon. Then the dish with the oranges was in her lap, then on the floor.

'I'll get it,' Peter said, beside her.

'I don't think I want any dessert,' she said, 'just now.' She got up.

'I don't either,' said Peter, and they left the table, Peter to go upstairs, maybe to his rabbit, she to stand before the bookcase where her eyes roamed the titles. She felt calm. She could choose a title as casually as Phil chose a magazine. Strange how calm and nervousness came and went. She chose a book, opened it, read a sentence, then closed it on her finger, as if keeping the place, wanting something in her hands, something to do with her hands while she spoke, that they might not simply hang at her sides.

She turned and spoke to him.

'Phil,' she asked, her smile open, friendly and calm, 'why do you dislike me so?'

Silence fell like a shadow. She glanced into the face of the clock, as if for a clue. It was minutes from striking. Now she looked back at Phil. His eyes were on her, cold as a reptile's.

'Please tell me, Phil.'

He said it before she heard it. She was braced for another pause, and instead his voice came. 'I dislike you,' he said, 'because you're a cheap little schemer, and because you get into George's booze.' He looked back at the face of his magazine.

She reached up to touch her hair. Then she turned. As straight as she could carry herself she drifted to the pink bedroom and closed the door behind her. Inside, her shoulders sagged, and she moved, touching furniture toward the big bed. There she lay face down, trying to refuse the words she'd heard. She was quite dry-eyed, and sick with cold although summer drifted in through the window. She lay like one in shock, passively absorbing the sounds of the ranch outside, the clink of the latch on the bunkhouse door, the report of a small rifle as the men played at the noon game of shooting magpies perched warily on the butcher pen, the shouts of triumph or failure — sounds that for a time kept at bay the sound of Phil's voice, his brutal calm, his chilly eye, the cruelly expressive word 'booze,' the scornful 'cheap' and her own wooden smile after he had left the table — meant to telegraph to Peter her ability to protect him. She felt suffocated in the void between her intention and her ability, and shattered by loneliness.

Now she heard Phil's firm footsteps pass the door, go down the hall. The recent protector of Indians, the erstwhile arranger of flowers, brought her fist to her mouth.

Upstairs Peter stood at the dormer window that looked on the sagebrush hill, his narrow thin hands one on top of the other. Turning, he went to the mirror over the bookcase where he kept his father's books, and there combed his hair carefully. Finished, he continued to watch himself, and dragged his thumb across the teeth of the comb. His lips formed a single word. 'Phil . . .'

12

Just as it was George's function to sit at the head of the table, to keep the books, to palaver with the buyers, to write letters, answer the telephone and keep the Reo running, so it was Phil's to oversee haying operations, to inspect the equipment and repair the eight mowing machines — four John Deeres and four McCormack-Deerings — the six buck rakes, the six sulky rakes, the two derricks, the cookshack and the dining shack — little houses on sledges they dragged from camp to camp. He had the twelve big canvas tents removed from the shed and unrolled and inspected for rips and tears. He directed where the water should be turned out of the main creeks in the early summer for irrigation, he inspected the growth of the hay; he set the date for haying to begin — as soon as possible after the Fourth of July — 'the Glorious Fourth' as Phil thought of it.

On the Fourth the migrant workers who gathered outside the poolhalls in Herndon had a last fling before hiring out as hay hands on the ranches that fanned out from the town.

One last fling: and to sustain them during the ninety days of haying they held the memory of flags in the streets, the sun glittering on the yellow brass of the Herndon Municipal Band that oomped and tooted on the smooth fragrant lawn beside the railroad station, the rodeo at the fairgrounds, dust and hot dogs, firecrackers popping the night before, bonfires and — if they were lucky — plenty of booze and the whispered excitements of some little lady upstairs. Sure, the law ran them in — the sick and disorderly, those infected with wobbly principles. The law ran them in as vagrants, and for a night or two they sang and wept and fought in the filthy cells in the rear of the courthouse. They came to the ranches pale with celebration, silent and contrite. They dropped off the stage at the Burbank ranch or hitched rides, or walked from Beech where they'd dropped off a freight. Ready for work, eyes bloodshot, hands trembling, but game and willing. 'Hello there, old-timer,' Phil would greet them in front of the house.

'Hello there, Phil,' they'd say, and Phil would shake hands with them, touched by their loyalty. Phil was moved by loyalty, and more than once felt a lump in his throat. He handled the men well, and they worked for him well, and said comfortably among themselves that he was common as an old shoe.

'Well, it's another year,' Phil would remind them, proud of the continuity, that there was yet something unchanging in life. He walked with them around the side of the house to the barn where the dogs, whose memories are short, bristled and barked.

'Pipe down, you mutts,' Phil would laugh, and shy a stone at them. Ki-yi-ing, the dogs retreated under the barn where their barking was muffled and defiant, and the hay hands unrolled their beds in the hay until all the men had gathered and the outfit moved down to the fields with the machinery, the horses, the tents and the cookshack.

One thing about Phil — he was no snob. He gave credit where credit was due — always had, and so he got the confidence of men who had never before spoken frankly to another human being. Year after year there returned a handsome whitehaired old man who had worked in a circus; he moved and stood like a boy, but his eyes mirrored those tragedies he had confessed to Phil. For all his good looks, he had been the lowliest in the circus: he carted away horse and elephant droppings. Without morals in those bad days, his merry eyes had seduced many young women. The last of them, having borne his child, had died.

This shocking death had brought him to his senses; he adopted a roster of strict new morals that were subject to only fleeting human frailty. He advanced himself to teamster and drew a scarlet cage of lions from town to town. He got himself a Bible and read it by lamplight, preparing himself to resist the next temptation and to become the father he longed to be.

Imagine finding that the little gold-haired girl — so lovely that performers sometimes touched her for good luck before going on the trapeze — was herself drawn to the trapeze and at twelve (and still gold-haired) was billed as the youngest aerial artist in the world! The father still carried in his wallet a limp handbill and it was this, carefully unfolded so as not to part it at the folds, that began the father's friendship with Phil. So Fate rewards those who clean up after animals with children who make them proud!

But Phil knew Fate punishes the proud, and dashes hope. One night before a thousand faces the child fell from the high wire, and was carried, broken, to her dressing room. It was this Phil saw in the father's eyes, and this that made the father desert the circus to wander from one brief job to another. After such tragedy he never complained, and Phil had found him a fine man with a team and admired him for his guts and stubborn devotion to the ragged Bible that had failed him, that he read at night by the light of a lantern, his huge shadow against the wall of the tent, his massive head bowed to the words of God, and Phil felt with him; for Phil, too, knew what it was to grieve.

Possessed of the most rigid morals himself, Phil seldom judged those more unfortunate than he in that department. Among those who worked for him and whom he was proud to call friend was an ex-con. The fellow need not have confessed to Phil, for Phil's shrewd sense told him all he needed to know — he saw the eyes, caught the bitter laugh, saw the terrible sunburn of one who has spent recent years in the shadows. Just as the old circus man carried a Bible as another might carry a side arm, so this ex-con carried a small limp-leather edition of Shakespeare's *Sonnets*. Phil was not one to inquire, not one to remark on the scar — it looked like a pocketknife — for who knows why people do the things they do, who knows the pressures? What mattered, what Phil admired, is that this man had carried something of value away from prison, the chilly strength to face with dignity the inevitable end of his life — death in some charity ward or Cabbage Patch, some shanty town on the edge of some Herndon, mourned only by another (perhaps) like himself.

This man called Joe had carried away from prison a remarkable skill, if a simple one — a fantastic artistry in working in horsehair, to twist and braid, an art so refined it had surely been got only at the expense of total despair.

This man called Joe was either young at forty or old at thirty, and in a cigar box he kept several watch chains woven of black and white hair, no thicker than a pencil. Phil's quick mind calculated that each chain contained a hundred yards of hair. Yes, a man given unlimited time can do anything.

The summer evenings after work were long; the sun lingered over the mountains, reddish-hued through the smoke of distant forest fires; and then sank suddenly, trailing bloody streamers. Phil liked it that there always followed on the heels of the vanished sun a stunning silence, an unearthly hush, and how into it crept little sounds — as night-things creep into the dark — the whispers of willow leaves and branches kissing, touching, water caressing and fondling the smooth stones in the creek, lazy human voices, close in friendship, seeping out through the canvas of the tents. That vanished sun brought forth a sudden coolness that caused the mist to lift and drift wraithlike over the creek, heavy with the scent of new hay.

After their supper had settled a little, the eight men who drove the mowing machines ducked out of their tents, paused to belch and stretch, and then wandered to the hitching racks where they had drawn up their machines before unhitching their teams. The mowing machine was a simple rig — two-wheeled like a chariot, but with a seat centered over the axle. Heavy but maneuverable, they were ideal vehicles behind half-broken horses so long as the cutter bar was drawn up vertically. But once the bar was let down to skim over the ground, all seven feet of it, the sharp sections sliding back and forth over the ledger plates, no more dangerous machinery existed. So innocent, so dangerous. Not a year passed but somewhere in that broad valley a man was thrown from the seat into the path of the cutter bar; he was lucky to lose only a foot or a hand as he screamed and bled or lay in shock. Because they handled half-broken horses and lived in danger, because after work when others loafed they removed the cutter bars from their machines and sharpened them on grindstones they straddled like bicycles, delicately holding the dangerous bar — because of this they commanded extra pay; they were accorded a quaint deference: their tents were the newest, their voices were listened to, they first picked over the platters of meat and claimed the finest steaks.

Phil sat cross-legged before the tent he was pleased to share with three of the old-timers, two mowers among them. He watched the mowers sharpening their sickle bars; the scream of steel on whirling stone enough to set a man's teeth on edge. The man Joe, the ex-con, had been a mower; and he had not returned.

And he had promised.

'I'll be back,' he'd promised Phil; they had shaken hands. The man was either dead or in prison. How else explain it? It could not be a simple betrayal, for Phil felt something between them, a recognition.

It was evening, the hour of speculation; Phil pondered how one man passes a gift on to another, how like the very chains and lengths of rawhide rope a man makes, human character is woven on a strand of this and a strand of that — sometimes beautifully and sometimes poorly. It was in simple homage to Joe and to Bronco Henry, those two braiders and plaiters, that Phil braided now. Each had taught him something.

Beside him, in a tin washbasin, he had a big handful of rawhide strips soaking in water. Bleached white from the sun, swollen in the water, they resembled stout worms.

Phil had at first no intention of braiding more than a foot or two of rawhide rope; he wanted only to prove to himself that he still braided well. Such a rope, dried carefully out of the sun and finished off with tallow, was as strong as hemp and more accurate in the corral — an intelligent serpent. The man Joe claimed he had refused fifty dollars for the thirty-foot coil he kept in a pasteboard suitcase and Phil didn't doubt him; he admired the man's refusal to sell for money the work made with his gifted hands: a scorn of money and a respect for time was something else the man had learned in prison; so had Bronco Henry learned a scorn of Death; and in that way, too, had removed himself from the usual tribe of men.

Phil had just begun the actual braiding when his sorrel, haltered at the hitching rack, suddenly raised his head, snorted, and whinnied. Phil was proud the sorrel had the keen nose, eye and ear of the wild thing, and in a moment, caught between the sudden silence and the scream of steel on grindstones, Phil heard the ring of harness chains.

George, then, in spring wagon. Phil knew those chains.

Yes, George all right, the spring wagon loaded with cartons of canned goods and a quarter of beef wrapped in a white shroud. But not only the canned goods and the beef, but other baggage — Rosie-Posie sitting straight up there beside brother George, and the sissy-boy sitting in the end of the wagon, his feet in new white tennis shoes just clearing the stubble. They were quite a sight, coming in through the willows into the broad park, George a bump on a log with his hat straight on his head, the woman with a red scarf tied around her head, twisted around, a scarf Phil supposed she thought attractive or — as women said then — 'stunning.' Stunning was right. It reminded him of nothing so much as what a squaw might wear. How hard that floozy worked at looking like Somebody!

The wagon squeaked slowly past the open tents; the men watched closely; the woman looked straight ahead, but Phil saw she had colored a bit. George drew the team up before the cookshack, and the cook, a thin old geezer with a towel around his pot walked out smoking a cigar; when he saw the woman, he tossed it away.

George clambered down grunting greetings to the cook. The woman started to clamber down, but before she got

213

started, the boy came around to give her a hand — Little Lord Fauntleroy helping Mama out of the carriage — a pretty little formality. Now the woman arranged the rag she had on her head, and then glanced down at the new high-laced boots bought, Phil supposed, from the catalog that came to the ranch from back East, a place where you bought compasses and guns and such, a place Phil humorously dubbed Abbie, Dabbie & Bitch, a place fancied by the Old Lady and the Old Gent at Christmastime.

Maybe the boy and Phil saw something in the woman that George hadn't, that she really needed to be helped down. Was she still boozing it up? A person had to fall down under George's nose before he noticed a thing like that. Frankly, it had surprised Phil that she was one to booze it up; and at first he'd thought maybe it was only that once she'd tried to speak up to him. But he had checked; Yup! She'd been watering the booze — the oldest trick in the world — and even snitched a couple of bottles. He'd bet six bits he could lay his hands on where she'd hidden them. All he had to do was wait now for the woman to hang herself; her personality was alcoholic, as she might have known from her husband's doctor-books. The very first time she got woozy on George's booze. Boozy-Woozy-Rosie!

Little Lord Fauntleroy was likewise dolled up in new duds. With the new tennis shoes, he sported a new pair of levis. Now, in that country the first thing a man did with a new pair was toss them in the creek for a few days with a rock to hold them down and let them soak till they shrank to size and lost the blue dye and the filler. You could tell a dude because a dude didn't do that.

Little Lord F. stood a moment beside his mama and then Phil saw him look across the opening toward a willow where a family of magpies had built them a ratty-looking nest of sticks and twigs. Then big as you please the boy suddenly began to walk across the space before the open tents, Phil guessed to investigate.

During lazy evenings down there, drowsy evenings fragrant with the smudges the men made of green hay to keep off the mosquitoes, Phil had told the men about the boy, how he shut himself in his room with his books and pictures, how the boys in Beech had jeered at him as one who didn't know a fly from a foul ball, how the boy made and arranged paper flowers, and the men doubtless resented — as they were bound to — this little monster not boy and not girl, this son of a two-bit sawbones who now rode in a Burbank wagon simply because his maw had a pretty face. Itinerant workers — many infected with wobbly principles — were quick to sense injustice.

Phil continued with his braiding and plaiting of the rawhide strips, holding each one up to let it drain. The cleverness of his fingers freed his eyes to watch the boy traverse the opening; at each step the stiff denim of the overalls went zip-zip-zip as leg passed leg. Stiff as a stick-man the boy moved with the slightest feminine twitch of hips Phil could hardly stand, the new tennis shoes vulnerable and white. The woman, a little apart while George jawed with the cook, watched the boy's progress, and Phil saw her stiffen when the first sharp whistle flew like an arrow as the boy passed the second tent; the whistle men give a girl. Why, the boy was better off dead than to attract such scorn.

That rude whistle, a result of Phil's stories and as audible to George and to the woman as to the boy, convinced Phil that the men looked to him and not to George as the boss of the ranch; for not only had the woman's presence failed to protect the boy, but so had George's.

Well-a-day!

But Phil would say one thing for the kid. He neither paused nor faltered in running that strange gauntlet before the open tents. He seemed not even to hear, but once past the watching, grinning men, he looked up into the willows at the tawdry nest, at the tottering, chattering young magpies who hadn't even the gumption to go to roost.

Phil watched, braiding. The kid didn't need to return to his mama in the way he'd come. He could walk behind the tents, and thus avoid the grins and eyes.

The kid turned, and began to walk right past the open tents again. Strangely, there were no whistles.

Now, Phil always gave credit where credit was due. The kid had an uncommon kind of guts. Wouldn't it be just interesting as hell if Phil could wean the boy away from his mama? Wouldn't it now? Why, the kid would jump at the chance for friendship, a friendship with a man. And the woman — the woman, feeling deserted would depend more and more on the sauce, the old booze.

And then what?

Here's what. The blowup between the woman and George would come sooner than ever; for old George, slow as he was, even George was bound to see in the woman's drinking his failure to make her happy.

It was almost too perfect.

And perfect in another, miraculous way. For at this very moment he held in his hands the means to the final solution, this just-begun rope, the gift of it the very means to begin wooing the kid away. This rope would be, so to speak, the bond between them. His hands paused and were still. He raised them from the rawhide and watched them opposed there, like two big spiders. He felt suddenly possessed, bewitched, and his whole mind was swelled with the idea; this very rope he held in his hands was the means to the end.

'Peter . . .' Softly.

The kid continued his stiff walk back toward the cook-shack where the last thin, exhausted smoke rose in vague threads from the twisted, rusted chimney and drifted and disappeared over the willows.

'Peter . . . !' Phil spoke a little sharper, because for a moment he thought the kid might dare ignore the summons.

The boy tacked suddenly like a sailboat and walked toward him, paused and shoved his hands into the pockets of the stiff new levis.

'You want me, Mr Burbank?'

Phil's face took on a mock puzzled look, and then he looked around, twisting his head on his neck to the right and left, as if searching for somebody. 'Mr Burbank, you say? I don't know any Mr Burbank. I'm Phil, Pete.'

'Yes, Mr Burbank,' said Peter. 'You want me?'

'Well now,' said Phil. 'I guess it's hard for a young fellow to get used to calling an old codger like me just plain Phil — at first.'

Then he lifted the new rope. 'Look at this, Pete.'

Peter looked at it. It seemed to Phil the rope was reflected in Peter's eyes. 'That's fine work, sir.'

'You ever do any plaiting or braiding yourself, Pete?'

'No, sir. I never did.'

'Pete,' Phil said, 'I've been thinking. We sort of got off on the wrong foot, you and me, at the beginning.'

'Did we, sir?'

'No, forget the sir stuff,' and Phil coughed a little. 'That was my impression. That sort of thing can happen to people, you know. People who get to be good friends.'

'I suppose it could.'

'Well, know what?'

'What — what, Phil?'

217

'Now you see? You did it. Called me Phil. I'm going to finish up this rope and give it to you, finish it up and give it to you and show you how to use it. Now, you're going to be here on the ranch, you might as well learn to rope a little, what? And ride? Sort of a lonesome place out here, Pete, unless you get into the swing of things.'

'Thank you — Phil. How long do you expect it would take to finish that rope?'

Phil again had the odd impression that the entire rope was reflected in Peter's eyes; the boy was interested, all right. Phil shrugged. 'Oh, I imagine working off and on I could finish it before you go back to school.'

Peter was looking closely at the rawhide strips soaking in the basin. 'It won't be very long then, Phil,' Peter said.

'You just stop by next time you come down here to camp,' Phil said. 'You come on down and see how I'm coming along.'

And the boy actually smiled at him, and turned and walked back to the wagon, his stiff new levis going zip-zip-zip, like scissors.

He's a peculiar one, Phil thought. Yes, sir. No, sir. Inhuman kid. Talked like a Victrola record. Thank you, sir; but like the kid said, it wouldn't be very long now.

13

Peter longed for his tidy room in Herndon, longed to play chess with his friend, the long, lanky bespectacled son of the high school teacher who, like Peter himself, had never before had a friend, who burst into uncontrollable giggles that left him weak and moist-eyed. He longed to talk with this friend of the possibility of God and to exchange descriptions of their futures, the one to be a famous surgeon, the other a famous professor of English. First as a joke and then quite seriously they came to address one another as Doctor and as Professor; but never in front of people.

These two had come to know a different Herndon, the Herndon of the nighttime, the houses dark except for a light in the hall, stores dark but for small, economical naked bulbs over the rococo cash registers; they knew of the men moving up and down the back stairway to the Red-White-and-Blue Rooms, of the prowl car of the chief of police turning a corner on some unspeakable errand. But especially they knew the railroad station, the stiff wooden benches vacant, the waiting room silent but for the murmur of water weakly bubbling out from the drinking fountain, and the sudden hysterical chatter of the telegraph in the cramped room where their friend, the night telegrapher, stared into space taking messages from God knew where. Lonely himself, this man welcomed these strange boys who came to drink the bitter black coffee he brewed over a Sterno can; to them he confessed his dreams to learn Spanish well and then go to Argentina, where there were opportunities. He was indeed studying Spanish by correspondence and they saw no reason why his dreams should not come true and they told him so.

'*Buenos noches,*' they learned to say when they came to him at night, '*Que tal?*' and he would rise from where he sat before the telegraph key, slip the lock, and let them in. No telling, if some railroad inspector should happen in! Nobody else in all Herndon was received in that room at night, that holy place; nobody else understood their longing for the far-off places the telegraph told of, the future professor and future surgeon.

That he and his mother might know those far-off places, Peter welcomed his new relationship with Phil; he must ignore the reproach in his mother's eyes. Few human beings, he thought, understood much; women least of all.

He stood in her pink room now, a room in which he would never feel comfortable, for there a stranger had the right to play husband, and part of Peter's plan or not, that man's things were side by side with his mother's things in the closet, his sharp straightedged razors beside her perfumes and creams — George's things, the things of a man who had not yet proved himself, had done no more than introduce his mother to the governor of the state at a dinner she didn't talk about.

He had come downstairs from his room where he'd been reading, and at the bottom of the stairs his mother suddenly opened the door and spoke.

'Peter, can't you come in and talk a little?' The shape of her mouth troubled him. He thought of a leaf in the wind.

In the pink room he stood looking into the rain that fell

on the haying machinery brought home now from the fields, at smoke drifting out through the doors of the shop where Phil worked at the forge, at the derricks, huge gaunt structures of poles that reminded him of gibbets. He stood looking so long she spoke again, and her eyes followed his. 'What do you see out there?'

'Only the rain. What shall we talk about?' He had long dreaded talks with his mother, for they now led inevitably to nostalgic references to the past, and whatever approached sentiment made him restive. He wanted to clench his fists.

'We can talk about anything. I guess I was lonesome. George is out riding somewhere.'

'You look cold,' he said. 'I'll get your sweater.'

'He was riding his bay horse,' she said. 'You've got to be quite friendly with Phil, haven't you.'

'He's making a rope for me.'

'Making a rope for you?'

'He's good with his hands. He's making it out of raw-hide.'

'What is rawhide?'

He was patient. 'Nothing much. Just dried strips of cowhide, and you soak them and — well, fashion them.'

'Fashion them?'

'Braid them.'

'Peter, I wish you wouldn't do that with your comb.'

He stopped dragging his thumb across the teeth. 'I wasn't aware.'

Fashion, she thought. Aware. He stood near the window, and the light from outside, pressing against her eyes, made her a little sick. He seemed always to be standing, never sitting, always ready to move, to listen, never to rest, never a part of any scene, any conversation, but simply patiently — patiently what? Waiting? He had brought into the room

221

with him a curious odor, somehow familiar. 'Little sounds like that. When I was little, I felt something in my spine when they'd begin to write on the blackboard. There was Miss Merchant.'

'Miss Merchant?'

'Yes, and she gave us stars after our names on the blackboard, I've forgot why, but for something we did right. I remember the stars, and how you could choose what color you liked, and Miss Merchant picked up the right chalk and made the star without once lifting the chalk from the board. Why, she didn't draw the star, she wrote it. I wonder now why it was always stars we got, and why not diamonds or spades. Why not hearts? I wonder why it was stars.'

He spoke quietly, his face in profile, and like a ventriloquist he scarcely moved his lips. 'Because they're supposed to be unreachable.'

'Yes, unreachable,' she said, afraid she had slurred the word. She talked little these days, afraid of the slurring, the treacherous words like unreachable. She spoke slowly. 'But now, they weren't unreachable in the sixth grade. And Peter,' she went on, 'we used to have a valentine box, and they'd get this big box, somebody would bring it from home, and we'd cover it with white crepe paper and paste big red hearts on it, lopsided hearts, some of them, because all of us didn't understand about folding the paper so both sides would match. Some drew them freehand.' She wondered now if it was the cold light that pressed against her eyes that made her a little faint or the odor that surrounded him.

'And you got a great many valentines,' he said, his lips scarcely moving.

'A great many?'

'Because you were beautiful even then,' he said.

How could he have said that, she wondered. How have

so misunderstood her, for she tried only to convince him and herself that she had once had identity, a desk of her own, a numbered hook in the cloakroom for her coat, a place on the class roll, a view out the window of swings and a board fence beyond. Or was he right in sensing that she boasted of stars earned and valentines received because she was — beautiful? How awful to lead a conversation around so that another was bound to say, because you were beautiful!

He had spoken with such unusual intensity that she stared at him, and noted the rare flush that suffused his clear skin. 'You must have known,' she said, 'some sound that made you shiver.'

'I don't remember,' he said. He did, of course — remembered the panic that pressed up like a lump in his throat when someone shouted sissy; he'd feared the bloody nose, the loss of breath if someone pinned him down. Once he'd been afraid to enter a room, or to leave it. 'I've got to go upstairs now,' he said. 'I've got something to finish.'

She rose carefully, and smiling reached over and passed her palm over his neatly combed hair. 'It's been a nice talk, hasn't it,' she murmured. 'To each other,' she said, and used the treacherous word, 'we're not unreachable.'

He lifted his eyes, and caught and held hers. 'Mother,' he said, 'you don't have to do this.'

She attempted to wrench her eyes from his, about to ask, don't have to do what?

But she dare not ask, for he would say, 'Don't have to drink.' And it would be out in the open.

His eyes still held her. 'I'll see that you don't have to do it,' he said.

She wanted to ask, how will you see to it? If she had spoken, perhaps their lives would have been much different, but God help her, she kept silent.

He left her then (no one could close a door more quietly than he) and she turned to watch the rain falling and falling and falling on the haying machinery. Of Peter there remained behind only the odor he had brought with him.

She whispered to herself, chloroform.

The rawhide rope was within six feet of completion; Phil might now have finished it off with a neat crown knot or a Turk's head; but he continued working on it; he had come to look forward to the boy's being near while he worked, braiding and molding, for Peter was a perfect audience, rapt as Phil told him of the early days, and so receptive and caught up in the gray web of the past that Phil had once laughed aloud, for Peter had let enchantment paralyze him. He was staring sightless, like one hypnotized, at the sagebrush hill out front. 'What do you see out there, old-timer?' Phil asked, amused to see the kid caught off guard. His hands were still.

Peter's eyes moved slowly to Phil; they looked like a sleepwalker's. 'Phil, I was thinking about the old days.'

Phil watched the kid's face, how it was caught in the sun that slanted in through the doors of the blacksmith shop. 'I'll bet you were, at that,' Phil said slowly. 'Don't ever let your maw make a sissy of you. There were real men in those days.' The kid nodded gravely. Phil told of a cliff he knew reared up lonely above the source of a spring, and there someone had carved initials and the date — 1805. 'Must have been some fellow from the Lewis and Clark expedition,' Phil said. 'Fifty years went by before any whites settled here for good. And Pete, when I was a fellow about your age, I found piles of rock out behind that hill yonder that seemed to lead somewhere. Never found out where, exactly; didn't follow 'em to the end. What say maybe sometime just you and me might look for 'em again? Follow 'em to the end?'

The sun — Old Sol, Phil called it — was retreating south: the nights grew cold, the morning frost was thick, and remained late, and its retreat was stubborn at the advance of the paling sun; storms in the mountains drove the cattle down to the fields, down to the brown stubble they would graze on until the snow flew. Almost any time you might raise your eyes and see a few cows, big spring calves at their sides trailing single file through well-worn paths in the sagebrush on the hill out front. Occasionally a cow had twins, but the extra calves were never enough to replace those left dead behind in the hills or on the flats — hamstrung, torn and eaten by wolves or bloated and dead from anthrax — blackleg, as they called it in that country. 'Don't worry, old-timer,' Phil told Peter. 'I'll have your rope done before you go back to school.'

Phil had taught Peter to ride, had turned over to him a gentle bay horse, and together they rode down into the fields where Peter helped him build pole fences around the haystacks, and at noon they ate their lunches of deviled ham sandwiches and apples while Phil told stories of Bronco Henry. 'We've had quite a time this fall, ain't we, old-timer?' Phil asked. And for a fact, Phil enjoyed himself.

'I won't forget it, Phil,' Peter said soberly.

The rope, the bond between them, Phil kept coiled like a snake in a sack as he worked at the unfinished end, feeding it, as it grew, into the sack.

Frankly, Phil had never expected to make any use of the hides that one by one were flung flesh-side out over the top pole of the fence as cows were butchered. Wary magpies cleaned off the bits of flesh left sticking to the skin, for the men in the bunkhouse were clumsy at skinning, so anxious to get the job over and done with and back to the bunkhouse where they could shoot the breeze and blow away at their fool harmonicas. Most of the hides were badly punctured, useless for anything, but until Phil got started on the rope, there was no use for them anyway. In a year's time there might be twenty hides hung there drying and shrinking in the sun and weather and then Phil would have the men pile them up, pour on the old kerosene, and burn them. What a stink they made!

Most Septembers before the burning, men would come around — in wagons in the old days, in rattletrap trucks these days — trying to buy the hides for a buck or a buck and a quarter, but Phil laughed right in their faces. The hides they bought here and there for that price they sold for twice, and made fortunes, some of them. Jews, all of them Jews after hides, Jews after junk, Jews with the eye for the quick buck, bargaining for rusty iron, mowing machine frames, rake frames, lengths of pipe and so forth that collects on a ranch; but rather than sell to these shysters, Phil let the junk collect and the hides dry and shrink on the fence until he got around to the burning. Phil had nothing against the right kind of Jews, Jews of intellect and talent, so long as he didn't have to mix with them. But Lord, these others.

These others, these Wandering Jews, as he called them, made fortunes out of junk. How do you think the fellow with the big department store in Herndon got his start? Why, Phil could remember when he was sitting up in the seat of a crumby spring wagon haggling for the hides of dead animals. And now what? Now he had this house in town, big white house with pillars, biggest house in Herndon, green lawn and sprinklers playing on it. Pierce-Arrow out front in the graveled driveway — parties with Japanese lanterns and such stuff — all got out of hides and junk and the eye on the old dollar.

Greenberg.

Called himself Green, now, for a fact. Green! Had got himself into Herndon Sassiety and hobnobbed with What's-his-name at the bank — George's pal. Phil chuckled, remembering. On a rare visit to Herndon for a haircut, Phil was leaned back comfortable in Whitey Potter's chair because he'd decided to go whole hog and get himself a tailor-made shave — much as anything because when Whitey shaved you he didn't talk so much: Whitey was one of those barbers who thinks you pay for the gab. Well, there was Phil lying back, his long legs and cheap black town shoes sticking out from under, and it was a Saturday, and the other two barbers were snipping away at the hirsute appendages of the townspeople and the place was lively with jabber and some reading the *Elks Magazine* and whatever else Whitey had in there for the customers' convenience and edification while they sniffed the old Lucky Tiger and so forth and so on.

A woman waited, too, all gussied up with a fur around her neck and a diamond rock big as a hen's egg on one of her pinkies — the Catholic girl Green (Greenberg) had married up with to take the curse off his own origins. Together he and the Catholic girl had joined up with the church there in Hemdon-town the Old Lady herself had fooled around with, and Phil guessed a whole generation was growing up who knew Greenberg and his wife for something else than they were. Well, a generation of new Greenbergs was growing up, anyway who thought they were Greens, and one of the kids, a girl, was with the woman, waiting for papa.

So you see the place was full, bright that Saturday with sun and mirrors and bottles lined up, and the men talked and joshed and smoked and read the *Elks Magazine* and kids ran in and out from the hotel where the old men sat, and suddenly old Whitey pulled the lever that let Phil up and back into the world that lying back and being shaved puts you out of, the dreamworld of old Lucky Tiger.

'That sufficient unto you?' asked Whitey humorously, remembering the very words Phil had once used on handing him the six bits for the haircut and a two bit tip. Quite a guy, Whitey.

Phil regarded his thin, naked, shaven, foxlike face in the big mirror that with the one opposite it reflected all infinity. 'Fine-O, me lad,' said Phil. 'That'll do for a sufficiency,' and then the man in the next chair spoke up to Phil.

'How are you there, Mr Burbank,' the fellow said in a big hearty Rotary voice.

A loud, beefy voice; a voice that loud, followed by the two or three seconds of Phil's silence made people look up from their *Elks Magazines*.

Then Phil spoke. 'Why, dashed if it ain't Mr Greenberg!'

Let me tell you, there was silence after that, and the woman's face turned as red as her dyed red hair. Greenberg? *Redberg* was more like it.

No, far as Phil was concerned, the hides could rot there on the fence and the scrap iron powder to rust before Phil would fall for their wheedling arguments, before he would let them use *him* and profit as they did from another's gullibility, carelessness or just pure out-and-out charity. It had got so that these jokers seldom stopped at the Burbank ranch, having heard through their grapevine that the Burbanks weren't suckers — a grapevine just like the gypsies have.

'Just Like a Gypsy,' as Woozy-Rosie played at on her piano.

Anyway so much for the Jews. And now it turned out that Phil had most excellent use of the hides after all. Who'd a thunk it!

For all Phil's patient instructions, Peter sat a saddle poorly, and Phil thought it pathetic and even engaging how the boy tried to hold his body straight, his hands easy on the reins, to rise posting at the trot.

'All you got to do is practice, Pete.'

But more than practice took Peter behind the hill to other hills that rolled and stretched out there; out there in the secret land he did a lot of thinking, a lot of searching and something close to praying, a praying that took the form of a petition, in his father's name.

He looked and looked, his gray eyes darting as swiftly as the tiny gray birds that darted from sagebrush to sagebrush. He found the skeleton of a horse with a bluebell growing up through the eye of the skull, and a lean coyote watched from a nearby rise; he found agate and flint of the sort the Indians used for arrowheads and whole patches of prickly pear, blankets of it, and a forty-four cartridge green with age and corrosion. He found a wedge of stone that looked like the work of a human hand and pocketing it he thought how it would flatter Phil when he asked him to identify it; but for a long time he didn't find what he looked for.

Then one afternoon he drew up his horse before a low outcropping of pale pinkish rock; it might have been a sport of nature except that beyond it he found another outcropping and then another, each exactly twenty paces from the last according to some human plan, some ancient ceremony, each a beckoning sentinel. These must be the broken stone piles Phil had spoken of, some almost sunk in the earth, and Peter followed them but the sun sank, the mountain chill crept down and Peter turned back before he reached the end of them. That night he had ample opportunity to report his find to Phil, for Phil spent the evening in his room plucking on his banjo, and the sound Peter knew was an invitation to come in and talk. But he kept his find a secret.

Next day he rode out early, followed the stones farther and farther, and at noon ate his lunch and watched the last remnants of cattle straggle down from the hills, watched them follow ancient paths that snaked through the tall sagebrush, then he mounted his bay horse and followed the rocks again.

As he rode, the heaps of rocks grew smaller and smaller, and he hurried as if to find the end of them before they vanished; and they did vanish, vanished at the brink of a dry ravine, the throat choked by rubble and rubbish hurled down from the heights by flash-floods-rounded boulders, gray porous roots of sagebrush, weathered gray boards from some abandoned shack. And tumbleweeds — those ghostly briars brought alive by the faintest breeze, those frighteners of horses. In that ravine, along whose side ran one of the ancient cow paths, Peter found exactly the dead animal he'd been searching for; he thought it fitting that it was Phil, in a way, who had led him to it.

He looked around as calmly as coyotes looked at him, and he listened; then he reached into his pocket and drew out gloves and drew them on as a surgeon might, got down from his horse, felt God smile, and went to work.

It was unthinkable that a man on the ranch, except for Sundays, should be idle, and that may explain why even the Old Gent, caught up in his own beliefs and having nothing else to do, paced the floor in stiff military fashion and wore

230

down the pile of the carpet with the same dogged purpose that another man might dig postholes or shoe a horse. It explained why George, who felt no man should be asked to do anything he wouldn't himself do, cleaned out the cesspool; it was a job nobody else could be asked to do. Rose watched him out the dining room window (the high beauty of the Rockies behind him) dipping a bucket nailed to a long thin pole down into the stinking reaches of the pool, and she watched him turn gagging each time he emptied the bucket into the basin of an iron wheelbarrow. She, too, then turned away.

And George was gone from her so much of the time. When Peter and Phil rode into the fields to fence haystacks, George rode away to do the same thing in another direction. Why couldn't it have been George and the boy who rode together! And how should she fill her pointless days — Lola doing the housework, Mrs Lewis cooking?

She drove often to Herndon — 'shopping' as the *Recorder* had it, and at Green's she was an easy mark for the salesladies, buying hats and gloves and shoes. Trying on dress after dress — frocks they were beginning to call them — frocks she was certain had been ordered for her alone. She began to look on clothes as costumes, disguises, masks to hide the useless and frightened self she was becoming. She charged everything, having little cash. It had never occurred to George to give her a checking account; like the Queen of England, his mother never carried any more money than enough for tips, and to Rose he handed a ten dollar bill or so when she drove off to town — something to put into her purse. Change, he called it. And with it, after charging perhaps two hundred dollars' worth of shoes and hats and frocks, she would go on the errand that had driven her to town — at first to the drugstore for a 'prescription' and later to a house on Kentucky Avenue she approached from the rear, loathing herself, a house covered in the summer with purple trumpet vines.

One afternoon she frightened herself by running off the road; she was helped by a neighboring rancher. She lied to George about the slight damage to the fender.

Her headaches continued. Fearing to expose herself to Phil's possible remarks — remarks that any time now might be made before George, she kept to the pink room and did her tippling there. She thought she now saw a pattern in Phil's pressures, certain he had said nothing to George about her drinking, feeling that Phil knew the thing unsaid is more potent than the thing said. Had she not caught him watching her with a curious, stalking patience?

Oh, but the house was cold! Insulated by its logs and the thick layers of earthy plaster, the sun had no chance, and up from the basement seeped the damp of the flooded cellar. She did not understand the furnace, nor the means of getting to it by stepping from one water-soaked block of wood to another, didn't understand its several drafts George talked of, and how much coal to shovel on, and when. Thus the fire often died those rainy days of late summer, and her attempts to rekindle it failed. She apologized to George for her failures, and when he went silently and uncomplainingly down the stairs to repair the damage she could scarcely bear the sounds down there, the banging of the iron door, the rasping scrape of the flat shovel over the concrete floor. Listening, she would move about the pink room dressing for dinner, arranging the mask, hoping to please him by her appearance, to draw his attention from her increasingly uncertain gestures, the little touchings of furniture as she moved about the room.

She had better luck with the fireplace, and began to burn

up bits of trash she found around the barn and the shop. Dressing herself in dark green jodhpurs she'd bought when she'd had the courage to think she might learn to ride, she hunted about for scraps of lumber, orange crates, apple boxes, short lengths of pole left over from making buck rake teeth, lengths of firewood brought from the shed to prop up machinery and abandoned there.

The supply of burnable trash getting low, she noticed that her efforts to keep warm and to occupy herself were achieving a certain order, a kind of tidiness about the place that gave her a sense of achievement. She had never understood why the grounds of the richest ranch in the valley must look like a junkyard, and now she had got together and piled in a cleared spot between barn and shop a remarkable array of trash, much of it cast-off clothing, socks and overalls, shoes stolen by puppies from under the beds in the bunkhouse, twisted and shrunken in the weather.

Some trash she could not manage, the grass-filled stomachs of a fresh-butchered cow supposedly buried by the men out back but dug up and dragged to the yard by the older dogs, trailing intestines. Neither could she manage the severed, disinterred heads.

'I don't mind,' Peter told her, and with a pitchfork he urged the guts and stomachs into the iron wheelbarrow with the silent heads and trundled them off for reburial. The dogs watched, the chief mourners.

She thought those hides thrown over the top poles of the butcher pen must make a bad impression on those who passed the ranch. What must they think of the magpies quarreling over bits of flesh?

'Oh, a little later, Phil burns the hides,' George said. 'He burns them once a year.'

★

Sometimes in the bunkhouse Phil picked up the funny papers. *The Katzenjammer Kids, Happy Hooligan, Maggie and Jiggs*. He had watched the men moving their lips as they read and wondered if the brighter among them saw beneath the crude humor to the social comment. Who among them saw in the Katzenjammer Kids the ultimate triumph of roguishness, the irrepressible spirit of youth? Could they identify themselves with Happy Hooligan, that moron with a tin can for a hat, whose armor was his stupidity? What did they make of Gaston and Alphonse who with their 'after you my dear Alphonse' and their 'after *you* my dear Gaston!' maintained that manners were more important than intelligence? He'd listened closely to their laughter over Maggie and Jiggs, at how old Jiggs sneaked off to Dinty Moore's for corned beef and cabbage when he was supposed to be at the opera. But did they see that the fellow who wrote the thing, who inked in the limousines and colored the fancy clothes that Maggie wore to some shindig was simply lampooning social climbers?

With this on his mind, who could wonder that Phil, watching George staring out across the flats to the mountains through the binoculars, had suddenly remarked, 'What's up out there, Jiggs?'

George had stood motionless, staring out. Then slowly he brought the glasses down, and turned. 'Jiggs?' he said. 'Jiggs?'

Thunderheads loomed and piled up over the mountains to the south. She dreaded the thunder and lightning that sometimes struck so close the telephone bell jangled and the air smelled suddenly of ozone. Fresh was the story George had told of the station agent at Beech who had been struck and killed as the train pulled in, of six head of cattle huddled against a barbed wire fence, all killed instantly when lightning struck the wire a mile away. Over the whole country this afternoon brooded silence that announced the first fall storm. Mrs Lewis had not yet come from her cabin to grumble and begin the searing of meat. Lola was upstairs with her *True Romance* magazine. She had pointed out to Rose the story she was saving for just such an afternoon, one called 'Why I Sold My Baby.'

Standing in the pink room, a sweater about her shoulders, Rose vaguely considered her 'costume' for the evening.

'You always look so pretty,' George used to say. 'I feel so proud with you.'

She worried about George and she worried about Peter down in the fields, and she wondered if she could endure it if the telephone jangled. Was it safe by the window? The wind shook the leaves of the sick cottonwood tree.

What was that? Dust?

Dust up the road! And out of it came a car, a shabby little truck that slowed, hesitated, and then crept into the yard and stopped.

She rose carefully. She had learned in the last months to walk cautiously, to move from chair to table to chair to wall, touching each, as if she found strength there. An unbroken trip across a room was impossible — she might falter and stumble. Carefully she made her way to the living room and looked out at the strange little truck. On the driver's side were the inexpertly painted letters HIDES, the pigment chalky with age, and the bed of the truck was piled with layers of hides roped down hard.

She blinked, amazed at the formal appearance of the man who opened the door of the truck and stepped to the ground; he wore a dark business suit, a dark, rather wide felt hat, and a beard that recalled prophets. Across his vest was stretched a gold chain, dull in the darkening air. As he passed through the little gate and started up the steps, she saw beyond him the other figure in the car. His son?

She opened the door before the knock.

He removed his hat, and made a little bow, 'Good afternoon, ma'am.'

What a gentle voice, she thought. What a welcome, gentle voice. 'Good afternoon,' she murmured.

'I wondered if you had any old hides?' he asked.

The question was rhetorical, for the butcher pen was in sight not a hundred yards away. 'Why, I don't know,' she said, and walked out past him onto the porch where she touched the chair and stood looking at the hides. Eyesores. 'I see we do,' she remarked. 'They burn them, you know.'

Distant rumble of thunder.

'Burn them?' The man looked at the dark hat in his hand and then at Rose.

'Yes, I understand they burn them.'

'Why not take thirty dollars for them, ma'am?'

'Thirty dollars?'

'I couldn't see my way to offer more.'

'Oh, it wasn't that,' she said, gripping the back of the chair.

'What is it, then, ma'am?'

She could not have explained to the man what it was, if it wasn't that. But thirty dollars was a strange sum. Thirty dollars had no meaning to the Burbanks. Thirty dollars would once have meant riches to her and Johnny Gordon, but a check for thirty made out to the Burbanks would find its way to a sheaf of other uncashed checks she had seen in a cubbyhole in George's office, refunds from mail-order houses, small tax rebates, a few dollars a man had paid for an old saddle, perhaps a hundred dollars in all, checks dated far back. Were such checks, like the hides, at intervals ritually burned? She smiled vaguely at the thought.

'What's that, ma'am?'

'Nothing. Did I speak?' She gripped the chair. When she went 'shopping' George always handed her ten or twenty dollars, and that was that. With the charge accounts she bought anything she wanted except what she got at the drugstore and that vine-covered place. Cash for that. 'No, that sounds like a reasonable sum.' She felt the silence was long, and spoke again. 'Make the check out to my husband.'

'To your husband?'

She felt tears spring to her eyes, and smiled to cover their import.

He said, 'What's that, ma'am?'

'Did I speak?' she asked. No, she thought. It's Phil who burns the hides. It's Phil who must have the check. He can burn the check instead of the hides. 'Make the check to Phil,' she said.

'To Phil, ma'am?'

'Why, yes, just to Phil.' Why, she wondered, did that seem odd to him? 'No,' she said suddenly. 'Don't do that.' If the check was to go uncashed or maybe burned, why must it be a check? Why not cash? She would have cash in her hands! 'Would you mind giving me the money in cash?'

'Of course not, ma'am.' Now she watched closely as he drew out a purse, long like a black stocking with a bright metal frame at the top that closed when one little ball slipped past another. He opened it and reached down, disturbing the silver there. Once when she and Johnny had first come to the country — long, oh, long, long ago — that country of the silver dollar, a patient had paid Johnny with two silver dollars and he had stood grinning and rattling them in his pocket. 'Nothing sounds like money more than silver,' he'd said. 'The pretty, pretty sound of silver, the pretty sound of silver, my pretty lady.' She watched the man bring out bills, worn bills that must have passed many, many times for one favor or another. He offered them; she took them. 'Thank you.'

'Thank *you*,' he said, and bowed his formal little bow, and turned and with an arm made a gesture to the other figure. Then he walked down without looking back. She watched him go, and watching him felt a queer urge to follow, to call out, to return the money, but her throat was dry, her tongue lifeless. And truly, the feel of the bills gave her a precious sense of security. Thus, she stood gripping the back of the chair and watched while the truck drove away from the house, made a slow turn and then proceeded rumbling across the pole bridge to the butcher pen. A cloud of magpies rose and settled like dirty ash, one by one, on a fence at a safer distance.

She turned carefully, steadied herself a final time on the back of the chair, and moved into the house. Inside, she began to laugh to herself. How strange it all was!

How strange, how strange.

Since she had married a Burbank she had become sly.

She had become dishonest.

She had become an alcoholic, a common drunk. She hadn't been entirely sober in weeks. Nothing but George's kindness had kept him silent. But in weeks he would divorce her. And now this final thing, when he found she'd become a petty larcenist for the sake of thirty dollars.

She forgot to remember the long, long distance from the door of the bedroom to the bed, and found herself with no handy chair, no trusted table. She tottered and fell halfway to the bed, lost a slipper, a fancy shoe, so fancy she'd never get used to them, shoes ordered especially for her, an excuse for a 'shopping' trip. Shoes for Mrs Vanderbilt, the Mrs Vanderbilt only in Johnny's mind, only in his. He'd believed she was, so she was. She couldn't be anything unless someone believed in her, nothing at all. She could be nothing but what someone believed she was.

She left the shoe and staggered to the bed, the big Burbank bed. Lying there, she brought her fist to her mouth.

And there George found her asleep, three ten dollar bills scattered beside her, like leaves.

14

Piles of poles were sanctuaries for small living things.

Under there gophers were safe from badgers who wished to eat them whole. There cottontails were safe from coyotes who worried the poles with their paws and teeth. Living there until men came to use the poles to build the fences around the stacks, the small living things knew every recess and cranny and brazenly insulted the big animals in their little voices. They shared their bastion with animals even smaller than themselves, with moles and mice, and helped make war with the smallest animals against snakes who threaded their way in, the skin whispering against the wood as they slithered in, hoping to eat another's young. A cottontail rabbit with its long hind toenails can rip a snake wide open.

It was a sport of ranch boys to rout out the gophers, the cottontails, the mice — to exhaust themselves lifting pole after pole to expose the hiding place of some terrified creature grown too confident. How moving it was to see it cowering, the eyes mad with fear, limbs trembling, hoping by stillness it might yet again escape. Often the boys let it scurry to another hiding place, and the boys imagined the slowly subsiding fear, the return of confidence. But then again the boys set to and moved the sheltering poles, worked with stolid patience until once again the little creature was exposed to unspeakable dangers. Some boys, tired at last, desisted. Some were perhaps diverted by a bird call, a killdeer pretending a broken wing, fluttering just out of reach to draw away from eggs or young. A few boys felt the first stirrings of conscience. Some boys — bored, disappointed in what they had hoped to be a more exciting sport — tortured or clubbed the creatures, and even that was sometimes strangely unsatisfying. Just so one learns how hollow is the pursuit of pleasure.

It was often said of Phil that he never lost a certain boyish air; you saw it in his eyes, in the step of his high-arched foot. He was forty, yet his face was innocent of lines except those around the eyes that hint of one who looks often and long into the distance. Only his hands had aged, and they only because of the baffling pride he took in going gloveless. Yes, he still took delight in boyish games. Idle for a moment in the shade of a willow, he might take out his pocketknife, open the big blade and the small blade, and holding it between thumb and index finger he would toss it to turn over once, twice or three times before it pricked the earth at an angle of exactly forty-five degrees. Thus he kept expert at an old game called mumblety-peg. If you lost, you were bound to root out from the earth with teeth a peg pounded level with the earth. You ate dirt. Many's the game Phil had played with George, and many's the peg George had rooted out of the ground.

Phil had astounded the young son of a cattle-buyer who represented himself to Phil as an expert at marbles, had indeed brought out a chamois bag of chinks, agates and flints and those lesser stones of baked, glazed earth. A fat little boy, Phil had thought, a greedy child, passing his precious bag of marbles from hand to hand so they rattled richly deep inside the pouch. George and the cattle-buyer, some new fellow, sat jawing on the running board of the buyer's fancy car. Phil had squatted on his haunches looking into the distance when the fat kid sauntered over and spoke up.

'Want to see my marbles?' he asked Phil, bold as brass.

'Why sure,' Phil said, smiling pleasantly.

How like a miser that kid looked, how he looked this way and that way before he drew the bag open, knelt, and then he poured out the precious marbles. 'There's two hundred of them,' the kid said softly.

'Well, how about that!' Phil said, listening at the same time to George's palavering with the buyer.

The kid scooped up the marbles and let them fall on each other. 'Did you ever play marbles when you were a little boy?' the kid asked.

'Oh, just a little bit.'

'Do you know what?' the kid asked.

'No, what?'

'I was champeen marble player this year at my school.' The kid's eyes challenged Phil.

'Well, how about that!' Phil said.

The voices of George and the buyer droned on. They weren't getting down to cases yet, Phil knew, and he could safely turn his attention to other things. The sun beat down mercilessly in the middle of the field where the steers they had brought the buyer to see — curious as steers are — stood at a distance, heads lowered, sizing up the fancy car.

'I was champeen two years in a row.' The kid was fat, so fat he felt the heat; needed some good exercise to get that fat off. He was a town kid, Phil knew, but he dressed up in boots and stetson like his old man. Funny rig, Phil thought, for the marble champion to sport.

'I expect you're mighty proud,' Phil said dryly.

Yes, the sun was hot. Looked as if George and the buyer were going to yammer for some time. The buyer had got out a pad of paper and was figuring. 'Want to try a game of marbles, mister?'

What cheek, Phil thought. 'Why, son, I haven't got any marbles.'

'I could sort of lend you some of mine.'

'Now, how could you "sort of lend" anything? I'll tell you. Suppose I buy a couple off you?'

The fat kid got a hooded look; you could see that fatty mind grinding and figuring. Just so the father wrote on the pad, mind grinding away. There were those marbles made of baked earth: he could sell them, win them back, and make a clear profit of whatever he could cheat out of Phil.

Sure enough, the kid pawed apart a few clay marbles.

'How much you want for them, son?'

His old man had taught him well. 'They're worth a quarter.'

They weren't worth a dime, Phil knew. 'All right, son.' And Phil took out the little purse he carried with him with its bits of silver and some double eagles in the depths.

'You go ahead and shoot first, mister,' the kid urged.

'My,' Phil said. 'I couldn't let a guest shoot second. You go ahead, son.'

The kid was pretty good. He got four of the marbles Phil had bought before it was Phil's turn. Phil picked up a little stick and ran it around the circle the boy had traced in the earth. 'Now it's my turn, huh?'

'Your turn, mister,' the kid said, and licked the sweat off his upper lip.

'Is this how to hold the marble when I shoot?' Phil asked.

'More like this,' the kid said.

'Oh,' Phil said. And then Phil got down on one knee,

like he used to, and my, if it didn't bring back being a boy again, the feel of the old sun, Old Sol, on your back, the grit of the earth on your knuckles, the breath you heaved before you whammed the marble into the ring. 'Here goes!' and he whammed out ten of the cheap marbles. 'Want to trade these ten for one of your flints and play flintsies?'

Round-eyed, stunned, the kid nodded.

Well, sir, Phil took every marble the kid had, and when he got them all before him, he scooped them up and put them back in the kid's bag. 'Now you take your marbles back,' he said. 'Your old man maybe showed you a few tricks about bein' sharp, but he didn't tell you the works by a long shot.' Now when the kid held the bag he didn't pass it back and forth, but just held onto it for dear life. Phil liked to teach people a lesson. He got to his feet and walked to the car where George and the buyer were still jawing. 'I figure you don't want these cattle,' Phil drawled, and put his eyes on the buyer. 'I figure you're just taking up me and my brother's time.'

Phil could still construct a kite, and fly it. Until lately he and George played a little catch out back, Sunday; used to be a crackerjack first baseman. He could spin a top. He was ageless, and never lost his boyish air. Others wondered what had happened, whence the rheumatism, the aching bones, the burgeoning paunch; and where was the lovely old flavor of the world they'd lost?

In a boyish mood Phil now drew Peter's attention to a cottontail that had skedaddled under the poles there where they worked, fencing haystacks. It was an old pile, unused for several years. The hired men had hauled new sharp-smelling pine poles in the wagon and piled them there; they hadn't yet hauled the old ones to the house for firewood. The rabbit had maybe had the poles to himself for some years, from his unconcern. He hopped around, mind you, as if he owned the place and Phil had first glimpsed him when he and Peter paused for lunch. The sun was bright, and so hot they had moved into the shade of the stack, backs against the stack, legs stretched out. Phil selected a cured blade of timothy from beside him and sucked and nursed the end of it, thinking how curious that Peter's face and arms seemed to glow. He coughed and removed the blade of hay from his mouth. 'You've got quite a tan there,' he said, and fell silent. Then, 'What it was about Bronco Henry, is he never did any roping, never any riding till he was anyway your age. Hey, look at that rabbit.'

It might have been tame so bold it was. Phil smiled, removed his hat, took aim, and shied it at the rabbit; like a hawk, the hat rose, its shadow a hawk's shadow, and it descended. The rabbit cowered at the shadow, then leaped for the poles. Phil unfolded himself and sauntered into the sunlight and retrieved his hat, knocked the dust off. Then, frowning, he stooped and shook the top pole of the pile, and the sound of it rattling, the heat of the sun and the smell of the afternoon made him smile and moved him to long, long thoughts. 'Hey, Pete,' he called. 'Let's see how long it takes before Peter Cottontail makes a run for the open.' That's what boys used to do, bet on how many poles they'd have to move before the animals ran for it.

Peter on one end of the pile, Phil on the other, they removed first this one and then that, and set it aside; at the end of the tenth pole the rabbit still cowered underneath somewhere, waited. Phil thought he saw it once; he probably had, for his eyes seldom failed. You can bet your sweet life on that.

'Gutty little bugger, ain't he,' Phil breathed. It was like pulling teeth to get Peter to talk. You had to toss the kid direct questions. When Peter spoke, he felt curiously rewarded.

'I guess he has to be gutty,' Peter said.

'I thought he'd've made a break for it by now,' Phil said.

They removed two more poles; the second disturbed the precarious balance of others that collapsed like huge jackstraws to a new pattern; then underneath there was a wild scurrying that was drowned out by a clap of thunder.

And what's this? The rabbit emerged with a broken leg; flopping, thrusting at the earth with the one good leg, it had a hard time of it. Phil watched while Peter picked the thing up, holding it in the crook of his arm. 'The poles fell on it,' Phil remarked.

'It seems they did,' Peter said.

'Well, put the thing out of its misery,' Phil ordered. 'I guess the quickest way, knock its head in. Funny, ain't it? If it hadn't been so damned gutty, it wouldn't have got itself hurt.'

'It seems to show the way things work,' said Peter.

So the kid was some kind of philosopher, was he? Phil smiled. 'It seems to show that you never can tell,' said Phil.

He watched Peter smooth his hand over the rabbit's head, calming it, and the next minute he was wringing its neck, and so deftly that Phil couldn't help but admire — he'd never seen anything quite like it. Now the rabbit's hind legs, free at the severing of the spinal cord from the tensions in the brain, relaxed and hung still in the boy's hand, the eyes glazing over in death. There was no blood at all! It was Phil himself who was bloody, hooked himself on some sharp thing.

Peter looked at the oozing blood. 'That's deep,' he remarked.

'But what the hell,' Phil said easily, and took out his blue bandanna and swabbed off the wound. The thunder boomed and echoed over the vast valley; black clouds hid the sun. Phil wet his index finger and held it up. His spit made it feel the slightest breeze. 'Won't get this storm,' he announced. 'Wind's south.' But he felt thwarted and grumpy. The rabbit thing hadn't worked out. He'd failed to capture the nostalgia his heart required; when they went around to the far side of the stack again to finish lunch, he spoke again of Bronco Henry. 'No,' he said, 'Bronco Henry came to these parts ignorant of every damned thing about riding and roping. Knew less than you, Pete old dear. Why, you're sitting up there these days on a horse good! But by God, he learned. Oh, he taught me things. He taught me that if you've got guts, you can do any damned thing, guts and patience. Impatience is a costly commodity, Pete. Taught me to use my eyes, too. Look yonder, there. What do you see?' Phil shrugged. 'You see the side of the hill. But Bronc, when he looked there, what do you suppose he saw?'

'A dog,' Peter said. 'A running dog.'

Phil stared, and ran his tongue over his lips. 'The *hell*,' he said, 'you see it just now?'

'When I first came here,' Peter said.

'Well, to get back. I think what a man needs is odds against him.'

Peter's knees were drawn up with his arm around them. 'My father said, obstacles. And you had to remove them.'

'Maybe another way to put it. Well, Pete, you've got obstacles, and for a fact, Peter-me-bye.' He sometimes lapsed into a brogue, for the Irish amused him, their pluck, their roguishness.

'Obstacles?' Peter's eyes were mild.

'Take your maw.'

'My mother?'

'How she's on the sauce.' Phil held his breath. Had he said too much? Too soon? Had he maybe alienated the boy before the entirety of his plan had unfolded? Continuing to smile in a pleasant and understanding way, he wondered why he had spoken as he did. Had he perhaps spoken from some motive he himself didn't wholly understand? Son of a *bitch*!

'On the sauce?' Peter asked, pretending, Phil thought, to look puzzled, as if he didn't savvy that old expression.

'Drinking, Pete. Boozing it up.' The boy winced at the word booze. A little too strong for him that word? But damn it, it was precisely that little old wince he needed to see. Maybe to gauge the wince, to judge it, and when he saw it, he knew he had not said too much, that it was *impossible* now to say too much. 'I guess you know she's been half-shot all summer.'

'Yes. Yes I know she has. She didn't use to drink.'

'Didn't she now?' A bit of the Irish accent again, to keep things on a light plane. But were they?

'No, she never did.'

'But your paw, Pete?'

'My father?'

'Father. Paw. I guess he hit the bottle pretty hard? The booze, Pete?' Phil's heart was racing a little. Said too much? Didn't the boy grow a little rigid? Phil tasted his upper lip.

'Until right at the end,' Peter said. 'Then he hanged himself.'

Phil started to touch the boy, but drew back his hand, and dropped his voice. 'You poor kid,' he said, and Peter made a faint smile. 'Things will work out for you yet.'

'Thanks, Phil,' Peter murmured.

The thunderheads rolled away as Phil said they would. Riding home through a little patch of sagebrush at one corner of the field they came on the abandoned nest of a sage hen, nothing left in it but a few shells. You hardly ever run across a sage hen's nest. You've got to keep your eyes peeled. Phil always did.

So good God, he noticed the hides were gone from the butcher pen long before they rode past there. Phil's mind was photographic; each detail that passed before his eye was etched deep in that dark recess where, for the rest of us, float and drift those pointless hairlike shapes, where lights flash off and on, and some amorphous shape slides across.

Phil saw the hides were gone, and Phil saw red. He rose in his stirrups. 'Well, I'll be damned!!' he said, and spurred his sorrel who began a long strong pace into the barnyard.

'Phil — Phil what's wrong?' Peter asked. 'Phil is something wrong?'

'Wrong? Wrong for Christ's sake?' Phil said. 'Every God damned hide is gone. She's really put her foot into it this time.'

'You think she did it, Phil — sold them?'

'You're bloody tootin',' Phil said. 'Or maybe *gave* them away.'

'Why would she do that, Phil. Why? She knew we needed the hides.'

'Because she was drunk. Pie-eyed. She was stewed. Why sonny, I'd think you'd know from them books that your paw left you that your maw's got a whatyoumacallit alcoholic personality. In them books of yours, it would come right under the letter A.'

'Phil — you're not going to say anything to her?'

'Say anything?' Phil barked. 'I won't say nothing. It's no skin off my ass, but sure as one good hell brother George will. High time that bozo got next to a few whatyouma-callit *facts*.'

They entered the long, dark barn that smelled of dust and manure and hay. Yes, and of years. Pale light knifed down from the crazy high windows.

'Phil?'

Phil's tongue had now swollen with anger. 'Mmmm?'

And then the boy touched his arm — touched it. 'Phil — I've got rawhide to finish the rope.'

'*You've* got it? What *you* doing with rawhide?'

And the boy's hand remained right where it was. 'I cut some up, Phil. I wanted to learn — to braid like you. Please take what I've got?' They were facing each other, and the boy's hand remained right where it was. 'You've been good to me, Phil.'

Take what I've got. You've been good. Phil, at that moment in that place that smelled of years felt in his throat what he'd felt once before and dear God knows never expected nor wanted to feel again, for the loss of it breaks your heart.

Oh, sure. Could have been the boy's offer was but a cheap means of getting his pretty little mother out of the soup. But wanting to *braid* like him! What reason for the boy to have rawhide but wanting to braid like him! To emulate him! Why else would he have cut up strips of rawhide? The boy wanted to *become* him, to merge with him as Phil had only once before wanted to become one with someone, and that one was gone, trampled to death while Phil, twenty years old, watched from the top rail of the bronc corral. Ah, God, but Phil had almost forgot what the touch of a hand will do, and his heart counted the seconds that Peter's was on him and rejoiced at the quality of the pressure. It told him what his heart required to know.

Please, was it not Fate (because a man must believe in something), was it not Fate that the boy had looked on him in his nakedness in that hidden place known only to George and to himself — and to Bronco Henry? Just so, he had looked on the boy's nakedness in that eternity when the boy had walked proud and unprotected past the open tents, jeered at, scorned — a pariah. But Phil knew, God knows he knew, what it was to be a pariah, and he had loathed the world, should it loath him first.

His voice was husky, 'That's damned kind of you, Pete,' and he slid his long arm about the boy's shoulders. Once before that day, he'd been tempted, and desisted, because he'd always sworn out of that old loyalty never again to make that move. 'I'll tell you one thing. Everything's going to be clear sailing for you from now on in. And do you know, I'm going to work and finish up that rope tonight. And Pete, will you watch me do it?' So that night the boy watched while Phil finished it off, scorning his fresh-wounded hand.

Peter was moved, too. In some astonishing way far beyond his pagan petitions, his poor mother had taken his own plan right out of his hands, and as he stood feeling the hand that gripped his shoulder, he seemed to hear a voice whispering that he was as special as he believed himself to be.

It was a matter of pride with Phil to be first at the breakfast table.

'Well, gentlemen,' he'd say with mock formality as they ambled in the back door. 'We got through another night. Good morning to yez!'

Or he might say 'Gut' Morgen' in memory of a Dutchman who once worked on the place. He delighted in dialect. He liked a good big breakfast, and had no patience with people who had but reluctant stomachs. 'Have another coupla eggs,' he'd urge a sick young fellow who could scarcely hold down coffee. 'Come on, now.' And he'd wink at the other men.

Oatmeal and cream, pancakes, fried eggs, rose-hued slabs of ham, coffee with thick cream. The meal never varied, and never would. No young fellow ever disobeyed Phil, and the men seemed to get a kick out of the show. Phil did like to josh people, and he liked to jolly people, too, and during breakfast he jollied them, including George.

George, a heavy sleeper, had not even in the old days appeared until the others were seated and fixed on their food, and his silence was as contagious as Phil's morning bounciness. Sometimes Phil found himself irritated with George, and he needled him.

'Have a bad night, George?' he'd ask, winking at the others. 'Get tangled up in the arms of Morpheus?'

George, since his marriage, might be five minutes late for breakfast, and the faster eaters had already cleaned up their plates and pushed back their chairs and begun rolling smokes.

Recently, when George was more than five minutes late, Phil had remarked, wide-eyed and innocent, "Strouble, George? Your old lady roll over on your nightshirt?'

Phil could laugh at the memory of the shocked silence, for to these men, these drifters, these homeless wanderers, there were but two kinds of women, good women and bad women. Bad women had no more right to respect than animals, and as animals they were used and discussed.

Ah, but good women! Good women were pure, sexless and as holy as God. Good women were Sister, Mother, and the childhood sweetheart whose glance melted the heart. The pictures and photographs of these good women the men kept in their suitcases, their icons and altar stones.

The little slip of a woman they saw occasionally in the yard, or recently tugging at pieces of trash almost as big as herself, a funny little hand around her head to keep the hair out of her eyes — she was a good woman, hardly to be considered in terms of beds and nightshirts.

George blushed in that silence that contained the mousy sounds of forks and knives and the plink of china. The men held their eyes on their plates, and the moment passed while Phil reached long across the table for the hotcakes — his boardinghouse reach, he called it, that caused the sleeve of his blue chambray shirt to slip far up on his wrist revealing skin that was shockingly white, such skin as might be found under a stone. How red and chapped his hands were, his worldly, scratched and damaged hands.

One comes to count on the usual and the expected, the appearance of the sun, the chilling voice of wild geese wedging south, the breakup of the ice, the shy green grass on the south slopes, the heady breezes that disturb the purple camas. Sun, geese, ice, grass and waving camas all point to the knowable future, and the world was well.

But now Phil was late. No cheery greeting for the cook, no 'Good morning to yez,' no good morning in any of the dialects that amused him.

Mrs Lewis brought in the first round of pancakes, slow and heavy on her unsatisfactory feet.

Neither George nor Peter had yet appeared. There was a curious animation among the men, a nervousness they hoped to conceal by continuing to belabor a joke that had sprung up a few moments before in the bunkhouse — some one of the men had got hold of a water snake, surely one of the last of the season, for the frost was now everywhere. The man — just who nobody yet knew — had put the snake into the bedding of a sleeping man. The man had waked, felt something, touched it, and knew a snake was coiled comfortably and torpid close against the hollow of his throat. He alone was now sullen and angry, taking it as the sort of joke you play on a child. Since his only achievement, so far, was that he had grown up, he was jealous of his dignity. When he found out who had done the thing, he had some plans of his own, and don't you forget it.

'I'll bet that old snake was sure sleeping there,' a man said, giggling a little. 'But it'd sure take a snake to do it. I sure wouldn't want to be the one sleeping with you.'

'Who the hell ever asked you to,' the man growled.

George walked in and said good morning.

Peter came in silently, and sat. He took a pancake. The fast eater at the table had now already finished, and had pushed back his chair and was commencing to pick his teeth.

The tooth-picker, perhaps a little proud that he had again finished first, was tempted to josh Phil at being late, and opened his mouth to speak, but closed it at once at what he saw in Phil's face. Phil had apparently not dried his face well on the roller towel in the back lavatory — or was it sweat? — and he had only inexpertly raked his fingers through his hair. He pulled out his chair and sat.

And simply sat. Mrs Lewis lumbered in with a steaming cup of coffee and set it before him. He reached out a hand, picked up the cup, and put it down again, and continued to look at his hand. He looked around the table with a curious, mild expression, pushed back his chair, rose, and left the room. He was not seen again until half an hour later when he sat in the doorway of the blacksmith shop. The sun, just risen above the sagebrush hill, was full in his face. The new frost on the ground began its retreat.

Next, Phil was seen walking with the slow, paced dignity of an old man back to the house. He went into his bedroom and closed the door. He made no sounds in there, nor did he answer when George knocked. George took a breath and did the unheard-of thing — he opened his brother's door without an invitation. 'I'll run you into Herndon,' George said.

'All right,' said Phil.

He had got himself arranged into his ill-fitting town suit; he had got into his shoes from the Army & Navy store. It had been long since he had sat in Whitey Potter's chair, and his thick hair had so increased that his hat sat high and comical, like a clown's. He seemed all angles as he walked through the living room and out the front door. Rose, at his approach, left the living room for the kitchen where she poured herself a cup of coffee with a shaking hand to give herself a more reasonable reason for having fled the room. She could not understand the yawning silence in the house, nor what was going on in it. The last she saw of Phil, he was walking across to the garage where the old Reo shot rings of exhaust smoke into the cold morning; Phil stood aside while George backed out the car. Over against the hill, all was shadow. She sipped her coffee; she had so frightened herself two days before in collapsing drunk on the bed that she had drunk nothing since, determined to be sober when George spoke to her, as he surely would. Why hadn't he spoken yet? Why? She was crushed by the irrational notion that whatever was going on that morning was her fault. Thus does guilt smother and sicken.

The Old Lady and the Old Gent both agreed there was nothing for it but to take the next train to Herndon where George had telegraphed he would meet them.

'No, she's good about it,' the Old Lady said. 'If the tip is big enough, they're good about it.' She spoke of the chambermaid who was good about coming in to water the geraniums that made their hotel rooms homelike. 'What time is it?'

The Old Gent in his vaguely Prince Albert topcoat reached into his vest pocket for his watch. 'Exactly five thirty-seven,' he said.

'I hate these tiny watches,' she said, frowning at the wee face of the jeweled one on her wrist. 'I always have. You can't see them and they don't keep time. We can get something to eat on the train.' Suddenly the Old Lady covered her face with her hands, and the Old Gent walked at once to her as if he had expected the gesture.

'Now-now,' he whispered.

'I'm sorry, I'm all right now,' she insisted. In a few minutes they left the room, closed the door behind them, and the Old Gent tried it once. They had already sent their bags down ahead into the lobby where, beyond in the dining room, a few transients, unacquainted with the rhythm of the great hotel, ate early dinners under the chandeliers.

'No, I'm perfectly all right,' she told the Old Gent as they followed the driver to the revolving door. 'I've been braced for some such thing.'

Phil was fortunate to have his town suit with him, for it was on a Sunday night he needed his suit, although of course Mr Green of Greens would gladly have opened up, under the circumstances. The weather was fine, Indian summer, really — lazy. And lazy out in the country, the air languid and perfumed by the incense of distant forest fires. The winter chore of feeding cattle had not yet begun so people were free that Monday. There was a representative from every store where the Burbanks traded, and even from the stores where the Burbanks did not trade — they having an eye to the future. There was a group from the bank, of course. The ranchers themselves came with their wives and children, the wives — some of them — in the furs of animals their husbands had trapped and had made up as Christmas surprises at a furrier's in the capital city — local animals, beaver, stone marten, red fox and so forth. Because the funeral was at two (the usual time in that country) they planned so they could have a nice lunch either at the Sugar Bowl or in the hotel and a nice little visit afterwards, for many never saw each other except on such pointed occasions.

To George, of course, had fallen the dismal task of choosing a coffin from among those out back in the Baker Funeral Home. But little light fell through the windows that faced the back alley; they had been purposely left dirty that loiterers might not easily look in upon the accouterments of the dead, the boxes of indifferent wood enhanced with fake silver. Here, too, was an expensive coffin of mahogany, bought perhaps with the Burbanks and two or three other such families in mind. 'No, don't turn on the light,' George murmured. 'I can see well enough.'

'Buck up, George,' Baker said.

'It's all right,' George said. 'I'll take the one here.'

'A fine piece of merchandise, George,' Baker said. 'Fit tribute to a fine man. I knew you'd want to do the right thing.'

The church smelled of coal smoke and old brown wood. Those who were not Episcopalians — Episcopalopians, as Phil used to call them — whispered that it was a shame that there was no eulogy. There was so much, they said, to say about Phil — so much about his intelligence, his friendliness, how common he was as an old shoe, his lack of side; and my, they did remember his banjo playing, his bright whistle, his boyishness, the works of his strong, scarred, chapped hands — the little carved chairs, the wrought iron pieces. Mrs Lewis, back at the ranch, shed a tear over a darning ball Phil had once surprised her with.

The Old Folks went directly from the grave to the railroad depot; otherwise they would have had to spend the night in Herndon. There was nothing to say to anybody, and they knew it.

'Don't look like that,' the Old Lady commanded the Old Gent. 'You had nothing, precisely nothing, to do with it. One is what one is, does what one must do, and ends as fate requires.'

'May I remind you of the same?' the Old Gent said softly.

'Oh, so many flowers,' the Old Lady remarked. Sufficient flowers to later perk up each room in the Herndon Hospital, even blooms for the charity wards.

'I was watching,' the Old Gent said, 'when you kissed Rose.'

'So now we call her Rose. You were watching? Well, of course. I hope for so much.'

'You can, of course. That's when I noticed you didn't have your rings.'

'My rings? Oh, yes.'

'I've always liked your hands. You know, you never needed rings.'

'And she least of all, I think. But sometimes they please. A symbol? But thank you, thank you kindly. I was watching how she got down from the machine, how she gave her hand to George, and suddenly looked at him. So good, both of them. So then I went to her, and I said, "Here . . ."'

As their accommodation was the single large drawing room on the fast olive-green train back to Salt Lake City, the Old Lady could weep a bit in private. When at last she stopped, the Old Gent rose, steadied himself as the train leaned into a swooping curve, and went and opened one of the bags and got out two monogrammed decks of playing cards and pushed the button for the porter who came and smiled and brought a table and set it up. There beside the window the Burbanks sat and played Russian Bank, and no matter how fast the car sped, the full moon floated easily beside them, a yellow balloon on a string.

'I suppose,' the Old Lady said, 'that I always knew something strange would happen.'

'. . . mystified. But you said you were braced. And remember you were always patient, you were always kind.'

She leaned suddenly forward in the seat, and began kneading her bare hands to stop their trembling. 'Kindness!' Her voice broke. 'What else in God's name is there?'

'Nothing, really.'

She smiled a little, and spoke softly. 'Do you know? We're to spend Christmas with them. At her specific request. I used to feel so old.'

'I swear you never looked it.'

'Indeed? But then, I always had you. Always had you, just as she has *him*. She's only thirty-seven.'

'Sometimes you're hard to follow.'

'Am I — really?' She lifted her chin and looked straight into his eyes.

Phil's doctor, too, was mystified. On Phil's admission to the hospital, he had taken blood samples and cultured them. The culture the samples produced — a little pale jelly in a test tube — he had already sent off to the State Hospital where they knew about such things. Phil's final convulsion, although mercifully brief, had been truly frightful. Well, he'd know in a day or two what had gone wrong. He thought the whole business, as he remarked to a nurse, the whole business of sending the culture off was rather like locking the barn door after the horse was stolen.

The culture in the test tube would tell him what one person already knew.

Peter, waiting patiently at the ranch during the funeral, had an interesting day. One of the dogs, a half-breed collie, followed him around from the barn and played a game with itself, snapping at its reflection in one of the basement windows there at ground level. It was the first of the dogs to adore him. His first friend. When he went inside, it whined for him beyond the front door. Then he spent some time soberly thumbing through George's pile of *Saturday Evening Posts*. Among them he found evidence of one of George's little dreams, a somewhat ragged brochure for Pierce-Arrow motorcars. His face came very close to a grin for he felt a sudden warm kinship with George. Who could help but admire those magnificent machines, the insolent sweep of the fenders and the headlights set into them? Those were the vehicles of the high and mighty, and he knew that only the Locomobile (fancied by old General Pershing, among others) rivaled the Pierce.

The sun had slipped around behind, and the shadow of the house lay black across the road and crept up the face of the hill. Peter browsed among the books in the case in the living room, looking close (for the light was failing), noting the range of their contents. Here the *Memoirs of the Russian Court* composed by a Grand Duchess, was smack against a copy of *Grasses of the Western United States*, and then a modern edition of Hoyle's *Card Games*, books for dreams, books for facts. And here was the *Book of Common Prayer*. He supposed it would be used that day in Herndon, and drew it out; it fell open to Psalms, Day 6. But this was the fourth of September, and he turned back, and since the shadow was already creeping up the face of the hill out front, he read the Psalms of Evening Prayer. The twentieth verse was weirdly appropriate, and moved him to turn to and read through *The Order for the Burial of the Dead*, equally appropriate, and a much shorter service than he'd imagined, hardly longer than the *Form of Solemnization of Matrimony* he had first read not nine months before. Not many words, he thought, to celebrate oblivion. Reading it slowly as the pale priest might, he found it took but fifteen minutes by the big clock to finish — counting appropriate pauses at the commas and periods; however, the coffin would have to be carried in and carried out, and it would be bulky. Thus, the entire service might take a good half hour.

From the windows of the neat, quiet room where he lived in Herndon he had watched a half dozen processions to the cemetery on the hill a mile away, had seen the sun fix and flash on bottles and mason jars that held the rotting stems of flowers; the hearse moved so slowly that it always took a good half hour, but in the wintertime they hurried it up a little. But this day was warm. Then there were the words 'appointed to be read at the grave' — about fifteen minutes' worth (reading as the old priest might) and then the trip back with the empty hearse, a blue Buick hearse, new that year. He'd read about it in the Herndon *Recorder*. Baker, the undertaker, and his family had driven the old hearse out to Chicago and taken delivery of the new one and had driven it back, picnicking along the way with many little adventures that the editor wrote up with a gentle humor.

Then there would be coffee and sandwiches somewhere, and greetings and good-byes, so it would be past five before the whole thing was over, and dark.

But what enchanting words those were in the Prayer Book, what majesty, what a roll they had. How his father would have loved them, had they been said over him, but they had not been, because his father had played God and removed himself. But oh, what words they would have been to read — to sing over his father!

It was long past suppertime when his mother and George got back. The girl came in from the kitchen and had spoken to Peter with respect. 'Do you want me to leave their places on?'

'Please,' he said. Then he went upstairs and washed his hands carefully, and wetted and combed his hair. Before long the dogs began their predicted barking and he combed his hair carefully and got up and opened the window and looked out. At first they were hidden in the shadow of the hill; he heard his mother's soft voice. Then they moved slowly out into the moonlight. How lovely she looked in the moonlight, how fine that George stood still, took her, kissed her! What but for this, this playing of a scene in the moonlight that marked the true beginning of his mother's life, what but for this had his father removed himself — sacrificed himself to lie under that other hill, in Beech, under a handful of paper flowers, faithful to his own book of dreams?

The dogs kept to the shadows, whimpered softly, then were strangely still. Peter was moved to whisper the line from Psalms that had so moved him, hours before.

Deliver my soul from the sword,
My darling from the power of the dog.

He wondered if that Prayer Book were often used, if he might not snip out that bit and paste it into place in the scrapbook, a far better final entry than the rose leaves that, still red, had lost their odor. For she was delivered now — thanks to his father's sacrifice, and to the sacrifice he himself had found it possible to make from a knowledge got from his father's big black books. The dog was dead.

In those black books, one August afternoon, he had found that anthrax — blackleg they called it out there — was a disease of animals communicable to man, and that it finds its sure way into the human bloodstream through cuts or breaks in the skin from a man's handling the hide of a diseased animal — as when perhaps a man with damaged hands will use a diseased hide in braiding a rope.

Afterword
by Annie Proulx

The Power of the Dog was published in 1967 by Little, Brown in Boston after Thomas Savage's editor at Random House asked for changes that the writer refused to make. It earned extremely good reviews, stayed on the *New York Times* 'New and Recommended' list for nearly two months, was five times optioned for a film (which was never made). It is the fifth and, for some readers, including this one, the best of Savage's thirteen novels, a psychological study freighted with drama and tension, unusual in dealing with a topic rarely discussed in that period — repressed homosexuality displayed as homophobia in the masculine ranch world. It is a brilliant and tough book and belongs on the shelf of hard-eyed western fiction along with Walter Van Tilburg Clark's *Track of the Cat*, Wallace Stegner's *The Big Rock Candy Mountain*, and Katherine Anne Porter's *Noon Wine*. Although Savage wrote strong and intelligent novels, some set in the east, some in the west, it is his Montana-Idaho-Utah books that ring truest and stick permanently in the mind. Something aching and lonely and terrible of the west is caught forever on his pages, and the most compelling and painful of these books is *The Power of the Dog*, a work of literary art.

Savage, though rarely included in the western literary lists, was one of the first of the Montana writers, an informal but famous regional concentration of writers. His novels are rich in character development, written in clear and well-balanced sentences with striking and important landscape description, imbued with a natural sense of drama and literary tension. As his writing matured it became clear he was a powerful observer of the human condition. Book critic Jonathan Yardley commented in his review of *For Mary, With Love* that 'over his long and notably productive career [Savage] has shown himself to be a writer of real consequence; it is a shame, bordering on an outrage, that so few readers have discovered him.'

Most of the reviewers in the late 1960s, even if they recognized the interior tragedy of *The Power of the Dog*, dodged the homosexuality issue by reporting a simplistic contest of good versus evil, cruelty versus decent kindness, or 'the wary war between compulsion and intelligence,' whatever that means.[1] Only one, an anonymous reviewer for *Publisher's Weekly*, though squeamish about a calf castration scene on the first page, understood what *The Power of the Dog* was about and said so clearly:

A taut and powerful novel with such an unnecessarily graphic brutality in its opening paragraph, however, that many readers will be put off by it. The scene is Utah in 1924 and against a rugged ranch country background Mr Savage spins a tale of two brothers, George, slow, clumsy, essentially decent, and Phil, a repressed homosexual. When George marries a widow and brings her back to the ranch, Phil makes life such hell for her that she takes to secret drinking. Then her young son, Peter, who is bright and strange, comes for the summer

---

[1] Eliot Fremont-Smith, *New York Times Book Review*.

and sees what is happening. While Phil is plotting a homosexual involvement with the boy, young Peter is plotting a diabolically clever revenge on him that is pretty chilling. Krafft-Ebbing against a regional Western setting, this has strong literary but rather less commercial appeal.[2]

The book earned much critical praise — 'a powerful tragedy,' 'taut and powerful,' 'the year's best novel,' and, wrote Roger Sale in *The Hudson Review,* 'the finest single book I know about the modern west,' but sold few copies. Emily Salkin of Little, Brown, the force behind the 2001 republication of this neglected novel, remarks that the publisher's sales records do not go back to 1967 but 'I can't imagine it sold more than 1,000 copies in hardcover.'[3] Though the novel is still occasionally found on ranch bookshelves, it is virtually unknown today to the general reading public, even to specialists in western literature. It is cause for rejoicing that *The Power of the Dog* has a second chance with today's readers.

Thomas Savage was born in 1915 in Salt Lake City, Utah, to a remarkably handsome couple, Elizabeth (Yearian) and Benjamin Savage. Elizabeth Yearian was the oldest daughter of a famous Idaho sheep-ranching family, and her mother, imperious and powerful and well connected, was known as 'the Sheep Queen.' The ranch itself had been founded a generation earlier when the clan patriarch discovered gold.

When Savage was two years old, his parents divorced. Three years later his mother married a wealthy Montana rancher named Brenner, and from that time he was

---

[2] *Publisher's Weekly*, January 2, 1967.

[3] Emily Salkin, private correspondence, October 10, 2000.

ranch-raised as Tom Brenner in Beaverhead County in southwest Montana. He was fortunate to be part of two eccentric and sprawling clans — the Yearians and the Brenners — which furnished him a wealth of character studies; fortunate to be part of two rich and notable ranches, the Brenners in cattle, the Yearians in sheep. Family mattered intensely, especially to the Yearians. In his autobiographical novel, the best known of his works, *I Heard My Sister Speak My Name* (republished by Little, Brown in 2001, under the title *The Sheep Queen*), he wrote:

> We all love each other. My aunt Maude, the middle aunt, once told me, 'You know, Tom, we've always liked each other better than anybody else.' It is not that we think we are better than anybody else but that we are better company, at least for each other. We like to have fun.[4]
>
> . . . We picnicked annually, sometimes as many as fifty of us, on the very spot where George Sweringen had discovered gold and we ate what he had eaten: beans and bacon and trout fried over the fire, and dried apple pies. We felt we could reach out and touch him and his wife Lizzie who had often sung hymns. We were proud of them and felt they would be proud of us. They would have liked us better than anybody else.[5]

Beaverhead County was a bronc-stomping Montana now long gone, rough and masculine in ethos, only one or two generations removed from pioneer days. It was a man's world of cattle, sheep, horses, dogs, guns, fences, and property. The

[4] Thomas Savage, *I Heard My Sister Speak My Name*, p. 138, Little, Brown, Boston, 1977.

[5] Ibid., p. 140. Sweringen is the fictional name Savage used for the Yearians.

open range still existed in living memory, as did confrontations with Indians. In the 1920s the Brenner ranch house enjoyed electricity (from a Delco generating plant, later replaced by a Wind Charger) and a certain amount of elegance. There were some automobiles in Montana in the '20s, and young Savage was passionate about the more prestigious equipages (his interest in classic automobiles is embedded in *Trust in Chariots*, his fourth novel, about the escapades of a man who fled marriage and toured the continent in a Rolls-Royce, linked to Savage's own purchase in 1952 of the Rolls-Royce that had been on exhibit at the 1939 World's Fair), but in ranch country the railroad continued to be all-important and the horse was still major transportation; men were valued for their abilities with horses. Most ranch diets were home-raised, rustled, or hunted meat, potatoes, beans. Coffee was swallowed black. Both the Yearian and Brenner tables featured delicacies and abundance uncommon in that day.

A powerful work ethic dominated western culture, and it took (and still takes) a tough cuss to make a go of ranching. This kind of rural life is more or less extinct in the American 21st century; most people cannot even imagine a society without paved roads, television or radio, cars, hot showers, telephones, airplanes. Nor can many know the combination of hard physical work and quiet wealth that characterized some of the old ranches. This was Thomas Savage's world for the first twenty-one years of his life. After graduation from Beaverhead County High School (where he claims to have learned little beyond speed typing) and two years at the University of Montana studying writing, he broke horses and herded sheep in Montana and Idaho for a few years, doing the ritual Saturday night go-to-town-and-get-drunk, 'where you sat on the running boards of cars and got sick.'[6] The horse-breaking part of that past was visible in his first published article, 'The Bronc Stomper,' for *Coronet* magazine in 1937 under the name of Tom Brenner, unremarkable except for its unusual subject matter. Years later Savage wrote:

> In 1936 I began to wonder what I was doing, wandering around, and perhaps to find a direction, I wrote an article about how to break a horse, sent it off to *Coronet* magazine and was astonished to receive a check for seventy-five dollars. Fifty of it I invested and lost in gold mining stock. The other twenty-five I spent on a red dress for a young cousin of mine who had been invited to a Junior prom. I didn't sell another thing for seven years.[7]

A certain restlessness was in him now, and the possibility of another kind of life than ranching began to glimmer in the distance. He enrolled as an English major at Colby College in Waterville, Maine.

> On my 21st birthday I woke up herding sheep in the Bitterroot Valley. I asked myself what in hell am I doing here, and my stepfather, the best of stepfathers, much in love with my mother, sent me off to Colby where I'd heard there was a charming girl who had been in high school in Missoula, Montana. We wrote all that summer, and I went back and we were married the summer of '39.[8]

---

[6] Thomas Savage, *I, Thomas Savage, am the author of The Power of the Dog*, 1967, p. 5, autobiographical essay used by Little, Brown for promotional purposes.
[7] Ibid., pp. 5–6.
[8] Thomas Savage, personal correspondence, September 15, 2000.

After Savage graduated from Colby he took an uncongenial job as a claims adjuster for a Chicago insurance company. Over the years he also worked as a wrangler, ranch hand, plumber's assistant, welder, and railroad brakeman. He taught English as well, at Suffolk University in Boston, at Brandeis, and more briefly at Franconia College in New Hampshire and Vassar College. Through all of these jobs he was writing steadily.

This marriage with Elizabeth Fitzgerald, later a novelist herself, endured until her death in 1988. They had three children, sons Brassil and Russell, and daughter Elizabeth. In 1952 the Savages bought property on the Maine coast and lived there until the February blizzard of 1978 washed the house off its foundations. 'It cost us $25,000 to fix that house,' Savage says ruefully. The next year Savage received a Guggenheim Foundation grant, which helped him write *Her Side of It*, the story of an alcoholic writer wrestling with demons.

In 1982 the Savages sold the Maine house and moved to Whidby Island in Puget Sound, where they built on property given to Savage by his long-lost sister, immortalized in *I Heard My Sister Speak My Name*. Today Thomas Savage, who left the island after his wife's death, makes his home in Virginia Beach near his daughter.

As a young man at Colby, Savage began his writing career with a short story about the importance of the railroad to an isolated ranching community cut off from the outside by a high pass and the intense Montana winters.

I sent it off to Ed Weeks, then editor of *The Atlantic*. He returned it, remarking that there were no human beings in it, and suggested I make a novel of it. . . . I wrote the first draft of *The Pass* at Colby. Dean Mariner allowed me to skip classes so long as I wrote.[9]

The Pass was published by Doubleday in 1944 under the name Thomas Savage, for, with the birth of his first child, Tom Brenner sent to Salt Lake City for his birth certificate and began the laborious process of having all his past job and education records changed to show his birth name, Thomas Savage, 'all difficulty, but eventually accomplished except for having my wife's Phi Beta Kappa name changed from Brenner to Savage, which they wouldn't do.'[10] This family complexity of names and identities, of east coast culture and western mountains, of manual labor and writing, of a lost past and private secrets, characterizes Savage's life, his novels, and the people in them. The tangle of abandonment, loss, broken families, and difficult emotional situations is in Savage's work and, to a considerable degree, is related to his own life. With intense human drama swirling about him throughout his childhood, and from the vantage point of outsider in the Brenner house, Savage developed an exquisitely keen eye for nuances of body language, intonation, silence. He has said a number of times that he does little research but relies on his own experience of life, memories, imagination. The 1977 autobiographical novel, *I Heard My Sister Speak My Name*, fictionalizes the extraordinary and true appearance in Savage's life, when they were both in their fifties, of an older sister neither he nor anyone else knew existed. His beautiful mother had been dead then for a decade, but the digging out of legal proofs and papers uncovered a long-ago temporary false identity, her secret

---

[9] Ibid.
[10] Ibid.

— that in 1912 she had borne a baby girl and, as in some antique melodrama, left the infant on a doorstep. This novel is particularly useful for a study of Savage's sources.

Savage's first novel, *The Pass*, is shot through with the deepest kind of landscape description which utterly controls the destinies and fortunes of the ranchers and Scandinavian farmers who settle on the prairie adjacent to a formidable pass. The people of the place love it beyond reason, the blue autumnal haze, the grassland stretched out, and they relish testing themselves against spring storms and baking drought. The novel is studded with brilliant portraits that already display Savage's masterly ability to show the inner lives of characters, especially women, who are treated with a rare depth of understanding. The language and thinking of the ranch people in *The Pass* is strikingly vivid, even today, and invites comparison with James Galvin's biography of place, *The Meadow*, and the brilliant and funny stories of the Chilcotin country by Canadian writer Paul St. Pierre, *Breaking Smith's Quarter Horse* and *Smith and Other Events*.

A sense of great longing and sympathy for the western landscape colors this novel, and it is hard to dismiss the idea that Savage, in the tighter confines of the east, re-created the country he came from for personal as well as literary reasons. But living in such country demands and takes everything. When a character freezes to death on his trapline in *The Pass*, a young wife says to her husband, 'The prairie killed him. He loved the prairie and it killed him.' There are more ways than one that hard country kills, as Savage shows in his western fiction. Some years after *The Pass*, Savage said in an interview:

I have always believed that the landscape shapes the people. A person will say, for instance, that there is something different about Westerners. And I think the moment you leave Chicago and go West, you find that people are quite different. For one thing, there is an openness about them. I think the difference in Westerners has to do with the fact that they feel it's impossible to look at the Rocky Mountains — or to look at the horizon, which is equally vast — and consider that there is such a thing as Europe or neighbors or anything else.[11]

The Pass and *Lona Hanson* and, to some extent, *The Power of the Dog* may be seen as late novels from the golden age of American landscape fiction, a period that falls roughly in the first half of the last century. In these novels landscape is used not just as decorative background, but to drive the story and control the characters' lives, as in the work of Willa Cather, Marjorie Kinnan Rawlings, Walter D. Edmonds, William Faulkner, Flannery O'Connor, John Steinbeck, and nearly all that Hemingway wrote, all resonant with the sense of place, a technique well suited to describing the then strikingly different regions of America, the pioneer ethos, the drive of capitalist democracy on the hunt for resources. By 1948, when Norman Mailer's *The Naked and the Dead* appeared, with its characters braced in adversarial and manipulative position to the raw land, that older landscape novel was disappearing.

The title of Savage's major book, *The Power of the Dog*, is a multiple-layered reference to a striking landscape feature that Phil Burbank can see but his brother, George, cannot. In fact, Phil uses this distant formation of rock and slope that resembles a running dog as a kind of test — those who

[11] Interview, Jean W. Ross, *Contemporary Authors Online*, The Gale Group, 1999.

cannot see it are lacking in intelligence and perception. For himself it is a proof of his sharp and special sensitivity.

> In the outcropping of rocks on the hill that rose up before the ranchhouse, in the tangled growth of sagebrush that scarred the hill's face like acne he saw the astonishing figure of a running dog. The lean hind legs thrust the powerful shoulders forward; the hot snout was lowered in pursuit of some frightened thing — some idea — that fled across the draws and ridges and shadows of the northern hills. But there was no doubt in Phil's mind of the end of that pursuit. The dog would have its prey. Phil had only to raise his eyes to the hill to smell the dog's breath. But vivid as that huge dog was, no one but one other had seen it, George least of all.[12]

In another sense the dog is Phil himself; alternatively he is the dog's prey. The dog is also a connection with the old, finer days. But most powerfully the title comes from the Book of Common Prayer:

> Deliver my soul from the sword;
> My [only one] from the power of the dog.[13]

The Burbank ranch is located in southwestern Montana near the cattle-shipping town of Beech, and it has been operated for many years by the parents of Phil and George, 'the Old Gentleman' and 'the Old Lady.' The elder Burbanks are moneyed easterners who maintained relatively luxurious

---

[12] Thomas Savage, *The Power of the Dog*, p. 67, Little, Brown, Boston, 1967.
[13] Ibid., p. 273. Psalms, 22:20, The New Scofield Reference Bible, Oxford U. Press, N.Y.

lives in their years on the ranch but who, when the story opens in 1924, have retired to a suite of rooms in a Salt Lake City hotel, following an undescribed contretemps with Phil. The Burbanks are the most important ranchers in the valley. When the story opens the two sons run the ranch, Phil forty years old, George thirty-eight. The two men share a bedroom as they have since childhood, out of tradition and habit.

On the ranch Phil is responsible for haying, roundups, ranch labor, trailing herds to the railroad, the daily work of a big spread, while George oversees the business affairs and finances, meets with bankers and the governor, and winds the clock on Sunday afternoon. In the rural division of labor, ranch work is man's work.[14] Phil spends much time in the bunkhouse with the hands, talking about the good old days when ranch hands were real men and the chief of them was Bronco Henry. Phil prides himself on his ability to get along with the cowboys and thinks there is something about George that makes them uncomfortable.

The brothers are a study in opposites. Phil is slender and good-looking; he is brilliant and enormously capable, a great reader, a taxidermist, skilled at braiding rawhide and horsehair, a solver of chess problems, a smith and metalworker, a collector of arrowheads (even fashioning arrowheads himself with greater skill than any Indian), a banjo player, a fine rider, a builder of hay-stacking beaver-slide derricks, a vivid conversationalist. He is also a high-tempered bully, a harping critic of all around him; he knows unerringly the cruel thing to say, relishes getting people's goats. He is, in

---

[14] Will Fellows, *Farm Boys: Lives of Gay Men from the Rural Midwest*, U. Wisconsin Press, 1996, 1998, well illustrates the rigid division of the sexes in conservative, rural America.

fact, a vicious bitch. He bathes only once a month in summer, not in the bathtub but in a hidden pool, makes it a point never to wear gloves so his hands are nicked and callused and dirty. He gets his hair cut rarely. He believes that people need obstacles in their lives that they may strive and rise above them.

George, on the other hand, is phlegmatic, slow to learn but with a good memory, feels sorry for people and never blames anybody, has little to say. George is stocky (Phil calls him 'Fatso' to irritate), steady against Phil's mercury, kind against Phil's cruelty. It is easy to see the brothers as personifications of Good and Evil, as Abel and Cain, as Weak and Strong, as Normal and Peculiar. To some extent all of these balance points fit, but both characters are far more complex.

In a barroom Phil, who himself drinks very sparingly out of fear of what he might reveal in a loose-tongued moment, humiliates and abuses the drunken town doctor, Johnny Gordon, who cannot resist liquor, with tragic results, for the doctor, corroded by humiliation, kills himself a year later. Phil is revolted by weakness and pride, and never misses a chance to lacerate another with his mean-spirited opinions. He humiliates not only the drunken doctor, but a Jewish department store owner who started out as a hide buyer, a boastful fat kid with a bag of marbles, and an elderly Indian; he spews hatred and scorn. So much does he dislike social-climbing Jews that rather than sell his old hides to the peddler, he wastefully burns them. He is particularly vocal and phobic about 'sissies,' still a word of choice in the west to describe effeminate boys and men. He is particularly scornful of Peter Gordon, the drunken doctor's sissy son, who has developed an unfortunate skill in making paper flowers. It is this son who discovers his father's body and who inherits the doctor's medical library. Less well known than his ability to fashion crepe-paper roses is the boy's omnivorous curiosity about medicine and wild plants, whose intricate leaf and root systems he draws in minute detail.

A character mentioned only a very few times and never described is of central importance to the novel — Bronco Henry, the ideal cowboy of Phil's youth. Again and again there is a fleeting reference to this hero, and gradually it dawns on the reader that Bronco Henry has a tremendous emotional grip on Phil's bitter and loveless heart. No one and nothing can ever match Bronco Henry. At some time in the past, we come to understand, Phil desired — touched — perhaps loved — Bronco Henry. And something very bad happened. We do not learn of the accident that killed Bronco Henry in front of the twenty-year-old Phil's eyes until nearly the end of the book. Nor do we learn until then that it was Bronco Henry who first saw the running dog in the landscape.

But it is not bitterness and loss that make Phil the mean-mouthed bully that he is. Bronco Henry's death does not explain Phil's almost pathological cultivation of nonsissy appearance — smelly, dirty, rough hands, deliberately ungrammatical talk, superabilities in such manly things as riding and braiding rawhide ropes. The major key to Phil's complex personality is, perhaps, that in wanting to touch and have Bronco Henry, he was forced to recognize and confront the enormous fact of his own homosexuality. His private obstacle became this thing that he knew about himself, something that in the cowboy world he inhabited was terrible and unspeakably vile. Following the code of the west, he remade himself as a manly, homophobic rancher. No one could mistake rough, stinking Phil for a sissy. In that light, his wounding tongue can be seen as preemptive

277

sarcasm that throws possible critics off balance and into confusion. '[H]e had loathed the world, should it loathe him first.'[15] He grew fangs.

Savage ratchets up the tension tremendously when he has George take an interest in Rose, the doctor's widow, and finally, secretly marry her. Hell breaks loose when he gives the news to Phil, who resentfully sees the widow as a schemer after the Burbank money. The couple moves into the large master bedroom once used by the Old Gentleman and the Old Lady, but Phil dedicates himself to making the bride's life a living hell in a thousand little mocking, secret ways, eventually driving her to secret tippling.

Then it is announced that Rose's sissy son, sixteen-year-old Peter, will spend the summer on the ranch. Phil is appalled and thinks:

> Was . . . George cogitating about the summer when the kid would come slinking in and out of the house, a constant reminder that Georgie boy wasn't the first one to put the blocks to her? He had a hunch George hated sissies as much as he did, and now there would be one such right there in the house, messing around, listening. Phil hated how they walked and how they talked.[16]

Phil prepares the bunkhouse hands for the sissy's arrival by describing Peter's mincing ways, the paper flowers. Peter arrives, and in the ranch house tensions thicken like glue and mealtimes become a horror. The boy can do nothing right. When he surprises Phil naked at his secret water hole, Phil flies into a shouting rage. But the boy is as sharp of

---

15 *The Power of the Dog*, p. 263.
16 Ibid., p. 126.

eye as Phil, and he sees what Phil is doing to his mother and much more. He has chill and watchful ways, a coldness that has always confounded Rose. In a gauntletlike roundup incident, even Phil recognizes something adamantine and courageous about Peter when the boy walks past the ranch hands in stiff new blue jeans after someone has mocked him with a wolf whistle.

Now, Phil always gave credit where credit was due. The kid had an uncommon kind of guts. Wouldn't it be just interesting as hell if Phil could wean the boy away from his mama? Wouldn't it now? Why, the kid would jump at the chance for friendship, a friendship with a man. And the woman — the woman, feeling deserted would depend more and more on the sauce, the old booze.

And then what?[17]

He anticipates that Rose's drinking will escalate and that George will finally cast her off. And so Phil makes the first overtures, offering to give Peter the rawhide rope he is braiding, offering to teach him to rope and ride, offering friendship, which Peter seems to accept. In all of this turn-around friendship (not unlike Long John Silver's grinning overtures to Jim Hawkins), he tells Peter about that extraordinary person from the old good days, Bronco Henry:

'Oh, he taught me things. He taught me that if you've got guts, you can do any damned thing, guts and patience. Impatience is a costly commodity, Pete. Taught me to use my eyes, too. Look yonder, there. What do you see?' Phil

[17] Ibid., p. 226.

shrugged. 'You see the side of a hill. But Bronc, when he looked there, what do you suppose he saw?'

'A dog,' Peter said. 'A running dog.'

Phil stared, and ran his tongue over his lips. 'The *hell*,' he said, 'you see it just now?'

'When I first came here,' Peter said.[18]

Accompanying the change in attitude there is a sense of rising sensuality, intensified when Phil, who never touches anyone, puts his arm over the boy's shoulders, an intimacy set off, as if in emotional parentheses, by Phil's fury at Rose for selling some old hides to the Jewish peddler. Peter listens stone-faced to Phil's vengeful rant, but he has his own secret plan, deeply chilling, more awful than any of Phil's sadistic cruelties, for Peter is already in the big leagues.

In reading Savage's autobiographical novel, *I Heard My Sister Speak My Name*, we see much of the raw material for the characters in *The Power of the Dog*. George Burbank is modeled on Savage's stepfather — stolid, steady, quiet. The Old Gentleman and the Old Lady are fictional illustrations of the elder Brenners. One of the Brenner brothers served as the model for Phil Burbank. The fictional Tom Burton in *The Sheep Queen* writes about their mother to the woman now proven his sister. He describes his mother's second marriage to the well-to-do rancher and the sly insults she suffered from the second brother, Ed.

Ed was a bachelor by profession, a woman-hater. He was brilliant, quick at chess, puzzles and word games. I recall that he knew the meaning of the word 'baobab.' He read

---

[18] Ibid., pp. 259–260.

widely in such top-drawer periodicals as no longer exist — *Asia, Century Magazine, World's Week, Mentor* . . . *Country Life* he tossed aside as directed at climbers and others who required the crutch of possessions.

He was lean, had a craggy profile under thick black hair he had cut no more than four times a year. He despised towns where hair was cut, where men gathered to engage in silly banter and chewed food in public. His long, sharp nose was an antenna quick to pick up the faintest rumor and send it on to his brain to be amplified . . . His laughter was an insulting bray; it crowded and pushed the air ahead of it.

He said many true words about other men. I never heard him say a kind one.[19]

Burton goes on to describe the stepuncle's devotion to his half sister:

The little girl became for Ed his chief instrument of torture; he began to woo her away from my mother. He did a fine job. . . . Ed talked to the little girl around my mother. That her daughter found Ed so lovable and so responsive to her will must have made my mother doubt her sanity.[20]

When Burton/Savage's mother played Schumann or Schubert on the piano, Ed would go to his room and counter with boisterous tunes on his banjo. 'His purpose was to destroy my mother, and that is what he did.'[21] This malicious act grew, in Savage's hands, as a black weed in *The Power of*

[19] *I Heard My Sister Speak My Name*, pp. 223–226.

[20] Ibid., p. 228.

[21] Ibid.

the Dog to great effect. Although young Savage often wished his stepuncle dead, he was too young to 'find the clue to his own weakness and destroy him.' In the end the man destroyed himself. While he was fencing a haystack using poles 'slick with cow manure wet from the fall rains,' a splinter jammed into 'the palm of his naked, horny hand.'[22] He was dead within days of anthrax, a deadly disease caused by *Bacillus anthracis* that can be transmitted from animals to humans through insect transmission, milk, and the handling of infected hides and tissue.

Savage's innate sense of literary drama let him construct a gripping and tense novel from these pieces of his Montana family history. It is one thing to have extraordinary raw material in your literary scrap bag, but quite another to stitch the pieces into a driving and classic story that forever fixes a place and an event in the reader's imagination. From the childhood memory of an odious man, with virtuoso skill Savage created one of the most compelling and vicious characters in American literature. In a curious way he has realized his childhood wish to see the man dead, for every time a new reader catches his breath at Phil Burbank's satisfyingly ghastly end, the child that was Thomas Savage re-kills him as surely as the fictional Peter Gordon removed his mother's nemesis.

---

[22] Ibid.

THE HISTORY OF VINTAGE

The famous American publisher Alfred A. Knopf (1892–1984) founded Vintage Books in the United States in 1954 as a paperback home for the authors published by his company. Vintage was launched in the United Kingdom in 1990 and works independently from the American imprint although both are part of the international publishing group, Random House.

Vintage in the United Kingdom was initially created to publish paperback editions of books bought by the prestigious literary hardback imprints in the Random House Group such as Jonathan Cape, Chatto & Windus, Hutchinson and later William Heinemann, Secker & Warburg and The Harvill Press. There are many Booker and Nobel Prize-winning authors on the Vintage list and the imprint publishes a huge variety of fiction and non-fiction. Over the years Vintage has expanded and the list now includes great authors of the past – who are published under the Vintage Classics imprint – as well as many of the most influential authors of the present. In 2012 Vintage Children's Classics was launched to include the much-loved authors of our youth.

For a full list of the books Vintage publishes, please visit our website www.vintage-books.co.uk

For book details and other information about the classic authors we publish, please visit the Vintage Classics website www.vintage-classics.info

www.vintage-classics.info

Visit www.worldofstories.co.uk for all your
favourite children's classics